A FATHER'S PROMISE

Books by Sandra Ardoin

Contemporary

Hidden Veil Hometown

A Musician's Heart
A Horseman's Mission
A Hero's Nature
A Father's Promise

Love at Christmas Inn

Love in Second Bloom
Leaving the Past Behind
Lost in Winter's Wonderland
Longing for Second Chances
Box Set

Stand Alone Books

A Love Most Worthy
Renee

Historical

House of Fire

A Lady Divided
A Lady Unveiled
(Next in Series)

Widow's Might

Unwrapping Hope
Enduring Dreams
Rekindling Trust

Barnes Brothers

The Yuletide Angel
A Reluctant Melody

Short Stories

Daphne's Day Out

A Father's Promise

Hidden Veil Hometown
Book Four

Sandra Ardoin

Corner Room Books

Corner Room Books, Salisbury, North Carolina, USA

For more information on this book and the author visit her website: www.sandraardoin.com.

Print ISBN: 979-8-9905848-3-9

Yet you, Lord, are our Father. We are the clay, you are the potter; we are all the work of your hand.
Isaiah 64:8

One

If he didn't get the hungover fool snoring in the passenger seat home soon, Sutton Vance might give free rein to his anger. He curled his fingers tighter around the old truck's steering wheel to keep from acting on his inclination. That fool was his father, after all.

A father in name only. A father who couldn't keep a promise if his life depended on it.

Sutton sped down the darkened ribbon of road, trees on each side nothing more than tall, ominous shadows at six o'clock in the morning.

He was an early riser, though not always out of the house yet. But this kind of thing happened with a drunk for a dad—a man who reeked of secondhand cigarette smoke and alcohol and had worn out his welcome at an all-night poker game. Who gets thrown out of a poker game?

But the answer was obvious. Dad had run out of money. Something else that drove Sutton's blood pressure through the truck cab's metal roof. He'd set that money aside for next month's payment on the tractor and, somehow, his father found it . . . and gambled it away.

Out of his peripheral vision, Sutton noticed his dad shiver, so he turned up the heat.

They passed Crooked Creek Ranch, home of his friend, Lane Becker. Could a child trade his parents for new ones? In a heartbeat, he'd trade John and Debra Vance for the responsible and attentive Cliff and Fay Becker, Lane's parents. Right now, with Sutton's fury, he might even consider a trade for Paige's parents. After all, the Hartwells proved they could keep a promise to their daughter by keeping her location from him years ago.

Sutton glanced at his dad. Some people lucked out in life.

"I don't believe in luck, man. I believe in God's blessings."

Hearing Lane Becker's voice in his head, he almost chuckled. But since those blessings had never come Sutton's way, why should he believe in them?

His mother had believed and received an early grave despite her faith. And her death sent his father on a downward spiral, affecting the lives of everyone he came into contact with, especially Sutton's.

Dad snorted and stirred in the seat. His eyes batted open and shut like a garage door opener gone berserk. "Where am I?" He glared at Sutton. "What are you doing here?"

"*Here* is inside my truck." Sutton shook his head. "I guess you don't remember getting tossed from the poker game."

Dad ran a hand down his whiskered face and groaned. "My money's as good as anyone else's."

"Until it's gone." Sutton gritted his back teeth. "We needed that money, Dad. How do I make the payment on the tractor?"

Sutton had babied the last machine until it died a slow, painful death—painful for him as the person who worked on it and had to scrounge up the money, first to replace parts, then to replace the entire machine.

After finding another used one a few months ago, Sutton had groveled, finally convincing the bank to trust him with a loan. In the end, it cost him a portion of the funds he'd saved for a house of his own. But the farm couldn't survive without a tractor.

His dad shrugged. "It'll work out. You'll see."

Sutton bristled at his dad's casual response. "How? Tell me how it will work out. We're not talking about owing on a piece of furniture, Dad. This is our livelihood, our ability to keep a roof over our heads." He wrestled with his temper. Talking to his father like that never ended well, but he'd reached his limit. What was the use? For twenty-odd years he'd failed to talk sense into the man.

They passed the Johnson house a quarter mile from the farm. In the growing light of dawn, the empty two-story frame structure stood like an old soldier determined to survive despite the wounds threatening its existence. Sutton's kindred spirit.

Once, he'd had such plans for that place—he and Paige. During their high school years, they often sneaked inside. They envisioned buying the house together one day. And yes, sometimes it was their make-out spot. But they stopped at kisses. While he would have taken things further, he'd respected Paige's wish that their enthusiasm not get out of hand. He'd felt no such moral constraints, but he'd loved her too much to cross the line.

And what had it gotten him? Nothing. She ran off after high school without a word.

From his days as a young teenager, Sutton had done his best to keep things together for his family. It wasn't easy on him, especially when an alcoholic father and often-ill stepmother left Sutton no choice but to be the breadwinner and parent figure for five younger brothers and sisters.

He'd decided years ago that he never wanted children of his own. He'd practically raised five already. His decision—one he didn't regret—lost him the only woman he ever wanted to share his life.

Sutton pulled into the farm's driveway and stopped the truck near the back door of the house. His father opened the passenger door, but Sutton latched onto his arm. "Are you trying to drive Debra away? Because if you are, you're doing a good job." He drew in a harsh breath and mumbled, "You're doing a good job of driving everyone away."

Dad stared at the trembling hands on his lap. "I don't mean to. I just . . ." His bottom lip quivered.

Aw . . . Don't do this to me.

If there was one thing he couldn't handle, it was seeing his father cry.

As a ten-year-old, Sutton had watched John Vance—the strongest man he had ever known—break down in tears when the doctor told him his wife had passed. Death took more than Sutton's mother that day. It took his father, too. It took the promise, spoken or unspoken, that came from a parent to a child to always care for them—their needs, their health, their hearts.

It deprived Sutton of the right to be the child and not the adult.

"I see the light on in the kitchen, Dad. Debra probably has breakfast and a pot of coffee made. You should apologize to her." Like an apology would change things.

Dad would miss another day at the janitorial service where he worked. Another job down the drain.

Once the door to the house closed behind his father, Sutton parked the truck next to the barn. He got out and scanned the yard. The farm owed its charm to the beautiful rolling landscape and its renovation to his hard work, resolve, and the help of close friends. Trey Abbott, Lane, and a few others had spent many an hour here sawing wood and pounding nails.

In the little town of Hidden Veil, neighbors helped neighbors, a characteristic Sutton appreciated, even if he never said it in terms beyond a hasty "Thanks."

Maybe he would talk to Ted Main, the local real estate broker, about what it would take for him to purchase the Johnson property—once he'd saved enough for the down payment. From a practical standpoint, its size was absurd for housing a single man, but he considered the place a business investment, a future office and a renovation example to show potential contractor clients the quality of his work.

An added plus was its proximity to the farm. The location would allow him to monitor what went on without living in the midst of the action.

From an emotional standpoint? He didn't want to think about why the place meant so much to him.

With years as a rental and occasional vacancies, the house looked rough inside, but the bones were good, and he'd heard the owner had updated the plumbing and electrical ten or twelve years ago. With time and muscle, he could bring the place back to its original glory.

His jaw tightened. Buying the Johnson house would take additional money. Lots of it. Money he didn't have and would never have if he kept bailing out his father, stepmother, and half-siblings.

Most of his brothers and sisters lent a hand around the farm, but the bulk of the work rested on him while they attended school. If it weren't for his construction sideline, the family would have gone under long ago.

Sutton worked as a farmer, but he thrived as a carpenter and builder. His long-term plan included owning a full-time contracting business. One day, he would accomplish it. Until then, he had to move out of this house and get away from the dysfunction that held the Vance family together like glue. They lived in constant crisis.

One day.

Trapped behind the steering wheel of the SUV, Paige Matthews rubbed her aching temple.

Liam turned in the front passenger seat and tried to yank the drawing pad from his sister's hands.

"Let go!" Seven-year-old Leyla lacked normal hearing but compensated with the volume of her voice.

"I just want to see it."

After six hours on the road, Paige couldn't decide which hurt worse, her head or her ears. She'd gotten the kids up at five this morning, intending to beat most of Atlanta's horrific morning traffic. She could have driven the northern, more scenic route out of the city but figured if they got on the road early enough the interstate would be faster. Best-laid plans had often failed her.

"Mom Paige, tell him to give it back."

Mom Paige. Almost three years and Leyla still hadn't decided whether she should call her Mom or Paige.

She cast a glance at Liam in the front passenger seat. He called her Aunt Paige—a term his biological mother promoted when she was alive—or, as most times, he called her nothing at all. She had given him time, but he still refused to acknowledge her adoption of him and his two sisters after the death of their mother, Paige's best friend.

"Liam, why don't you wait until we reach your grandparents' house, then ask Leyla if she minds if you look through her drawings. Okay?"

One would think that after rising early and spending hours in the car, the kids would nap. Only three-year-old Cassie had succumbed to fatigue. The other two expressed their tiredness through arguments.

"Fine." He twisted in the seat and tossed the drawing pad to his sister. "And they aren't my grandparents."

Paige sighed. Was it too late to return to Atlanta? Had she erred in thinking things would be better if she moved back to her hometown, if she had help in becoming the type of mother she'd dreamed of being? She needed that help because she had failed. Maybe, for their sake, she should have never agreed to adopt Marissa's children.

Regardless of whether they liked it, those three were a fulfillment of her greatest dream—

"Don't touch me!"

—and occasional nightmare.

A high-pitched giggle from the backseat eased some of Paige's physical and emotional pain. She hadn't failed completely. Cassie appreciated her, relied on her, and called her Mommy. Then again, to the child, Paige was her mother. She was too young to remember her biological parents.

Ten-year-old Liam, however, remembered them well, and he never let her forget it. Leyla seemed torn. One moment she was content to be in Paige's care. Next, she followed her brother's lead and raised a wall.

No, Liam was her greatest challenge. When he was small, they were buddies. He adored her. Her throat tightened. Then life's worst happened, and their relationship changed. Somehow, she had to win him back.

The drum in her head and chest beat harder as she drove the highway that would take them through the heart of Hidden Veil. The fancy wooden sign at the side of the road increased her anxiety.

Welcome to Hidden Veil, Home of Southern Charm and Good Neighbors

Good neighbors? She knew someone who would dispute that claim about her.

According to her family, her hometown was changing—attracting more and younger people, new businesses. Residents credited the current mayor, her old elementary school teacher, Mrs. Hildenberg, with the growth. Or they blamed the woman, depending on their outlook toward change.

Paige passed several familiar businesses on Main Street, like the antique store and the adjacent drugstore, though the soda shop was new. She'd also noted the coffee shop, Jo E's, owned by Jo Ella Callahan. Paige had known her from school as Jo Ella Ledbetter.

Paige's sister Reagan had said the empty storefront on the other side of the street would become the hub of a catering business owned by Macie Becker, a relative newcomer to town. After years away, Paige felt like a newcomer herself.

She slowed in front of In Harmoni, a handmade soap and candle shop, and made a mental note to contact the owner about selling some of her soap dishes and candleholders there.

Paige crossed the intersection with the only stoplight

downtown.

"That was it?" Liam's head swiveled from right to left, and his voice mocked what he saw.

"I know it isn't Atlanta." She pointed to the building on the left. "That's where I went to high school. Looks like they added a section." The recent addition expanded the building by about a third. Hidden Veil really had grown. She wasn't sure how she felt about it.

"Where will I go to school?"

"They built a new elementary and middle school west of town." Newer, anyway. "We'll go Monday morning and get you registered."

"Whatever."

She ignored the grumpy response. He was a fine student and took his studies seriously. "People are friendly here, Liam. You'll like it. And according to your aunts, the town is more interesting than when I left."

"More interesting than in the old days."

She flashed a grin. "Old to you." Bygone days to her.

"And they aren't my aunts."

Paige restrained the scream that struggled for freedom. What would the future hold? She would soon find out.

Two

Paige pulled into the gravel driveway leading to the brick ranch-style house where she'd grown up. Even in mid-fall, her mother's front garden with its yellow and blue pansies still reflected seasonal change. Evergreen shrubs hid the foundation of the house and expanded into a curved landscaped space.

With her sister Brianna still living at home, four more people could threaten to burst the poor little house's seams. Paige and the children would stay only until the movers delivered her things to her new house. Surely, it could hang on until then.

An inner groan clenched her stomach muscles. Had that been another mistake? Buying the Johnson house? Would memories of days past make her miserable each time she crossed the threshold? Why insist on making her home with the kids in that house? She could imagine Sutton's opinion. *Did she buy the place to torture me or because she wanted to be close to me?*

No, and no.

She hoped not, anyway.

Paige glanced in the rearview mirror at the girls in the back seat. She had no worries about renewing a romance with him. Her sisters insisted Sutton's opinion about parenthood hadn't changed. Hers hadn't either, even though that part of her life hadn't turned out as she'd planned.

And after the way she'd run off years ago, he would run in the opposite direction to avoid her now.

Her parents walked out the front door to greet them. After removing Cassie from the car, she shivered in the November chill. With the temperatures up one day and down the next, dressing was a guess. At least the sun brightened the sky.

Paige hugged her mother, then turned to her father for a hug. Her parents' huge smiles eased some of the tension that had knotted her muscles.

"How was the drive, honey?"

She glanced at the kids. "Let's just say we're all glad to have arrived, Dad."

"Of course you are." Mom crouched and held her arms out. Cassie ran to her, and Mom lifted the child, cuddling her. Paige's parents had met the children during trips to visit her in Atlanta, so they weren't strangers. "Let's go inside where it's warmer. I have a chocolate cake waiting to be eaten."

Since Mom had faced Cassie when she spoke, Leyla gazed up at Paige. "Did she say cake?"

Paige checked Leyla's ears, then looked her in the eye. "Where are your hearing aids?"

Leyla frowned and pulled them from the orange backpack that often rode like a baby monkey on her back. Only after she pushed them in her ears did Paige respond to her question. "Yes. Cake inside." With those words, the girl took her grandmother's hand and skipped toward the house. Liam followed at a distance, his shoulders hunched. He hadn't said a word to anyone.

Paige's dad watched them. "She still hates wearing the hearing aids?"

"She has some hearing, and she's good at reading lips if she faces the person, so she relies on the latter."

"I noticed her speech has improved."

"The speech therapist has done wonders. She recommended one nearby. I've made an appointment for Leyla to see her in a couple of weeks."

"I admire you, kiddo. Mom and I know what it's like to raise three children—not that any of you caused us genuine grief. Well, maybe Reagan a time or two."

Paige could think of one big headache she had caused her parents, but she laughed and pulled her sweater closer around her neck. "Reagan can be a handful. I don't envy her fiancé trying to keep her in check."

"Trey does his best. He's a great guy."

Paige expected her dad to add, "Unlike your ex-husband."

"They'll be here tomorrow to say hello."

"I'm looking forward to meeting him. I confess to peeking at the clinic's website and saw his photo. Reagan found a cute one."

Her father rolled his eyes at her assessment of her future brother-in-law and helped her pull suitcases from the back of the SUV. "To finish my thought from before, we didn't deal with your circumstances."

"I've accepted those circumstances. I just . . ." She sighed. "I wish things were going smoother, you know?"

"I understand."

"The kids have gone through changes that would be hard on an adult."

They had been hard on Paige. Her best friend, Marissa, died from cancer—Marissa's police officer husband already gone after losing control of his cruiser in a high-speed chase.

Years before Paige married Dustin, she had agreed to adopt the couple's children should the worst happen. The promise had rolled off her tongue like it would from any young person who never imagined the situation becoming a reality.

"Liam resents me, Dad."

"I doubt that's true. Sure, he misses his mom and dad. You can't blame him for that. Sometimes, he'll express it negatively, but he'll come around."

She decided not to remind him it had been nearly three years, along with six months of failed family therapy.

Dad carried Leyla and Liam's bags to the porch with Paige hauling hers and Cassie's. So much had changed in all of their lives. Some for the good, like her career as a potter. In the last four years she'd worked hard, and God had blessed her with a business that had taken off despite the necessity to adjust her hours to fit the children's schedules.

Some things had changed for the worse, though. While she tried to hand those troublesome problems over to the Lord, she inevitably snatched them back to worry over.

Her father stood at the door, a scowl furrowing his forehead. "Sometimes, I want to pay Dustin a visit to let him know what I think of his running out on you."

After Marissa passed, the children came to live with Paige and Dustin. Her husband moved out a few months afterward. "He had certain expectations that weren't possible. I wasn't heartbroken, Dad. Shouldn't that bother me?" Only one man had ever broken her heart.

"To be honest, honey, I always doubted the suitability of you and Dustin. I could kick myself for not speaking up before the wedding."

"I could kick myself for agreeing to a wedding." She had never pictured herself divorced, and Dustin wasn't a bad guy, just not the guy for her, because he wasn't . . . "Besides, how can I complain about someone running out on me after what I did?"

Dad's lips pinched, but he said nothing.

"Let's talk about something less maudlin. If you don't mind watching the kids tomorrow morning, I should run by the house. The moving van arrives next week, and I want to be sure everything is ready."

She'd made a to-do list for tomorrow. It included picking up the keys from the realtor and stopping by the store for cleaning supplies.

"About the house, Paige—"

A car door closed behind them, interrupting whatever her father had planned to say. Paige turned to see her sister, Brianna, rush up the driveway. "You're here!"

The two women hugged, and Paige grinned, glad to see more family, especially the baby sister. "I thought you had classes today."

In a stage whisper, Brianna leaned in and said, "Don't tell Daddy, but I skipped my last class." She cut her eyes to their father, who shook his head. "Where are the kids?"

"Mom has them in the kitchen. She's stuffing them with cake and ruining their supper."

"Ooh, I'd better get in there if I want some of her cake before it's gone." Bri rushed off, but Paige figured she wasn't as eager to eat dessert as she was to see her nephew and nieces.

Dad set the bags on the front porch. "We should discuss the house, Paige."

"I know, Dad. It's been empty for a while. I'm sure it needs intense cleaning, and the kitchen is a throwback to the seventies.

The inspector found a few things to fix, too." He'd found more than a few. His report comprised six pages, but she'd expected it. Looking at the house on Google's recent street view, it appeared surprisingly nice considering its past treatment, though nothing could have stopped Paige from buying the place. It was close to her parents and perfect for her family. "Don't worry. It will be fine."

"It's going to take plenty of work to get the place in shape. Most important, there's the matter of its location."

Even though she saw only treetops, Paige glanced at the vast wooded land behind her parents' house—the woods she'd often traipsed through years ago to get to the Vance farm.

To get to Sutton.

Now, if she hiked through those same woods and turned toward town, she would end up on her new property. Okay, so the location a short distance down the road from the Vance farm wasn't as ideal as it was in the past. They would be neighbors, but that didn't mean they had to be neighborly.

"Don't you think you owe him the courtesy of letting him know you're back before he sees you at your sister's wedding next month?"

She shrugged. "People talk. He'll find out sooner than later, and I don't intend to hide inside my house." Reagan and Bri had already invited her to join their friends, even though the group included Sutton. "That's been over for a long time, Dad. We're grownups now, and I'm sure he's moved on. We can handle it." She hoped. "And you and I know that once he learns about the kids, he'll run in the other direction."

Oh, did that sound as sour to her father as it did to her?

"Sutton, since you're going to town, would you mind picking up some things from the grocery store?" Before he could sneak out the mudroom door off the kitchen, Debra's voice wheezed his name.

For years, his stepmother had battled asthma, bronchitis, and pneumonia. The medicine she took left her overweight and sometimes weak. But she loved her children—even him—and cared for them all when and in whatever way she could, which involved cooking. Sutton complained about plenty of things in his life but never about Debra's gentle personality and talent in the kitchen.

He counted the money in his wallet. "Sure. Do you have a list?"

She handed him a sheet of paper with about a dozen items on it. Nothing too expensive or elaborate. She cooked plain but delicious meals. "I hate to ask you to—"

"Don't worry about it, Debra."

She grimaced each time he used her name instead of calling her "Mom," like the other kids. While he respected her, he just couldn't do it. He'd had a mother. She died. Dad remarried. End of story.

"Can I go with you, Sutton?" His sister Jenna brushed past her mother. "There's an amazing new makeup I want to try."

He pointed to the purse she carried. "Do you have money in there?"

"Some."

"Well, unless you have enough to pay for it, the answer is

no."

"Ugh! You are so mean to me!" Her blonde ponytail ticked back and forth with her ire. She didn't tell him he wasn't in charge of her. She knew better.

Sometimes, he hated being the responsible provider, especially when he had to say no to his siblings. He might be a guy, but he still understood a sixteen-year-old girl's desire to look older and impress the guys. Yet it wouldn't hurt her to go without the latest "amazing" foundation for her skin.

"Jenna, we don't have extra money for frou-frous right now."

"Frou-frous? What century were you born in?"

"The last, and when I wanted something, I worked for it." Sutton turned and bolted from the house before she could cajole him into taking her with him and spending unnecessary money.

When the Johnson house came into view, Sutton slowed his truck. On a whim, he pulled into the drive. It wasn't a long drive, but it needed new stone. After a good rain, like they expected tonight, a vehicle's tires would slide or sink into the mud.

He parked and walked around the structure, peeking in the first-floor windows. The place needed work, but nothing he saw discouraged him from wanting to make it his. Once he figured out how to pay the tractor payment, he'd visit Ted Main. Learning the specifics of the purchase would cost him nothing, and with the shoddy condition of the house, he expected to snatch it up at a bargain, provided Fitz Johnson would sell.

Sutton returned to his truck and continued the short trip to the barbershop in town. He'd put off getting a haircut for long enough. Half an hour later, he walked down to Goodwin's Hardware. Bobby Goodwin stood at the cash register, talking to his redheaded co-owner—his son Roy.

"What can we do for you, Sutton?" The eighty-something Bobby grinned at him.

He hated the idea of admitting his desperation. With only a couple of minor carpentry jobs on the calendar, ones that wouldn't take long to complete, he had no choice but to drum up business however he could. "Hey, guys. You know things are slow on the farm right now. I wondered if you'd heard of anyone needing some carpentry or construction work done?"

The two Goodwins eyed one another, both frowning as they thought. Finally, Roy said, "We've gotten no inquiries lately, but if someone asks us for a recommendation, we'll send them your way."

Sutton tapped the old wooden counter, original to the business and close to sixty years old. It represented the type of quality work Sutton strove to achieve in his jobs. He forced a grin. "Thanks."

After driving to Johnson's Grocery and picking up the items on Debra's list, he returned to the truck. The total came to a little more than he'd counted on, which meant he would miss meeting his friends for lunch after their church service on Sunday. They tried to get together once a month. At least he'd see them for their Thanksgiving meal the following Sunday.

He loaded the bags into the truck and pulled out of the parking space as a woman approached the store's double doors. Brunette, tall, slim. He couldn't see her face, but an alarm went off inside him. A sense of recognition gripped him—the unexpected and shocking kind. The kind he would experience if he ever saw—

Sutton shook his head, clearing out the ridiculous notion that filled it as the woman disappeared inside the store. Man, if he was acting this crazy—assigning a certain identity to a stranger—a month from the wedding, what would he be like when Paige Hartwell rolled into town next month to see her sister married?

Three

Paige parked in the driveway of the two-story structure. The wheels of her SUV had spun in the mud from last night's rainstorm, reminding her to order a load of stone.

Cuddled by an amazing array of towering oaks, hickories, pines, and a few cedar trees, her new house sat on over two acres. She leaned sideways in the seat and stared at the frame structure through the vehicle's windows. In the past few years, someone had painted the exterior of the home white, giving it a bright facade.

The size and columns and covered porch spoke of past charm and romance. At the thought of romance, she stiffened her neck to keep from following the impulse to glance toward the Vance farm.

Nope, not thinking about him today.

She picked her way across the brown, wet, autumn-dead grass to the backyard and the cement block workshop behind the house. Ted Main had sent her photos, saying it was perfect for her pottery studio. But how much work was necessary to make it suitable?

Paige entered the building to find a large open space in need of a deep cleaning to remove the dust and cobwebs. She sniffed, and a smile curved her lips. Faint scents of oil, paint, dirt, but no smell of mold or sign of moisture. Dampness could ruin her clay.

Her gaze wandered from wall to wall and from floor to ceiling. Three windows offered plenty of natural light and various spots to set up her wheel and work table. Shelves, cabinets, and a workbench already installed would save her the cost of adding her own.

She whispered into the air, "It's perfect." Just as Ted had assured her. When the movers delivered her things, they could bring her pottery equipment straight into the building.

Still, before resuming work, Paige would hire an electrician to check the wiring for safety and install a receptacle with the proper voltage for her kiln. She'd also ask whichever contractor she hired to install a hole in the building's side to set up the ventilation the kiln required.

She considered the ability to work from home—to be available when the children returned from school—worth every penny she had paid for the property.

Paige locked the building and returned to the front of the house. Puddles of rainwater pooled in warped stair planks, and she dodged a hole in the porch on her way to the door. She wouldn't risk broken legs, so she pulled a notebook and pen from her purse. An immediate replacement of the broken boards went on the to-do list.

A chilly breeze met her back, and she huddled deeper into her sweater, thankful that Mr. Johnson had added central heating and air-conditioning to the house at some point in its history. Her changes would be mainly cosmetic.

After turning the key in the lock, she pushed on the front door. It gave a centimeter and stuck. She pushed again, harder this time, and the door reluctantly opened inward, creaking with each inch and scraping the floor. She'd have Dad look at it, but the door probably only required the bottom to be planed and the hinges oiled. What old house didn't settle over time?

An entrance hall lined with six-inch crown molding and baseboards stretched from the front to the back of the house. She ran a finger over the stairway newel post, dragging a thick layer of dirt with it.

Peeling wallpaper. Scuffed flooring. Dirt and old light fixtures. Her father had warned her that the condition inside might be more than she could handle, but she wasn't afraid of employing some elbow grease and hiring someone for the more demanding renovations.

As Paige looked around, a tidal wave of memories rose to transport her back in time. In her mind, she was no longer a struggling single mom in her early thirties. She was young and happy and in love. Her life revolved around her family and Sutton Vance.

With this move to Hidden Veil, one thing remained true. Her life revolved around her family.

She wrinkled her nose. The house needed a good airing out to remove the dusty smell of disuse. Fitz Johnson could have sold it long ago to someone who would appreciate its character and maintain it. Evidently, he'd waited for someone like her to make him a ridiculous offer.

In the dining room. Paige pictured her mother's faded flowered tablecloth spread out on the floor. She heard the laughter of two teens toasting the end of the school year with plastic glasses filled with soda. She smelled her favorite hamburger from the Red Dog Diner. She felt the touch of Sutton's sweet kiss on her lips.

Shaking her head shook away the image from the past.

A connecting doorway led into the kitchen. Scratched dark cabinets. Ancient appliances. It contained a stove but not much countertop space. The fireplace, a pass-through shared with the dining room, gave the kitchen its character and charm.

This wouldn't be a cheap fix, but she'd learned a few things from Dustin, an architect, and her artistic side saw tremendous potential. By the time she'd finished, it would be both functional and stunning.

Added to a hundred times before, she said a quiet "Thank you" to God for his provision. On the second floor, she found three bedrooms and another bath. Every room had a fireplace.

As she explored her chosen bedroom—a space large enough to be two rooms—Paige glanced up and spotted a wet area on the ceiling. Her stomach sank with the recollection of last night's wind and rain. She rushed back into the hall and up another flight of stairs to the third-floor attic. Her body trembled at the sight of leaf and limb poking through a jagged hole in the roof.

Dustin—whether through guilt or to buy her goodwill—had given her a divorce settlement that still boggled her mind. Because her business did well, she had almost declined the offer, but her attorney convinced her to take it. She could kiss both men right now.

"He's stomping on my last nerve, and I don't know what to do about it. I can't keep dealing with his issues." Sutton propped his back against a stall door in Lane Becker's barn, tired from a night of tossing and turning after imagining he'd seen Paige at the grocery store yesterday. He'd needed to vent, and who better to vent to than his best friend? But he'd chosen a different subject to talk about, something as equally vexing as visions of Paige. "Dad is on a one-way trip to destruction and taking everyone else with him."

Lane tossed a section of hay into the crib in Jasper's stall. The chatty Appaloosa whinnied before he chowed down. "I wish I knew what to tell you. As for the tractor payment, I could probably—"

"No!" Sutton regretted his sharp response, but if his father had taught him one thing of value in life, it was that a Vance accepted nothing from others. Not lip and especially not charity. "Thanks, but I'll work it out."

If anyone knew what Sutton had gone through and the way he'd grown up, it was Lane. They had met in first grade, and until Macie arrived, they spent most of their spare time together. Now Lane had found his soulmate, whereas Sutton had lost his and bucked at the idea of replacing her. Not that he'd become a hermit. He dated, but never women who would remind him of Paige Hartwell.

The sound of heavy boots scraping the concrete aisle of the barn announced Trey Abbott's arrival. "Hey, guys."

"Thanks for coming, Trey." Lane removed his work gloves to shake the vet's hand. "Smokey's in the arena. He's been off his feed the past couple of days."

After asking a few routine questions, Trey said, "Let me examine him, then we'll talk."

Sutton tagged behind the other men on their way to the arena. Lane babied his roping horse—all his horses—but a health emergency could come up at any time. Sutton hoped his horse, Rocket, would remain healthy. He couldn't afford a vet bill right now.

While Trey examined the horse, Sutton asked him, "Has Reagan turned into a bridezilla yet, Vet Boy?"

Trey and his fiancée planned to marry the weekend after Christmas. Sutton dreaded it. Trey was the last of his close friends to walk down the aisle. Worse, Paige was sure to attend.

He was determined to find a knockout date before the event. No way would he let Paige think he still pined for her.

"Keep it up, Farmer Boy, and it'll be dueling syringes and needles at noon."

"Scary."

Their laughter didn't take away from his need to know if he'd seen the ghost of his past yesterday.

The woman he saw at the grocery store couldn't have been Paige. It was too early for her to arrive for the wedding. Still, one person here could confirm that he had imagined her walking into the grocery store.

"So, when did Paige get into town?" Okay, he'd put the blunt question out there, even though he expected Trey to tell him she was miles away, and his tone sounded casual enough.

Lane whipped around to face him. "Paige is back?"

"I stopped by Johnson's and picked up a few things for Debra. As I pulled out of the parking lot, a woman who looked a lot like her went into the store. But it's been years. I couldn't swear it was her."

Trey moved to the other side of the horse, continuing his examination. He had to have heard the conversation. Was he already influenced by the Hartwell clan to keep Paige's presence in Hidden Veil a secret?

Lane laid a hand on his shoulder like he figured Sutton had lost his mind and needed to be brought back to reality. "I'm sure you saw someone who looked like her."

"I never said I saw her. I just . . ." Man, he kept digging himself in deeper. Bringing it up was as much a mistake as thinking he'd seen Paige.

Sutton had often considered asking Trey if he knew where she lived but always shut that thought down. Why give anyone the idea she still mattered to him? And he didn't want to put his friend in an awkward position . . . as he'd just done.

Trey remained quiet, occupied with his work. Finally, he turned from the gelding and pushed his glasses up his nose. Sutton held his breath, waiting for confirmation of what he'd seen. "Lane, Smokey has an abscessed tooth. I'll have to pull it. Let me show you."

And just like that, his friend avoided the subject. What did that mean? Could he have been right after all?

Naw, it was likely Trey's way of telling Sutton to leave him out of it.

"I'm headed home. See you guys later." Before they could even say "Bye," he was halfway to his truck and feeling two pairs of eyeballs on his back. Talk about a horror show.

Hopefully, the fliers he'd posted at various Hidden Veil businesses today would prove fruitful, and his phone would buzz with calls for work. He could use the distraction, as well as the money.

Sutton turned down the road leading to the farm. Once more, the Johnson place drew his gaze. This time, a car sat in the drive, one with a Georgia license plate. The last he'd heard, Fitz Johnson had moved to the Outer Banks. So whose car sat in the driveway of Sutton's future house?

The only way to find out was to apply the neighborhood watch ploy. Ask the person what he was doing there, tell him he was trespassing, and then order him off the property.

He parked behind the SUV—a fancy white Lexus—and slammed the door of his truck, hoping to get the attention of whoever owned the vehicle. No one came to meet him. Maybe the person was out back.

As he walked around the front corner, avoiding puddles from last night's downpour, movement in his peripheral vision and feet tramping across the boards caught his attention. He whirled to confront the intruder. Before he moved more than a couple of steps, a shrill scream pierced the air.

Sutton hurried to the porch. His feet slid to a halt in the mud, and his arms windmilled as he worked to keep his balance. His heart jumped to his throat, making the one word that passed his lips sound like it came from a hissing cat. "Paige?"

Four

Still dazed by what she'd seen in the attic, Paige had lumbered down the stairs, unable to believe her first trip to the house ended with the sight of disaster.

The door of a vehicle slammed, and Paige peeked out the sidelight to discover who had pulled into her driveway. Her stomach somersaulted like a gymnastics star. After all these years, it only took a moment for her brain to acknowledge what her eyes saw.

Unprepared to speak to the man who crept around the corner of the house, she panicked, flung open the door, and dashed outside. Two steps later, she screamed.

Now trapped—half on and half under the porch—like a rabbit in a snare, she stared into the jumbo-sized, brown eyes of Sutton Vance. Could they get any bigger?

Pain shimmied up her leg, reminding her of her physical predicament. In her haste to escape, she had forgotten the broken porch board.

Her emotional predicament left her with a different pain. No, more like fear. Not of Sutton, but of herself, her reaction to him.

"Paige?"

She struggled to climb out but managed little more than a sharp gasp at the sudden twinge in her left foot and sting in her calf. And who knew what crawled around under the porch? She shivered at the thought of a spider inching up her pant leg or a raccoon sniffing her foot.

"Why sneak around? Did you hope to scare me to death?" Paige recognized her sharp response for what it was—a defense mechanism against the memories barraging her.

"Sneaking? I'm not prowling around where I don't belong."

Although he could mean one of two things, Paige believed he meant both—she didn't belong on the property, and she didn't belong in Hidden Veil. Well, he was wrong on both counts. She belonged on this property and in her hometown.

Scowling and gorgeous and no longer looking like a wannabe man—a target he'd met in spades—Sutton glared at her as though he expected her to respond. She practiced her yoga breathing. Deep inhale. Deep exhale.

"You're growing a beard? I've never seen you with a beard." *Great, Paige. Any other brilliant observations to embarrass yourself?*

He ran his hand along the scruff on his face like it would confirm what she'd seen. "You wouldn't haven't seen it, because you haven't been here."

She deserved those grumbled words. "Help me out of this hole, please?" See, she could control her reaction to him and treat him as any other person who stood there like a big lump with an owlish stare.

He stomped up the steps, the full weight of his six foot-plus, muscular frame rattling the planks. She almost laughed at the thought of both of them getting stuck in broken porch boards.

Almost.

"Are you hurt?"

"It's my left ankle. I don't think it's broken. Sprained maybe."

He bent forward. "Take my hands."

Paige hesitated. When she had asked for his help, she hadn't taken into consideration the need to touch him. With that touch, would more emotions and memories rush back, tempting her to throw away her hard-fought independence from him?

"Come on, Paige. I don't have all day."

She frowned. Why worry about falling again for His Crabbiness?

She grasped his hands, his palms and fingers hard with calluses. A workingman's hands. In contrast, she babied her potter's hands with lotions to minimize the damaging effects of working for hours with water and clay.

With a gentleness contrary to his snarling manner, Sutton lifted her from the hole and helped her gain her balance. She tried to put her weight on the injured foot but cried out. Her eyes teared up with pain and frustration. And maybe some guilt and regret over the past?

Her injury was his fault. What was he doing here, anyway? She hadn't been ready to see him again. In fact, despite what she told her father, she'd hoped to avoid Sutton until the wedding.

He crouched and pulled at her pant leg. She hopped back on one foot. "What are you doing?"

"Blood is running down your leg. Don't you feel it?"

Paige had wanted to ignore the sting in her calf, suspecting it came from a deep cut. She grimaced at the tear in her best pants. Spotting the blood he'd mentioned, her body swayed.

"Whoa." Sutton sprang up and caught her before she fell.

"Still woozy at the sight of blood?"

Paige shut her eyes and nodded. Now that she couldn't see it, she should be fine. But the dizziness remained, and she had a horrible feeling it had nothing to do with the blood and everything to do with whose arms held her upright. She reminded herself that he had only kept her from falling. It meant nothing. Not to him.

When she regained her balance, he released her but stayed close. "You should go to the clinic. That cut probably needs stitches. While you're there, they can X-ray your foot."

Paige glanced at the Lexus. She should be able to drive herself to the clinic, right? Or, Dad could pick her up and take her. "I'll be fine."

Sutton stared off in the distance, then a hiss escaped his lips. "Come on. I'll take you."

"I told you. It will be fi—" She took a painful step and her breath caught.

He swooped her off her feet and carried her down the steps before she could finish her sentence. In fact, he left her no choice but to wrap her arms around his neck and settle in for the ride. And what a ride!

Paige forced her head up to keep it from resting on his shoulder as he marched through the yard. His firm steps spoke of frustration, even as he held her with all the tenderness she would expect from someone who—

No. No. No. He didn't care for her. Not any longer.

"This is ridiculous. Put me down, Sutton. I can walk."

"We'll take my truck. I'm sure that expensive car of yours has leather seats that wouldn't appreciate spots of blood. At least my vinyl covers clean up easily."

Bitterness permeated his tone. Nope, not someone who

cared.

She had often said she didn't want to know, but her sisters sneaked in comments about the state of Sutton's family life. She didn't fault him for the bitterness. The manhandling, yes, but not his resentment. He'd had a hard time since his mother died.

Neither of them spoke during the five-minute drive to Hidden Veil's medical clinic. For his part, he looked lost in thought. As for her, she couldn't think of anything to say to pacify his anger over her leaving years ago. She could ask about his family, but that was a sore subject, too.

What about his work? Given his earlier sour attitude when mentioning her car, it didn't seem a calming subject.

That left silence.

Sutton pulled into the clinic—new since she'd moved away. He reached her side at the same time she opened the truck's door. "If you'll help me down, I can walk inside."

He stood close enough to catch her if she lost her balance but didn't touch her this time.

The pain in her ankle had subsided some, but she hobbled to the counter and explained her injury. The receptionist handed her a stack of papers. "Fill these out, please, and we'll work you in. Keep in mind, it will probably be half an hour or so."

"That's fine." In Atlanta, she might wait a couple of hours or more.

Paige turned to thank Sutton and let him know he could leave. She found him ready to help her to a seat in the waiting room. She sighed, grasped his arm, and limped to a vacant chair. He took the adjacent one, tapping the arm with short, dirt-stained fingernails, his facial features tight.

"You don't need to wait. I'll call someone to pick me up." She dug into her back pocket. "Oh, I left my phone in the house."

She'd obviously lost her mind to run out of the place as she did, or she would have remembered to get it before she left. "I don't suppose I could borrow yours?"

He said nothing for a few moments, then swiveled in the chair. "What were you doing at Fitz Johnson's house?"

"No 'Sure, Paige, not a problem' or even 'When did you arrive in Hidden Veil'?" When his lips strained as though he barely held on to his temper, she said, "I bought it."

"You what?" Sutton's booming voice echoed in the room, drawing everyone's attention—probably for miles.

Paige glanced around the room. "Indoor voice, please."

Did she just correct him with a command to use an indoor voice?

Sutton's chest rose and fell with the effort to regain control over both his temper and the conversation.

She held out her hand. "Your phone?"

He dug his phone out of his back pocket and dropped it onto her open palm. When she curled her fingers around it, he checked out her ring finger. Bare. His stupid, treasonous heart acted like that was a good thing.

"Thanks."

He hadn't believed his eyes when he saw her on the porch, in pain and caught like a wolf in the jagged jaws of a trap. Now, he couldn't believe his ears. She *bought* the house? *His* house! She bought it out from under him! For the second time in his life, she had ruined his plans for the future.

Did she intend to renovate and sell the place for a profit? Was that how she afforded a Lexus and the expensive-looking clothes she wore? His sister would turn green if she saw them. Maybe she was one of those types Debra watched on TV, the designers that turned ugly houses into showplaces.

"Why?"

She frowned. "I told you. I left my phone in my car, and I want to call—"

"Why did you buy that house? You no longer live here, Paige."

Her chin rose, reminding him of his sister. It dropped again, and she sucked in her lips, looking away. "We—I'm back. For good."

Sutton slumped in the chair. He'd never expected her to return to Hidden Veil "for good." So, after all this time, why had she? From the minute Sutton discovered she'd left town, he had refused to entertain the idea that she would marry someone else, and since she wore no wedding ring, who did she mean by "we"?

After tapping numbers on the keypad, Paige grinned, showing the world a cheerful face. "Hey, Dad. There was a slight accident at the house . . . No. No, I'm fine, but I am at the clinic and don't have my car. I'll need a ride back to pick it up."

Sutton glared at her. She didn't want him to take her home? Of course not. She wanted to run away from him as soon as possible. *Guilty conscience, girl?*

"No, don't come now. They haven't called me back yet. I'll call you when I'm done, okay?" She listened. "Great. Thanks, Dad."

Thanks, Dad. The words repeated in Sutton's head after she returned his phone. She'd always been able to depend on her parents when she needed help. In that, their lives were extreme opposites.

"You don't have to wait, Sutton."

She'd said that before. Did she hope he'd leave before her father arrived?

For living in such a small town, Sutton hadn't talked to Brian Hartwell in fifteen years, not since his teenaged-self had all but begged the man for Paige's address, or at the least, her phone number. A worthless effort. And he didn't relish seeing the man today.

So why *was* he still here? It wasn't as if he didn't have a thousand chores waiting for him at the farm. Only one answer came to mind. He was a loser. The same loser who had waited years for Paige's return.

Still, something perverse took hold of him. He crossed his legs, settling into the seat as though he owned it. "You'll need help getting back to the exam room."

Paige opened her mouth and shut it again. He grabbed a magazine from the side table, hiding a smile of triumph behind the open pages. Speechless. Would wonders never cease?

She giggled like the girl he used to know.

Now what?

He glanced at her, and she pointed to the magazine in his hand. "Since when did you take an interest in cooking?"

Cooking? Sutton eyed the large photograph of some Italian-looking dish on the magazine's page. Heat climbed his neck. He'd meant to grab the outdoors-themed magazine he'd seen on the table earlier.

Truth or deflection? Deflection. Every time. "You don't cook?"

"Of course I do. I just didn't realize you did."

He shrugged. "Debra likes to try new things." Sometimes. Most of the time, she cooked with a limited collection of recipes.

He shut the magazine and asked the question gnawing at him. "You said 'we' a few minutes ago? You and who else?"

She stole the magazine from his lap and flipped through the pages. "Did I?"

"You know you did."

"Paige Matthews?"

Paige turned her attention to the nurse calling out from near the doorway leading to the exam rooms. "Here."

He gaped at her, a boulder in his stomach. Matthews? Not Hartwell?

"Thanks for the rescue and the ride, Sutton." She handed him the magazine, pushed up from the chair, and limped across the room. Alone.

He'd told her he would help her, but all Sutton could do was stare at her back. He'd been wrong. She *was* married.

Five

Paige ended the call with the insurance agent and faced Reagan. "The good news is they'll cover the roof repair."

"And the bad news?"

"My premiums will increase, and I'm not even moved in yet."

Paige sat on the stairs in the hallway. On Saturday, she'd left the clinic exam room with a bandaged ankle and instructions to ice it and let it rest. In addition, she received six stitches in her calf and a tetanus shot. After three days, her leg felt almost normal, but with too much activity this morning, it ached.

"Maybe I should pay for the repair myself."

"Dustin was generous, but do you realize how much cash you'll need to make this place livable?"

Paige didn't bother answering what she assumed was a rhetorical question.

Reagan had stopped by to see the house on her lunch hour while Paige was there to clean and prepare for the movers to arrive on Thursday. As much as she appreciated her sister, Paige didn't always appreciate Reagan's outspokenness.

"I know from updating the house Grandma left me it isn't cheap." Reagan's glance bounced from one wall to the other.

"This place is three times the size of mine."

Her sister had a point. "Seeing that disaster in the attic took my breath away. I am so grateful to Dad for helping me remove the tree limb and lay a tarp over the hole in the roof." Paige grinned as she motioned around her. "Isn't this something?"

Reagan's gaze swept the parlor walls, then went from the scratched floor to the dull ceiling. "It's something." She propped her hands on her hips. "I hope you know what you're doing, Paige."

"I thought you'd be pleased to have me back and close by."

"I am, but couldn't you have bought a house on the other side of town?"

"This is the house I wanted. I fell in love with it when . . . when I was a teenager."

"When you and a certain farmer rendezvoused here, you mean?" A teasing glint lit Reagan's eyes.

"You knew about that?" She and Sutton thought they had been cagey in meeting here. "How?"

"I followed you through the woods one day."

Paige's cheeks flamed. Why wasn't she surprised? "The house was empty and unlocked. It was a good place for Sutton to escape his family's drama. But nothing happened." She graced her sister with a crooked grin. "Much."

Reagan laughed. "Don't worry. I didn't spy on you. Much."

Paige covered her face with her hands. She and Sutton had done nothing wrong, nothing more than kiss. Okay, they did that a lot, sometimes too enthusiastically, but she'd made sure it didn't go further, and he'd respected her wishes. In those days, he'd respected *her*. She couldn't say that was the case anymore. Not after she'd run away without a word.

She'd done something similar on Saturday. The interruption

by the nurse had given her the perfect opportunity to avoid answering his question about her slip-up in saying "we" when referring to her return to Hidden Veil. By the time she reentered the waiting room, her father had arrived, and Sutton was nowhere to be seen.

She hadn't told Sutton about the kids, but surely he knew by now. Even with the recent growth, the small town supported a healthy grapevine.

"When I said I hoped you knew what you were doing, I was talking about the nearness to that certain farmer."

"You can say his name, Reagan. I won't pass out. Besides, Sutton and I have gotten past that awkward first meeting."

Reagan cocked her head as though she doubted that statement. "One meeting isn't the same as being neighbors."

"We're adults. We can handle it." Hadn't she said the same to her father? And yet, she hadn't handled it well on Saturday. "I've always loved this house and wanted to be near Mom and Dad. They'll be a good influence on Liam. He misses having a father figure." She may as well tell the truth. "To be honest, he resents me."

Reagan frowned. "Why? You've given him a home and kept the siblings together. He should be grateful."

"I'm not looking for gratitude." She was looking for love. "He's ten years old. He doesn't understand all that's happened to him, and he's fighting against his circumstances."

"I guess you're right. Ooh, if I could get my hands on Dustin!"

"You'll have to stand in line. Dad called first dibs." Paige rose from her seat on the stairs. "Come see the rest of the house." She led her sister through the rooms upstairs and down, saving the kitchen for last.

"Whoa." Reagan stopped in the doorway. "I see a lot of work here. Are you sure you want to tackle such a big job?"

"It's too late to change my mind now, but I don't need to do it all at one time. Along with getting the workshop in shape, this is the critical room." Paige walked to the center of the space. "I see a modern farmhouse style in here with cabinets in a gray-green color and white quartz counters." She turned toward the back wall. "A big farmhouse sink will go here, under the window, so I can look outside while I'm doing dishes. I'll add a dishwasher, of course, a new gas stove, and a large island in the center of the room, big enough for the kids to eat breakfast and lunch."

"I have to admit it. Your plan sounds terrific. Expensive, but terrific." Reagan bent over to look through the fireplace on the interior sidewall. "I can see into the dining room."

"Isn't it great?"

"There's definitely potential, Paige. This is a lot of renovation while working and caring for three kids, but I'll be here to help when I can."

"I know it won't be easy, but a little at a time, right? And you have enough on your plate with your wedding and making Trey happy."

"I'll find time."

Paige needed to get to work in the studio soon. She had orders to fill. "I saw the soap and candle store downtown."

"In Harmoni?"

"Is there more than one?"

Reagan laughed. "No."

"I thought I'd approach the owner about stocking some pieces that would coordinate with what she sells. What do you think?"

"Harmoni Basinger owns the shop. She's Shaina Weber's aunt and roommate. You remember me telling you about my co-worker, Shaina, don't you?"

"I do."

"I'm guessing Harmoni will jump at the chance to sell some of your pieces, especially since she makes so many of her own products, too. Be prepared. She's pretty shy and doesn't talk much. Would you rather I asked her?"

"No, I'll do it." Paige glanced around the kitchen. "Now that you've seen the house, I'd love to get more decorating opinions from you, Bri, and Mom."

"You know I'm always ready to give my opinion."

So true.

"Trey's kitchen is terrific, but we plan to make some changes to other areas, so I'm also open to suggestions. With Bri renting my house after she graduates and starts working, she wants to finish the renovations I began, putting her own touches on it, of course."

"Looks like we need an interior decorating party." Paige pulled a face. "I won't put all this work on Dad, so I intend to hire a contractor." Once more, she was thankful for Dustin's financial contribution to her new life.

Reagan bit down on her lower lip, a clear sign she had something to say. For once, she seemed to debate saying it.

"What's wrong?"

"I know someone you might hire."

"Who?" Based on her sister's unusual reticence, Paige's stomach bottomed out. She walked down the entry hall toward the front of the house. "Nope."

"I thought you were adults."

"I'm comfortable being neighbors who don't communicate

and barely see one another, but I don't think either of us would be comfortable working together." Paige saw herself approaching Sutton and asking him to work on her house. The vision didn't end with a harmonious kumbaya.

"I've heard he's good at what he does."

Paige had heard it, too, when she'd inquired of the real estate agent. "I'm sure he is, but I can't even imagine he would take the job."

"Maybe not. Then again, it isn't his busy season, and I hear he's looking for work. You'd do him a favor, Paige. It might help to make up for . . ."

"For what?"

"For the way you left."

Reagan disapproved of what she'd done? "You're mad too, because I left?"

Her sister's shoulders relaxed. "I'm not mad. I understand why you felt you had to leave, but I can't say I agreed with it."

Had Paige really expected a ringing endorsement of her decision?

"What I don't understand is why you insisted on the secrecy. I doubt Sutton will ever consider the Hartwells as friends, but he is Trey's friend and the one who prompted Trey to confess that he loved me."

Paige's eyebrows rose. "Sutton did that?" He'd always shied away from speaking of what he termed "emotional mush." Yet he had never needed to speak the words for her to know he loved her.

"In his gruff way. The point is, he's finally reached a place where he doesn't walk away when Brianna and I are around. He isn't a bad guy, and I don't enjoy seeing him hold a grudge like I did with Lane."

For years, Reagan blamed Lane Becker for his brother's death in Afghanistan over a decade ago. She and Matt Becker had been engaged. In truth, as Reagan admitted several months ago, she blamed herself, but Lane made the perfect scapegoat for her.

"Paige, a project like this could help everyone heal from old hurts."

She made a show of studying her sister, looking her up and down. "Are you sure you're Reagan Hartwell?"

Reagan rolled her eyes. "Don't dismiss the idea."

"Why would Sutton work for me? For one thing, he hated the fact that I bought this house, and he begrudged my nice car." When Reagan opened her mouth, Paige raised a hand. "I know he and his family have struggled. I admire him for his sense of responsibility to them, but I won't let him place me in the role of the bad girl because I can afford certain things and he can't."

"You aren't the bad girl." Reagan glanced at her phone. "Oops. I'd better get back to work. Trey may be my fiancé, but he's still my boss. Come to think of it, it isn't Trey I should worry about. Ever since he made Shaina the office manager, she's grown into a tyrant."

Paige didn't take Reagan's words seriously. Few people bossed her sister around. "I'm looking forward to meeting her. Anyone who can cause Reagan Hartwell to quake in her sneakers is someone I want to get to know."

"You'll meet her on Sunday. You are coming to the meal, right?"

The Thanksgiving meal with the gang that made up her sister's friends. "I don't know. I shouldn't leave the kids."

"Mom loves spoiling them and figures it's a good way to get to know them better. Besides, she mentioned that she and Dad would like to take the kids Christmas shopping. That would be the perfect day for them to do it. Come on, say yes. Jo is eager to see you again."

Jo Ella Ledbetter—Callahan now—had been a couple of years ahead of her in school, so they weren't best buddies, but they got along well. Yet she wouldn't associate with just Jo that day. "I'll think about it."

"Don't let the past keep you from living life here, Paige."

"I won't. I'm not." Wasn't she, though? "Okay. I'll attend for a little while, but I don't want to impose on Mom and Dad too much."

"Like that could happen." Reagan laughed as she opened the front door. She looked back. "I'm glad you're home, and I really do hope you'll be happy here."

"Thanks." Once she left, Paige shut the door and sighed. "Me too."

She hobbled back into the parlor and grabbed the dustrag from the fireplace mantel to finish cleaning the empty room. Before she could swipe it across the wood, her phone chirped, and she dug it from her pocket.

"Hey, Mom."

"Oh, Paige. Thank goodness. I don't know what to do."

With the rushed words, her mother sounded on the verge of tears, prompting a pit to form in Paige's stomach. "Slow down and tell me what's wrong."

"I put Cassie down for a nap. When I returned to the kitchen to clean up from lunch, Liam and Leyla were gone. I've looked everywhere, Paige. They're not in the house or yard. I can't find them."

That pit expanded into a bubbling cauldron of fear.

Six

With lunch behind him, Sutton grabbed the blue ball cap hanging off the back of the breakfast room chair. Dillon, his oldest sibling, had given it to him last Christmas after Debra had machine-embroidered it with "Vance Farm."

Slapping the cap on his head, he adjusted its position on his way to the mudroom. "Thanks for lunch, Debra."

"Honey, you don't need to thank me every day. It's the least I can do for you." She smiled up at him from her spot at the table, tired eyes belying the cheerful smile on her face.

He glanced at his father, who shoved food in his mouth, gave his stepmother a nod, and walked out the back door.

Almost seven years ago, after giving birth to Sutton's youngest sibling, Patrick, Debra was so sick she could barely walk, but she found the strength to make them all a good meal each day. Expressing his appreciation then seemed the right thing to do, and it had stuck. If only his father said those words occasionally . . . to anyone.

Sutton rolled up the long sleeves of his shirt, ready to return to work in the mild November weather. He'd take low seventies any day over working outside in the sweltering summer heat and humidity.

Loud, childish giggling echoed from inside the barn, stopping Sutton a few yards away. All the Vance kids were in school, so who trespassed on the property?

When the giggling continued, Sutton strode through the open doorway. Sunlight streamed inside, and dust swirled in the glow. His boots kicked up more dust as he drew closer to the two children bent over to peer through the rails of Rocket's stall. Not even Sutton's brothers and sisters had the interest or temerity to touch his horse. The only kid he had let get near Rocket was Alex Newman, Lane's stepson, and only because Alex loved horses.

"First, who are you? Second, what are you doing in here?"

The boy, who looked to be about the age of Sutton's sister Ariel, shot to attention and came close to banging his head on the one-by-four rail of Rocket's stall. His eyes grew large, and he tapped the little girl next to him on the shoulder. When she spotted Sutton, her eyes expanded even larger than the boy's. Neither said anything. They just stared.

"Well? Where'd you come from?"

The boy gathered his wits and scowled. "We were just looking at the horse. We didn't touch him."

"That isn't what I asked." A slight sting to his conscience pricked Sutton when the little girl shrank behind the boy. Because children made him want to break out in hives, it didn't mean he had the right to frighten them, even when they invaded his personal space.

Rocket hung his head over the top rail, his lips nibbling at the boy's blond hair in a way that said he wanted to be friends. *Traitor.* Still, the kid's willingness to let him do it and not pull away in fright impressed Sutton.

"We came through the woods." The boy reached toward Rocket's muzzle but stopped and looked at Sutton, as if asking for permission. The horse gave it when he rubbed the side of his face on the kid's arm. "We've never been on a farm."

So they wanted a tour? "Didn't your parents teach you to stay off private property?"

The boy's jaw hardened. "My dad was a policeman."

"Then you should know better." Sutton stepped closer. "Where do you live?"

The girl, about his brother Patrick's age, wore a small orange backpack and bright yellow rubber boots. She said, "We're staying with Grandma and Grandpa Hartwell until Mom Paige says we can move into our new house. She's there now, and she won't like you being mean to us."

These kids belonged to Paige? Sutton studied the girl, then the boy, seeing no resemblance in either of them to their mother. Their light-colored hair and fair skin reflected nothing of her dark hair and olive complexion. They must take after the father. Sutton couldn't bring himself to even think the word *husband.* It left a bad taste in his brain.

But if these were Paige's kids, the cheeky child was right. She wouldn't like him getting grouchy with her children, even though they trespassed on his property.

Her kids. His gut twisted. Her kids . . . and the cop's.

Of course, they had to belong to *her.* They couldn't belong to a stranger down the street. After learning her last name was now Matthews, he should have anticipated children. Marrying and having kids had been her greatest dream. That dream had put an end to their future together.

But Mom Paige? And something the boy said struck him. His dad *was* a cop? He wasn't any longer? Maybe with the move, he quit whatever force he'd worked for in Georgia to start over doing something else here.

Sutton rubbed the back of his neck. "Let's go."

"Where?"

The boy crossed his arms, the rebellion on his face bringing a faint smile to Sutton's. How had mild-mannered and cheerful Paige raised two such sassy kids? Again, it must be the father's influence.

"I'll take you to your mom." And tell her to keep a closer eye on them. He turned to leave the barn, waving his arm to encourage the trespassers to follow him.

"She's not our mom."

Sutton stopped dead in his tracks. As slow as a sloth, he turned.

The little girl tugged on her brother's shirt and nearly shouted, "What did you say to him, Liam?"

The boy faced her. "I told him Aunt Paige wasn't our mom."

"But she is. She's Mom Paige."

"Come on, Leyla. Let's get out of here."

Liam took his sister's hand. With a last look of longing at Rocket, he hiked past Sutton, dragging his sister behind him. Sutton curled his fingers, preventing himself from reaching out and pulling a dead leaf from Leyla's hair. Why had Liam needed to repeat what he'd said? And why did the boy insist they weren't Paige's children?

He knew where to find the answers to those questions. "Get in the truck. I'll drive you to the house."

"No, thanks. We can walk."

"That wasn't an offer, kid."

Liam glared at him. Too bad. He refused to be the one who lost Paige's kids.

Paige ended the call with her mom and stood in the middle of the parlor, where she'd paced the floor while listening to the news that Leyla and Liam had wandered away from the house. She rubbed a hand over her forehead, digging deep, as she pondered her next move. "Where could they be?"

She would call the police, then go to her parents' house for the search. No, she would call 911 as she drove to the house.

A vehicle door slammed, and she ran to the parlor's front window to find Sutton standing next to his truck. She had no time to deal with him right now.

Before she reached the door to tell him so, it opened, and Liam stalked inside, a black expression marring his face. Leyla followed him.

Seeing them safe, though, Paige released a heavy, relieved breath. "Where have you two been? You've had your grandmother and me worried sick!"

Leyla grabbed her around the legs in a hug. "Sorry, Mom Paige. We wanted to see the horse."

She raised her daughter's chin, noting she didn't wear her hearing aids. After pulling a leaf from Leyla's hair, she asked, "What horse?"

"Mine." Sutton stepped inside and leaned against the door frame. "I found them in my barn with my roping horse. They'd cut through the woods." He paused, the smirk on his face bringing heat to hers. "I think you know the path I mean."

She wouldn't shrink from the challenging gleam. "I'm surprised it's still there."

"A little rough with no use for fifteen years, but yeah, it's there."

"You know this guy?"

Paige startled at Liam's intrusion into her past. "Mr. Vance and I grew up together. We were neighbors, which you know since you cut through the woods."

"He isn't very nice." Leyla glowered at Sutton.

Crouching in front of her daughter, Paige caught Leyla's eye. "Can you blame him? You trespassed on his property. Not to mention, you ran off without telling your grandmother. She's been frantic. We both have." Paige pulled out her phone to let her mom know the kids were back home and fine.

"I'm sorry." Leyla peered at her with those soulful blue eyes that could melt Paige's heart.

Paige waited for Liam to apologize but didn't hold her breath as he sat on the stairs to the second floor, pouting. "Go get something to drink. I brought some bottles of water. They're in the cooler in the kitchen."

Leyla ran in that direction, the ever-present backpack flopping. The sound of the yellow rubber boots clomping on the wood floor followed her.

Liam rose from the stairs as if he were an old man. He looked from her to Sutton and back to her. Then he rounded the newel post, ambled down the hall, and disappeared into the kitchen.

She turned to Sutton and pasted on a smile she didn't feel. Being in his presence, being the target of those intense brown eyes . . . She could say it was harder than she'd imagined, but she had a pretty good imagination.

Paige cleared her throat. "Thanks for bringing them back. I'd just gotten off the phone with Mom, who panicked because they disappeared. In fact, let me call her now."

Once she hung up with her relieved mother, Paige found Sutton staring at her. The smirk had fallen from his face, replaced by disapproval. "What?"

"That's it? Go get some water?"

"What did you expect me to do? Send them to bed with nothing to eat or drink? Maybe lock them in the closet?" She shook her head. "I'm sorry. I shouldn't snap at you. I was worried."

"Seems like a good reason to impress on them not to run off."

Like mother, like children? Maybe she was being too sensitive.

He remained at the door but glanced toward the kitchen. "Looks like you got the kids you wanted."

"I did."

"Except the boy—"

"Liam."

"Liam said you're not their mother."

Another round of heat burned Paige's face and neck. Though she would have preferred to explain in her own time, perhaps the truth would help them feel more at ease in one another's presence. After all, Sutton's newfound knowledge of her motherhood put a period to the past. They could start over as friends, both assured their differences meant nothing else would come of it.

"Let's go in here." Paige led Sutton into the parlor and slid the pocket doors shut. She turned around and nearly ran into him, not expecting him to be standing so close. She sidestepped to put some space between them. "They're adopted. Their biological mother was my best friend. She died of cancer. Their father—"

"The cop?"

Paige nodded. "He died shortly before in the line of duty. The two oldest have gone through too much pain in their brief lives. Liam has taken the changes the hardest. He refuses to acknowledge that I'm his parent."

"You said the two oldest. How many are there?"

"You've met Liam and Leyla. Cassie is three."

Sutton winced, but she couldn't tell if it came from the number of children in her care or his ability to relate to them over their shared parental losses at such young ages.

A heart of gold used to beat under that muscular exterior—unrefined gold dulled by the experiences of life. If that precious heart didn't still exist, Sutton would have left the farm—left his family—long ago and not looked back.

"What about your husband? If he isn't their father, who is he? You didn't leave here with the name Paige Matthews."

She cocked her head at his use of her married name until she remembered the way the nurse at the clinic called to her. "Dustin is no longer in our lives."

His jaw tightened. "Let me guess. You ran out on him, too."

Paige sucked in a breath. She hated being divorced, but Dustin had made his choice after she couldn't give him what he wanted. Just as she had run out after Sutton couldn't give her what she wanted? How immature and selfish she had been to disappear from his life as she had.

It's probable she'd reaped what she'd sown. And maybe Sutton's heart of gold wasn't so pure.

He stuffed his hands in his pockets and shifted his feet. "I didn't mean to say that out loud."

"I don't blame you for expressing your unhappiness with me, Sutton." Even though the snark hurt. "I understand it, and I deserve it." Before he could expound on that unhappiness, she pushed open the pocket doors. "Thanks again for seeing them home."

His stiff jaw worked back and forth, as though he wanted to say more but mulled over whether it was a good idea. It wasn't.

He walked out the front door, and Paige watched as his long legs and brisk, resolute pace carried him to his truck. He slammed the door and backed out of the driveway.

A question had persisted in her mind since seeing him on Saturday. In running back to Hidden Veil, had a part of her thought to run back to Sutton?

If so, the joke was on her.

Seven

Paige entered her parents' kitchen behind Leyla and Liam. After Sutton left, they drove the short distance in silence, Paige worn down mentally and emotionally.

"Mommy." Cassie ran into her arms, re-energizing her.

"Hey, sweetie. Have you been a good girl?"

"I'm always a good girl."

Paige squeezed her in a tight hug. "Yes, you are."

The house smelled like an Italian restaurant, and a stab of guilt immobilized Paige. She'd relied too much on her parents these past few days.

"Mom, I'm so sorry about today. I can't tell you how grateful I am for all you and Dad have done. Now and in the past."

"You know we'll always help you. We're happy to have all our girls and our grandchildren home."

Liam marched into the den without a word. Leyla trailed behind. Paige's mother watched them go. "They scared me to death."

"Me too. I can't believe they found their way to the Vance farm."

"Why not? You blazed the path yourself."

Paige drew back. "You knew?"

"Oh, please. You'd think there aren't windows in this house." Her mother sighed. "I'm sure Sutton had his say when he dropped them off."

"He wasn't happy." Mostly with her.

Leyla's multi-decibel scream jolted Paige's mom. Paige had gotten used to it, but her parents jumped each time.

"Please don't take this wrong, honey, but your children need boundaries."

Boundaries? "Don't worry, I've told them they're never to go back to the farm."

"I'm not talking about physical boundaries, Paige. Although after today, it's clear they need those too. I'm talking about discipline and setting guidelines for them to follow."

"Is this about Liam and Leyla's disappearance?"

"That's one example. You just heard another."

"Mom, it isn't Leyla's fault that she can't hear well and compensates with a loud voice."

"It is when she refuses to wear the hearing aids after you've told her over and over to put them in her ears. You waited a long time to be a mother, but honey, there's more to motherhood than providing children with hugs and a roof over their heads. You do them and yourself no favors by letting them act as they please and treat you with a lack of respect."

With her mother's warning, Paige saw herself as a child again, lectured over an error she'd committed.

Mom squeezed her arm. "Dad will be home soon, and we'll be ready to eat supper."

On the heels of Sutton's disapproval of her parenting, Paige stood in the middle of the breakfast room floor, holding Cassie and mulling over her mother's criticism. She concluded that, like

Sutton, her mother didn't understand all Liam and Leyla had gone through. If they did, they would realize children needed time to adjust to a new parent and a new life.

It would all be fine. Eventually.

She prayed so, anyway.

The double doors whooshed open, and Sutton followed Dillon into the discount store. Christmas music blared from the speakers in the ceiling, and Sutton grimaced at the sound. Who needed a reminder of the upcoming holiday?

Christmas meant gifts, and gifts meant spending money the Vances had little of to spare. Why should they go broke celebrating a god they didn't worship?

Sutton grabbed a cart—of course, one with a bouncing wheel. He'd bet Paige had no problem buying gifts for her children. Three children. She had gotten the very thing she'd left him for—motherhood.

He shut down that topic running through his head. He hadn't thought of Paige since she threw him out of her house on Tuesday. He hadn't thought of her much anyway.

Okay, his many thoughts of her hadn't been charitable. Truth was, what he'd said to her kept popping into his head. *He* hadn't been charitable.

They'd had their time, and it didn't work. End of story. *Get over it, Vance. Get over her and concentrate on what you're doing.*

Sutton's brother had sprouted at least two inches over the summer and filled out. Debra had altered his clothes as best she could, but there were some things she couldn't alter.

"Why not go to the mall? They have everything I want." His brother grinned at a girl about his own age, who returned the grin.

Sutton pushed the cart toward the men's section. *Pa-plunk. Pa-plunk. Pa-plunk.* "This place has everything you need." And it was cheaper here.

Paige would probably think nothing of shopping for her kids at the most expensive stores in the mall.

"But—"

"I'm losing time from work, Dillon, but I can turn this cart around and you can come back later with your mom."

"*Eww.* No way. She wants me to buy new underwear. I don't want someone I know to see me buying underwear with my mom."

"Then let's get this over with." And save as much money as possible.

Sutton shoved the cart down the aisle, picking up the pace. Somehow, he'd find a well-paying construction job before the end of the year, something to provide for the tractor payment and a few of their regular expenses.

His thoughts continued to spin around Paige and his visit to her house. She couldn't call it a home until she hired someone to get the place in shape. Had she contracted with anyone for her renovation? He'd only seen the front portion of the interior but guessed it was the type of major project he needed.

His feet hit the brakes. No, he'd spend months in her presence if he accepted the job.

And why would she hire him in the first place, given the way he talked to her yesterday? Even if she did, she would likely fire him before he completed one room. Most likely for good reason.

He couldn't keep his mouth shut.

Dillon rushed to a rack and grabbed a tee shirt, its front emblazoned with the image of some musician—based on the guitar—that Sutton had never heard of.

Peering in a nearby mirror, Dillon held it against his body. "This is awesome." He tossed it into the cart.

Sutton picked it up and put it back on the rack. "If I let you bring that home, Debra would have both our heads. You're here to buy school clothes."

"That is what we wear to school these days. Man, you are ancient."

Dillon reached for the shirt, but Sutton grabbed his wrist. "No." He wasn't but fifteen years older than his brother, but maybe he was old before his time, even though he'd worn similar clothing at Dillon's age. He glanced at the shirt. Fifteen years and getting older by the second. "If you want it, ask your mom first."

"You know, she is *your* mom, too." His brother backed off, disgust spoiling what the girls in Dillon's circle might see as a cute face. "Why don't you call her that? We're a family—a team—but you don't act like a team player any more than Dad does."

"And you do? When have you done chores around the farm without me dragging you outside, kicking and screaming like a two-year-old?"

"That's what happens when you treat me like a two-year-old."

"I don't do that." Sutton glanced up to find a woman and her child watching them. He'd better lower his voice before they were both kicked out of the store.

"Then why don't you give me chores that mean something,

instead of telling me to pick weeds or muck Rocket's stall? Let me run the equipment and the tractor or drive the truck during harvest or something. I have my license, you know."

He was too young. Or was he? Sutton thought back. When had he started doing those jobs?

At fourteen.

Dad had fallen far enough into the bottle by then that, had Sutton not intervened, they would have found themselves on the street with the Vance farmstead—the one that had passed from generation to generation—sold to a stranger.

Sutton conceded Dillon's point. Even he hadn't hopped on a tractor seat instinctively knowing what to do. Before his mom passed, he had joined Dad in the fields. Sutton had watched, fascinated by the equipment around the farm, soaking it all in. He hadn't known what a blessing that would be for them.

A blessing? He'd hung around Lane too long. Now, he was using Christian-speak.

"Look, Dillon, everyone starts at the bottom and gradually builds responsibility and skill."

"That's what I'm talking about. I've been at the bottom. You're my big brother. Teach me to build my skills. I want to be a farmer."

"Since when?"

"Since a long time ago. You just don't listen."

Dad drove the truck during harvest. Tried, anyway. Inevitably, Sutton would hire someone to take his place or risk having his father plow through the corn rows rather than drive alongside them.

"I guess you can help me harvest the winter wheat when the time comes."

"I guess I can." Dillon grabbed a plain blue, long-sleeved tee shirt off a sales rack, a place Sutton would not have expected him to look. "This will work."

For the next hour, Sutton followed his brother around the store, letting him shop and inserting his opinion only when Dillon tossed something too outrageous or expensive into the cart. The kid rattled on about school—friends and teachers and classes. Graduation in the spring. The two of them compared notes on teachers they'd had in common. Overall, the time passed quickly . . . and not too unpleasantly. When had his brother turned into a confident young adult rather than a needy child?

They reached the checkout line and began emptying the cart.

"Hey, Sutton."

He looked up. Nicole Overbey flashed him a flirty smile from her place at the cash register. Honey blonde hair. Gorgeous face. Legs that reached the moon. His lips curved, remembering their past dates. What he couldn't recall was the reason they had stopped dating. Oh, yeah. She got engaged.

"Hey, Nicole. I didn't know you worked here."

"Just started a few months ago. How've you been? I have really missed seeing you." As she spoke, she passed UPC tags over the scanner for each piece of clothing, her gaze never leaving his face. "We should get together sometime."

As the scanner beeped, Sutton glanced at her ring finger. Bare. "Where's your husband?"

"I called it off before the wedding. He was a jerk. He was nothing like you." She stopped scanning and leaned forward over the conveyor belt, showing off more than her skill at ringing up products without looking at them. "What do you say? I have nothing going on this weekend."

Sutton stood mute. At any other time, he wouldn't have

hesitated to say yes. He would have met her halfway over the belt and flirted for a while.

He could ask her to the dinner on Sunday, but Paige might—

Why worry about Paige? Sure, she was back in town. It didn't mean his love life had to suffer. If he were smart, he'd relegate their time as a couple to the past. Nicole was the now. Plus, he'd told himself he'd find someone to take to Sunday's gathering.

He leaned in. "I'm getting together with some friends this weekend. You remember Lane Becker and the others from the lake party last summer?"

The sparkle in her luminous blue eyes dimmed a little. "Sure. If you're busy—"

"We're having an early Thanksgiving dinner at Jo E's Java Sunday afternoon. Want to go?"

Those eyes glowed again, and her cheeks rose with a bright smile. "Of course."

"I'll call you tonight with the details."

"Okay. You still have my number?"

"Never deleted it."

Sutton paid for Dillon's purchases and made his brother carry them to the truck. Dillon climbed in, snickering from his spot in the passenger seat.

"What's your problem?"

His brother's voice rose into a falsetto. "You still have my number?" He deepened his voice. "Never deleted it." The kid broke into laughter. "Forget the farm. I'll go with you on Sunday. You can teach me more about getting girls."

Sutton shoved Dillon's shoulder. "Shut up." But he fought to contain a grin.

They passed the Johnson house on the way to the farm. A moving van took up a good portion of the front yard and emphasized Sutton's loss. The place belonged to Paige now . . . for however long she stayed.

Dillon leaned across the truck seat to peer out the driver's side window. "I'd heard we had new neighbors."

"Yeah."

"It's about time somebody bought that house. It was getting to be an eyesore."

Like the Vance farmhouse before Sutton fixed it up.

"I wonder if they have a girl my age." Dillon chuckled. "I'd like to try that 'I'm getting together with some friends this weekend' line."

Trey called last night to give Sutton a heads up—Paige would be at Jo's on Sunday. He tried to imagine her reaction when he walked into the coffee shop with the beautiful Nicole at his side. But rather than the expected sense of gloating, a sense of loss consumed him.

Eight

Paige entered Jo E's Java with the buttermilk pie she'd prepared in the old oven, praying the entire time that the thermostat in the appliance still worked correctly.

Couples who laughed and conversed—good friends enjoying one another—filled the coffee shop's front room. Paige felt like a fish out of water. Some people she knew but hadn't seen in years. Others she had never met.

The smell of coffee must permeate the interior on a normal day. Today, roasted turkey dominated the other aromas in the room.

She scanned the space for Reagan and Trey or Brianna and her date but didn't see them. No sign of Sutton either. Her sisters had warned her he would be here, though.

This morning's sermon involving forgiveness convinced Paige she should apologize for ushering him out of her house last week. She would wait to see how well he behaved before deciding whether to do it today.

"Paige!" Jo waddled toward her, looking rosy-cheeked, blissful, and ready to pop from her pregnancy.

For a moment, Paige battled a sudden spark of envy but

shook it off. "Congratulations."

"Thanks. I'm so glad you came."

"So am I. I'm sorry I haven't been by since the move, but I'm still getting organized."

Boxes and miscellaneous furniture sat in the dining room and in the office/guest room, waiting to be unpacked. So far, she'd only set up the bedroom furniture. After all, they needed to sleep on something other than the floors that begged to be refinished.

"Moves are hectic."

"You look wonderful and happy. I am surprised you agreed to host this dinner. When are you due?"

"Two weeks." Jo rested a hand on her swollen middle. "Kyle thought I should skip it this year, but this is only our second get-together at Thanksgiving, and I was determined not to miss it. I didn't do much, just set the tables after Kyle arranged them in one long row."

Paige guessed she had done more than that. Kyle had lined five four-seater tables across the middle of the room. Another, longer table at the far end sat six people. Place settings for sixteen covered colorful fall mats. Centerpieces highlighted six-inch pillar candles with dried mums, asters, and pansies embedded on top. "It's spectacular."

Her gaze took in the cozy décor of the coffee shop—its warm wood and soft lighting. "The whole place is wonderful . . . so un-Hidden Veil-like."

They both laughed.

"Where are your children?"

"Shopping with my parents."

"I'm sure they love having you all back. You've noticed that much of the town is different since you left?"

"I've heard reports from family over the years, but yes, it isn't the same antiquated hometown." Still cozy, but trendier. Sort of.

Jo pointed to the dessert. "Would you like me to take that?"

Paige handed over the pie. "Thanks."

"I'll put this in the kitchen for later. I doubt you've met everyone, so I'll be back in a minute to introduce you." She disappeared through the doorway behind the counter.

At a tap on her shoulder, Paige turned to find Lane Becker behind her, standing next to a petite and pretty blonde.

"It's good to see you, Paige."

"Lane." She hugged him. "I'm happy to see you, too."

He wrapped his arm around the woman's waist and pulled her closer to him. "I'd like you to meet my wife, Macie."

"It's nice to meet you." Paige eyed the woman to see if she'd made the wrong move in hugging Lane, but Macie's smile put her at ease.

"You too. Lane said you had an accident soon after you arrived. Are you okay?"

Had one of her sisters told Lane? Or was it Sutton? The guys had always been tight.

She smiled. "The ankle was sore for a couple of days, but the stitches in my leg came out last Tuesday, so I'm back to normal."

"Good. I understand you have a son about the same age as our Alex. We should get them together."

Grateful for Macie's friendly invitation, Paige said, "I'm sure Liam would love it. For the past week, he's only had his little sisters to keep him company."

"Then we'll do it. Does Liam like horses?"

"For days, he's raved about Sutton's horse."

The couple exchanged a look, then Lane asked, "Sutton let

him near Rocket?"

Why had she brought that up? The Beckers must wonder how much contact she'd had with Sutton. "Not exactly. Liam and Leyla—"

"They snuck onto the farm last week." Sutton joined them. At his side stood a gorgeous younger woman.

Paige's sisters hadn't mentioned that Sutton was seeing someone. She caught herself studying his date. The woman's dark roots screamed that the blonde color came from a box. The sight brought Paige shameful satisfaction.

"I found them in my barn and returned them to their proper place."

Paige pasted on a smile that didn't brighten the hollow spot inside her. He acted as though her children had drawn graffiti on the horse's coat.

Before Paige could respond, Lane turned to the fake blonde. "We didn't expect you, Nicole." He jerked when Macie elbowed him in the ribs. "Uh . . . But we're glad you're here."

"Come meet my husband, Paige." Jo scowled, first at Sutton, then Lane. She led Paige away from the others to a tall man by the counter. "Kyle, this is Paige Hartwell. She's—"

"It's Matthews."

Jo appeared confused, then shook her head. "I'm sorry. I forgot. Reagan said you had married." She tapped the side of her head. "Pregnancy brain."

Jo's husband stepped forward. "It's a pleasure, Paige. I've heard a lot about you."

It seemed she was the talk of the town. She was sure Reagan and Brianna were the prime sources. Paige's sisters had kept her secrets for years, so what if they gave out information now that Paige had returned? It was nothing Paige herself wouldn't mention. "All good, I hope."

"All good."

She eyed the tall guy with neat blond hair almost to his shoulders. "I understand you're a musician."

"Struggling, but yes. These days, I write Christian country music."

They spoke for a couple of minutes, then Jo introduced her to the others. Shaina Weber mentioned that Reagan and Trey would be late. An emergency had come up at the vet clinic. A moment later, Shaina shot out of her seat when the door opened and Brianna and her date, Tucker, walked in.

The potluck's main dishes covered a folding table against one wall. Paige's mouth watered at the sight of casseroles, vegetables, and sliced turkey. She'd been so busy during the past week—cleaning, removing wallpaper, painting—that she had eaten little.

After Kyle's prayer, everyone filled their plates and carried them to the tables. Since the only other single person in attendance was Harmoni Basinger, Paige took a seat next to her—at the opposite end of the line of tables from Sutton and his blonde, giggly girlfriend. Reagan and Trey sat across from Paige, with Bri and Tucker sitting across from Jo and Kyle.

Paige leaned to the side to strike up a conversation with Harmoni, but it was like slogging uphill in concrete boots. Not that Harmoni was unfriendly, but her obvious shyness made it difficult to carry on a prolonged chat. How did the woman run a business?

Though Harmoni may not say much, Paige noticed her sneaking peeks down the row. At Devyn McCall or Trey's brother Kaine? She wasn't certain. Maybe few saw the potential in Harmoni, but Paige believed the woman with her cute pixie cut and oval face would dazzle if she allowed herself to relax and smile more often.

Jo sat on Paige's other side. "Did Harmoni tell you she made the candles for the tables?"

Paige turned to Harmoni, not much older than her niece, Shaina. "No. They're beautiful and smell wonderful. I'm a potter, and I'll be getting back to work shortly."

Harmoni's eyes widened. "You're Paige from The Potter's Hand. When you walked in, I told Shaina you looked familiar. I went to your website recently and saw your photo. Your work is incredible. Artistic yet functional. I plan to place an order for some of your candlesticks."

While the praise warmed her heart, it was the perfect opportunity to broach a business topic. "How sweet. I'm grateful. It also makes it easier to ask you—"

"Would you consider selling some of your pieces in my shop?"

Paige grinned at their mutual line of thought. "Yes, I would."

Harmoni spoke for what must have been five minutes about her work, Paige's work, and ideas to collaborate on local marketing. Reagan stopped eating and gaped at the talkative woman. Who would have guessed their common artistic endeavors would bring out Harmoni's chatty side?

The meal passed quickly as Paige did her best to keep up with conversations and questions addressed to her. When she wasn't talking or eating, she watched friendship in action. The dinner was a touching occasion. Everyone had accepted her today, just as they had accepted the dates of those in their circle, but she had earned no part in that circle. Not really. Not yet.

Raucous laughter at the other end of the table drew Paige's attention. Seated on the opposite side, Sutton lounged in his chair, resting his arm along the back of his cackling date's chair. Paige only caught snatches of conversation, but it sounded as though he told a story about one of his siblings. Obviously, it was amusing, but she knew his opinion about children well enough to bet it wasn't flattering.

Off and on during the meal, her gaze slipped to him. No denying that his physical maturity attracted notice. He looked relaxed, as if her presence didn't matter.

He must have sensed her interest, because he stopped talking, and his eyes caught hers. She tried to look away, to pretend someone else held her interest, but she couldn't move. His stare spoke of regret and longing. And a question? Or maybe he was simply a mirror reflecting her own longing, desire, and confusion.

Before she could decide which was true, he broke the connection and smiled at the woman snuggling closer to him. Yet the smile he gave Nicole never moved farther north than his mouth.

Questions broke into Paige's thoughts like a battering ram. What if he still had feelings for her? Could they turn back time and try again? Would she want to? Even if she did, their success as a couple required Sutton to see her children as a blessing and not trespassers into his life. Convincing him to become a father had proved an impossible mission years ago. What made her think he would accept her children as his own, especially when *she* barely managed her role as their mother?

Nope. She wouldn't attempt it and risk failure, putting the kids through yet another loss.

"Have you started the house renovation yet, Paige?"

She turned to answer Kyle's question. "I'm looking for a contractor. I've called a couple of people, but our schedules didn't work out."

Reagan cleared her throat in a wordless *I told you who to hire.*

"I'm sure Sutton could do the job for you. He helped us renovate our kitchen. You're pleased, aren't you, Jo?"

Jo's cheeks warmed. "Yes."

Paige didn't miss her silent appeal to her husband to drop the subject. He obviously understood, because he finished the last of his mashed potatoes smothered in gravy without saying another word.

Would it be so bad to hire Sutton? From all she'd heard, he did excellent work. Besides, it meant nothing more than an employer/employee relationship.

Paige glanced down the line of tables again and restrained the urge to wrinkle her nose at the gaze of adoration the phony blonde aimed at Sutton. Delight rippled through her when his smile reflected more appeasement than admiration toward his date.

She tamped down that delight. *A working relationship, Paige. Nothing more.*

After dessert and cleanup, people gradually left the coffee shop. Before she lost her nerve and Sutton disappeared, Paige walked up to him. "Do you have a minute? I'd like to ask you something."

He hesitated, then told Nicole, "I'll be back."

Paige led Sutton to the other side of the room. "I need a skilled contractor, and I've been told you're the man to hire."

He said nothing for a moment, but Paige saw temptation in his expression. Then he stiffened, his lips drawn into a stubborn line. "Not available." He turned to walk away.

"That isn't what I've heard." As soon as the blunt words left her mouth, she regretted them.

He froze, then rotated to face her, his hardened expression causing her to retreat a step. Maybe she shouldn't hire him. "What exactly have you heard?"

Paige exhaled a breath. "Only that you're looking for work." On top of Reagan's remark last week, she had stopped by the hardware store the other day and noticed the card Sutton had tacked to the bulletin board, and Mr. Goodwin mentioned Sutton's eagerness to find construction jobs. "I'm looking for someone to renovate portions of my house. Provided we can work out satisfactory financial details, I'm offering you the job."

"*Your* house." Sutton breathed a humorless chuckle. "The answer is no, Paige." He turned his back on her and walked away. Within seconds, he'd wrapped an arm around Blondie and exited the coffee shop.

She hadn't really expected him to accept, had she?

Reagan approached. "What happened?"

"I did as you suggested and tried to hire him. He turned me down." Once again, she got the idea that he resented her purchase of the Johnson property. "Reagan, do you know if Sutton has ever shown an interest in buying the house I'm in?"

"Not that I recall. Lane would probably know. Why?"

The last person she would ask would be Sutton's best friend. Actually, the last person would be Sutton. "I just thought, since it's so close to the farm . . ."

"I don't think anyone knew it was for sale."

"It wasn't until I made my offer."

If Sutton had wanted to buy the house, had she offended him with her proposal?

Nine

After entering the kitchen Thanksgiving morning, Sutton headed straight to the coffeepot on the counter for some fresh-brewed caffeine. He filled his insulated mug, and the warmth from the steam moistened his face.

Debra sat at the breakfast table, her eyes glassy and red. He took his cup and slid into the chair next to her. "What has Dad done this time?"

She rubbed her eyes with the heels of her hands and passed him a sheet of paper he recognized as a credit card bill. "Joel pulled this from the mailbox yesterday."

Sutton skipped to the total at the bottom. His loud and coarse response drew a wince from Debra. Only two people had access to the farm's credit card. Sutton and his father, so it was a no-brainer to guess who racked up almost eight hundred and fifty dollars in charges.

"Your dad bought Christmas gifts."

Along with liquor at the ABC store.

"Expensive gifts. How drunk was he when he did this?" Sutton tightened his fist, crushing the paper. His father's drinking had gotten worse over the past two or three years. It had to stop before they ended up in the proverbial poorhouse and he rested in a grave. "Where is he?"

"In bed." She coughed and pushed out of the chair. "Please don't lose your temper with him, Sutton. He meant well."

"Those good intentions have put us in the red. We agreed to draw names, with one gift per person. How are we supposed to pay our bills, Debra, if he keeps going out and spending money like he has it?"

Sutton marched to the sink. He stared out the window at the far tree line and the limbs as bare as his future. He should leave. Right now. Pack his bags, hit the road, and not look back. He would walk away from the farm, his family's financial problems, and a life that wasn't his own. If he stayed, he'd look back in twenty years and wonder what he'd accomplished. Probably nothing of importance.

Debra inhaled a labored breath and coughed several times, taxing her breathing.

He ran a hand down his face to the bottom tip of his beard—the one he would shave off before the wedding—striving to get himself under control. This wasn't Debra's fault, and he hadn't meant to take it out on her. It only added more stress and could send her to the hospital, the last thing they all needed. And he couldn't lay on her the responsibility of providing for the family.

"Do you want your nebulizer?"

She reached into a pocket in her pants and pulled out an inhaler. "This will do for now." She wrapped her mouth around it and pressed the plunger, inhaling the medicine.

"Why don't you head upstairs and lie down?"

She offered him a slight smile. "I just got up. Besides, it's Thanksgiving. I have things to do."

"You don't need to bear all the responsibility. Let the kids make the meal." He had five siblings. Together, they could knock out edible food. He hoped. His words reminded him of his conversation with Dillon at the store. "Except Dillon. He can help me."

"He looks up to you, you know."

Dillon looked up to him? He doubted it. That meant showing him respect, something none of his siblings knew how to do.

Except for that day of shopping for Dillon's clothes. The time he'd dreaded had turned into an unanticipated time of relaxed contentment.

He pressed the top onto his mug and carried it toward the back door. "Let Dillon know I expect to see him outside in twenty minutes."

In the meantime, he'd mull over how to pay both the tractor payment and the credit card bill without filing for bankruptcy.

On the way to the barn, his phone buzzed, and he dug it out of his pocket. *Nicole.* He read and then ignored the text, shoving the phone into the back pocket of his jeans. He regretted taking her with him to the Thanksgiving get-together. She hadn't left him alone since.

In a way, it had been worth it to see Paige's face when she spotted his date. She choked as though she'd swallowed a fly but gathered herself and laid on the charm. His pleasure was short-lived, though, since he spent too much time the rest of the afternoon casting subtle glances in Paige's direction. Would he ever get over her?

Based on the depth of his sense of loss the day he pulled the wood slat from the wall of the barn, the one with their initials carved into it—PH+SV—he figured the answer was a hard no.

He still felt the rough, dried wood on his fingertips as he'd traced the letters. He couldn't bring himself to toss the childhood relic onto the pile to be burned in the den's wood stove. Instead, he hid it in a corner of the hayloft with the carving facing the wall.

Thinking of Sunday brought to mind Paige's offer to hire him. Work for her? Why not just slap his face? Renovating that house would achieve the same insulting effect.

He stuffed a section of hay in the hayrack in the corner of Rocket's stall and filled the water bucket with fresh water. Afterward, he opened the door that led to the corral to give his horse fresh air and exercise.

All the while, his thoughts returned to Paige's offer. He'd gotten a couple of minor jobs from his card on the hardware store's bulletin board. The net he received might pay the credit card bill, but the tractor payment remained.

Sutton visited Paige's website after hearing Harmoni gush about the quality of her work on Sunday—more words than he'd ever heard the woman say. It surprised him to discover Paige was a potter. Well, it did, and it didn't. He'd always known she was artistic, but the awards she'd garnered for her work showed how much he'd underestimated her talent. She even had her own online shop.

Still, no one bought a house like that without intending to update it. For a contractor, even a part-time one, it provided an opportunity for a decent payout. He could work well into the spring before completing the project and not worry about tractor and credit card payments.

But could he work for Paige day-in and day-out?

Sutton shut his eyes and focused his mind on recalling the pages of her website. Then, there was the successful business. The car worth ten of his trucks. The pricey clothes worn by her and her kids.

He nodded and opened his eyes. It might work. As long as he remained focused on their differences. He had no other choice. And her nearness might prove his memories of her were just that . . . memories with no connection to the people each of them were today.

And if those remembrances turned into present-day reality? He'd remind himself that what he could provide would never satisfy her.

Dillon ambled into the barn. "What are we doing this morning? Can I drive the tractor?"

"No. While I'm gone, you can muck Rocket's stall and clean out the chicken coop."

Dillon's jaw fell. "You promised."

"Not today." Sutton pulled the truck keys from his pocket as he walked toward the barn door and his fate.

"Where are you going?"

"To run an errand."

Man, this was gonna hurt.

The jarring, garbled sound of Paige's doorbell reminded her to replace it with one that provided video.

She set her coffee cup on the laminate kitchen counter—something else she couldn't wait to replace—and glanced at her smartwatch. A little after eight? Who on earth would ring her doorbell this early on a holiday?

She yawned as she shuffled down the hall and opened the front door. Seeing her visitor, her jaw dropped even lower.

"Sutton?"

"The doorbell needs fixing."

She scowled. "Tell me something I don't know."

A hint of a smirk tilted his mouth. "Is Perky Paige always this grouchy in the morning?"

"Only when other grouchy people interrupt my gradual wake-up time." She stifled the groan working its way into her throat and stopped herself from glancing down at the pajama pants she wore. Leyla insisted she buy the pair with the romping unicorns during a recent shopping trip. Why call more attention to them? "What are you doing here?"

He stood on her porch, holding a zippered portfolio and fidgeting with his keys until she wanted to reach out and snatch them from him. "Can we talk?"

So far, talking had produced nothing but hard feelings between them. Even so, she had prayed that would change. Maybe her prayer was being answered? "Sure. Come in." She shut the door behind him. "Coffee?"

"No, thanks. This isn't a social call." Sutton rubbed his forehead. "I mean, uh, I want to talk business."

Business? Did this mean he'd changed his mind and would complete her renovation? After his refusal on Sunday, she'd put her efforts into preparing the studio and doing what minor repairs she could do herself around the house. She hadn't looked for another contractor yet.

Now that he was here, though, second thoughts rush through her. She may have erred in her rash decision to hire him on Sunday. Could they get along for the months it would take to finish the job, or would their relationship deteriorate even more than it had before she returned to Hidden Veil?

"Well, if we're talking business this early in the morning, I need my coffee." She passed him on her way to the kitchen. He followed, which was fine. They may as well start their discussion in the room requiring the most work. Once he saw it, he might change his mind. Again.

Paige picked up a coffee pod from a wire basket and held it up. "Are you sure? It's hazelnut."

His brow creased. "I left my cup in the barn earlier."

With effort, she tugged open a sticking cabinet door and grabbed a mug. She set it on the base of the coffeemaker, then popped in the pod and hit the brew button. In moments, steam rose as liquid filled the green-glazed mug. The aroma of fresh hazelnut coffee made her want to sigh with pleasure. She handed him the mug and picked up her own.

Rather than drink the coffee, he did a 360-degree study of the cup. "One of yours?"

"Yes. I sell a lot of them in specialty stores and through my online shop."

"Nice work."

The sincerity of his compliment warmed Paige. As long as they both kept things professional, they could get along. "Thanks. I'll need to get back to that work soon." Curious or anxious—or both—she said, "Since you're here with that," she pointed to the portfolio, "I guess you've changed your mind about the renovation."

He shrugged. "I figured it wouldn't hurt for us to talk about your plans."

She waved an arm. "As you can see, the kitchen is horrible and the priority room. I'll also want to update the first-floor bathroom, build a closet and master bathroom upstairs, and refinish all the hardwood floors."

Sutton walked around the room. He examined the condition

of the walls, ceiling, flooring, and cabinets. "What did you have in mind here?"

"I want a modern kitchen without destroying the historic farmhouse feel."

"Are you keeping the wainscoting on the walls?"

"Not this. I thought a tall board and batten style on this wall and this one." She pointed out the two walls that lent themselves to the design. "What do you think about a backsplash of white subway tiles to keep the vintage look?"

He glanced around the room as though trying to picture it. "Sure. They were popular in the 1920s. Still are today."

The wistful quality in his voice and the admiration in his eyes stunned Paige. Did he still see the house as they had envisioned it together? Or had he, as she suspected, hoped to buy the house for himself and researched its renovation?

Paige had hired a designer to draw plans to fit her vision for this room, an updated version of their teenage discussions, and her bedroom. She would give them to him if—once—they worked out the employment details.

"What about the hardwood flooring in here? I'm surprised no one put down vinyl in the past."

"I won't be the first to do it. But you can see the wood needs to be refinished."

Sutton unzipped the portfolio and removed a tape measure. "Grab an end?"

She held the tape measure as Sutton stretched it out across the room. He took several measurements, wrote them in his notebook, and then snapped photos with his phone.

"Custom cabinets?"

"Yes. Will you make them?"

"I could, but the time required will slow down the rest of the work. I know a couple of people with the right computerized tools. I'll text you the numbers. You should order the cabinets as soon as possible."

He made additional suggestions about the counters, cabinets, and appliances. Most she agreed with. Some she would give more thought.

"I'd advise you to hire a plumber if you want to add a dishwasher. This house has never had one."

Oh, yes. She'd forgotten it would need to be plumbed for that. "Okay, I'll find a plumber and cabinetmaker." She saw dollar signs on every surface and said a silent prayer of appreciation for God's provision. "Let me show you the rest of the downstairs. The kids are still sleeping upstairs."

At the mention of her children, Sutton frowned. "Don't you think it's time they got up?"

It was Paige's turn to frown. "Why? It's a holiday. They have no school."

He tipped his head in an offhand manner that said, "They're your kids."

She stared at his back as he stepped across the hall. Yes, the children were hers . . . even if two of them didn't agree with her.

He was right, though. She should get them up soon. It was Thanksgiving, and Mom and Dad expected them all at eleven.

By the time he'd toured the inside and outside, taking photos and pointing out a list of repairs she hadn't noticed, Paige's head spun. Had she been too idealistic in her purchase of the house? It depended on Sutton's estimate. "Any idea of the cost?"

"Why don't you look for the finishes you want, and we can meet next week. Afterward, I'll prepare an estimate." Concern must have shown on her face, because he added, "I have an interest in seeing this job done right. I won't cut corners or run up the bill, Paige. But if you find I'm too high, you're free to contact other contractors."

She hadn't meant to imply that she thought he would cheat her or inflate the price. "I'm sure that won't be necessary, but thank you, Sutton."

She saw him out a few minutes later, and once he left, Paige climbed the front porch steps, dodging the upturned planter she had placed over the hole in the floor. Her father said he'd help her lay new boards where necessary this Saturday. That would be one job she didn't need to pay Sutton to do.

His eyes lit up as he went from room to room, examining everything, tapping the notepad and thinking. Knowing him, she was sure he didn't see dollar signs but a finished product that pleased him.

Why hadn't he bought this house long ago if he admired it so much?

Ten

Rather than hit the department stores to hunt for clothing and Christmas gifts like so many others, the Hartwell women spent their Black Friday hunting for home improvement items. After two hours, they had found flooring samples for Trey's half-bath and quartz counter samples for Paige's kitchen.

Paige had looked forward to this shopping trip with her mother and sisters. They strolled up and down the aisles, stopping when something caught their attention. She made notes of desired kitchen appliances and snapped photos on her phone of light and sink fixtures, but she hadn't expected the necessity for confession to overcome her in the tile department.

"I'm hiring Sutton to renovate my house." There, she'd said it. She should have announced it at dinner yesterday but chose today without her dad or children present.

"You're what?"

Paige's reflexes snapped into action. Before it crashed to the floor, she caught the piece of subway tile that slipped from her mother's hand and set it back on the store's shelf. Mom stood frozen on the concrete floor, and Paige almost laughed at her saucer-sized eyes. Thankfully, common sense stopped her.

"I haven't officially hired him. He hasn't given me an estimate yet." But once she'd shown him around the house, discussed details with him, and heard the enthusiasm for her plans in his voice, Paige couldn't imagine hiring anyone else to do the work.

"It isn't a bad idea." Brianna laid a hand on Mom's shoulder. "Working together will give them a chance to put the past behind them. Who knows?" She winked at Paige. "Sparks may fly from more than a welding torch."

"Yep. Then you can write a book about your experience, Paige. I can see the title now." Reagan waved a hand in front of her face. "*A Marriage of Contracting Convenience.*"

Both of her sisters cackled, attracting the curious attention of a nearby employee. Even her mother's lips twitched.

"Don't expect a marriage, convenient or otherwise." Paige scowled at Brianna. "And there will be no sparks." Her children came first. Her life had no room for men who didn't want them—men like Dustin . . . and Sutton.

"Mm-hmm."

"We still have choices to make." Paige grabbed a different tile—an unsuitable one—under the pretense of considering it for one of the bathrooms. Anything to change the subject. She wrinkled her nose. But this tile in her house? Never. It didn't fit any better than she and Sutton fit together.

The four of them moved on to a main aisle. With her hands on her hips, she stopped and spun in a slow twirl, glancing at all the products—the possibilities—around her. "I love too many tiles, too many paint colors, too many flooring materials for the bathrooms and laundry room."

"You're an artist, Paige. Choose one room at a time and focus on your desired result."

She closed her eyes and did as Reagan advised. Like a computer, her mind sifted through the five tile samples she'd chosen for the downstairs bathroom shower and narrowed it down to two. She compared them to the idea she had in mind for the sink. Either of them would work. "You're brilliant, Reagan. Let me put these other three back."

Paige hurried back to the tile department and found the proper shelves to replace the samples she would purchase. She returned to where she'd left her mom and sisters, but they had disappeared. As she looked around, a tall, familiar figure moved into her line of sight. He stopped in the fixtures area to look at a white farmhouse sink—the same one she'd admired earlier.

For what seemed an uncomfortable eternity, Paige watched, debating whether to speak to him or find her family. He ran a gentle hand along the inside of the sink. She could almost feel that tenderness against her cheek. He could be gruff, especially after dealing with a problem at home, but with her, he'd taken care to be tender.

"Paige?" Reagan called to her from the aisle to her left.

Turning, she hustled toward her sister's voice. If she couldn't even say hello to him in a crowded store, how would she survive months of close contact as he worked on her house?

Sutton kept his head down, even when his neck muscles protested the restraint.

He glanced at the time on his phone. Eighteen minutes. He'd walked through the door of Jo E's Java eighteen minutes ago and had nursed his cup of Red Eye coffee while waiting for Paige to arrive. Eighteen minutes of listening to Christmas music from the ceiling speakers and smelling the scents of gingerbread and cinnamon from the red candle flickering on the neighboring table. He'd blown his out after sitting down. What was wrong with smelling good, strong coffee? Why add holiday scents to mask the product sold here?

He'd known Jo E's did good business, but it hit home with the cool breeze that chilled him every time the door opened and closed. Hidden Veil's residents went in and out, but none of them were Paige.

Each time the door opened, Sutton tightened those neck muscles against the impulse to see if she had come inside. Why give people the idea that he was eager to see her?

Frankly, he still smarted from her hasty retreat from him at the store on Friday. He'd bet she didn't know he'd seen her, but how could he not? When it came to Paige, he had a sort of sixth sense that alerted him to her presence. While he'd stood in front of the sink, he was sure she would choose for the kitchen, that sense—he used to tease her by calling it his "Paigey sense"—had flared with a tickle that ran up his backbone.

Over the weekend, Sutton had come close to calling and telling her to find someone else for her renovation. Two things stopped him—the credit card bill, and the longing to be the one to bring that house into the twenty-first century.

The door opened, and light, hurried footsteps crossed the floor, stopping at his table. "I'm sorry I'm late. I had to finish throwing an order of candlesticks for the contract I have with a Dallas store. Then Cassie pitched a fit when Mom picked her up to take her to the park. She didn't want me to leave her. I can't blame her with the way life has been for all of them." Paige took a breath.

Sutton stilled the quirk of his lips at the way she went on and on. "Done?"

A snort of laughter ripped from her. "I hope so."

"What do you want to drink?" He pushed back his chair.

"I'll know it when I see it." She stayed him with a hand on his shoulder, one that sent a flash of heat through him. She plopped a full tote bag onto the seat beside her, the contents clanging and clacking. "I'll be right back."

While she ordered her drink at the counter, Sutton opened his notebook and pulled out the detailed drawing he'd done of her kitchen. She had emailed him the specs for the appliances she'd already ordered, along with a few more kitchen ideas. He was a contractor, not an artist or designer, but software was his friend. She might not like his design, but they met here to hash out the details.

She returned a few minutes later, carrying a mug topped with at least three inches of whipped cream and a caramel drizzle. The sweet smell alone could give him diabetes. "Is there coffee in there, or did you only order whipped cream?"

She set the cup on the table and removed her coat before sitting down. "Caramel macchiato." She took a sip and licked her lips. "Mmm . . ."

To keep his mind off the imagined sweetness of those lips still dotted white, Sutton pushed the sheet of paper he'd printed off toward her. "It's based on what we talked about last week and the modifications you emailed. I used the measurements I took last week and the specs of the appliances you picked."

Paige set down her drink, wiped her mouth with a napkin, and lifted the paper. After studying it for a moment, those sweet lips ticked up. She dug into the tote bag, pulled out her own sheet of paper, and turned it around for him to see.

"Huh." Paige had hired someone in Charlotte to design the room, and it almost looked like a copy of his draft.

"I had it drawn to be sure my plans would work. Great minds thinking alike?"

"Seems so." Or great minds using the same software.

Only a couple of differences stood out. First was the island in the middle of the room. She wanted it to seat four, two on each side. The designer had positioned hers running width-wise versus his running the length of the room. Second, on a bare wall, she had added a cabinet and labeled it a coffee bar.

He tapped the cabinet with the tip of his index finger. "Is this a built-in?"

"No, it's freestanding. I found a Hoosier cabinet at Yesteryear Antiques. It's perfect for the look of the room and functional for the purpose. Garnett Clark is holding it for me until the kitchen is done."

"Okay." Sutton studied the sheet again and suggested storage in the island.

"Good idea." She made a note on the paper, then dug into the tote and pulled out various materials. Picking up a flooring sample, she said, "When you refinish the hardwood flooring, I'd like it to be lighter. Like this."

"Fine."

"As for the counters, including the top of the island, I'm trying to decide between this quartz pattern and this one." She put both on the table. "What do you think?"

What did he think? He thought they both looked the same.

"I don't want anything too trendy. I want it to last. The pattern is bolder in this one." Paige pointed to the quartz sample on her right—a light cream with gray-brown veins. Somewhat conservative but noticeable. She ran a finger over the second sample. "This has a softer look with a faint, wavy vein, like sand art in a glass."

"You have time to decide."

"But which one would you choose given the overall plan?"

Why ask him? Sure, he knew which one he'd pick, but . . . Well, since she asked. "I'd choose the second one."

She grinned. "Done."

Women would forever baffle him, especially this one. Did she plan to base all her choices on his opinion? His own budget would tap out at laminate. "You realize it doesn't matter that I like your choices." Okay, that didn't sound bitter at all.

Her face fell. "Of course not. I'm asking various people for opinions."

Good going, Vance. Get yourself fired before she's even hired you.

Paige continued to pull sample after sample out of the bag, proving how seriously she took this renovation. "I've already chosen one of the companies you recommended for the cabinets. With the upcoming holidays, they're estimating twelve weeks until they're available for installation."

Sutton picked up the photo of her chosen cabinet style. She had great taste. Except for him, she always had.

Paint cards—for walls and cabinets. Photos of lighting choices. Wall tile. Cabinet hardware. No wonder the bag rattled when she moved it. With each one, she sought his thoughts. Sometimes they differed from hers. Many times, they matched. When it didn't matter, he deferred, not caring either way.

Thankfully, he'd gotten his contractor's license a couple of years ago in the event a project like this came along. Even so, a voice in his head nagged that he'd bitten off more than he could chew with the size of this job. He also had a farm to run. Maybe the desire for a construction company of his own was nothing more than a pipedream.

With her design plans and the additional repairs to be made, he didn't see himself finishing before spring planting if he continued to work solo. While he'd prefer to work that way, it wasn't practical or a good business. He had to hire help.

"Well, isn't this a sweet surprise?"

Paige jumped up. "Mrs. Bevins. It's great to see you."

Vera Bevins hugged her. "You, too. Jo E said you had returned." When Sutton bent to rise from his seat, Jo's grandmother laid a brown-spotted hand on his shoulder, and pushed him back down. "She didn't tell me you two were back together."

"We're not." The words shot from Sutton's mouth in a volume that drew looks from the two women at his table and half the customers in the coffee shop. He couldn't help it. If he didn't nip that impression, word that they had reunited would travel through Hidden Veil like paper blown by a tornado.

"I've hired Sutton to renovate my house. We're going over some kitchen ideas."

Although the smile remained, an edge had crept into Paige's voice. He couldn't decide if it was anger or embarrassment. Possibly both. And both were his fault.

Vera's fingers bit into his shoulder until he wanted to wince. The eighty-something-year-old still managed quite a grip. "It was nice seeing you again, Paige. Don't be a stranger now, you hear?"

"No, ma'am."

"I'll let you two get back to your meeting."

The pressure on his shoulder eased, but he bet the imprint remained.

After Jo's grandmother left, Paige took her seat again, and they went over a few more details, but the atmosphere surrounding him had cooled.

She finished her drink and gathered her samples. "I think we've gone over everything, don't you?"

"I have enough to work up a budget."

"Good." Paige rubbed the bridge of her nose, a sign she had something to say and wondered how or if she should say it. In his head, he urged her to spit it out. "I should have mentioned this before. I saw you at a store on Friday."

Sutton appreciated hearing the admission, because it was her silence that hurt. "I know."

"You do?"

"I heard Reagan call your name. Why didn't you say hello?"

"My family was looking for me." Her chin tilted up. "If you saw me, why didn't you say something yourself?"

She put it back on him? "You were on your way to Reagan." A partial truth.

Paige paused. "There's something else. Maybe I shouldn't admit this, but I almost called you and canceled the job."

His heart turned over faster than the engine on the new tractor. When they were together, Paige often wavered in her decisions—what food to order, what movie to see. Once she chose, though, she stuck to her decision. Had that trait changed in the time she'd been gone?

"I almost called you, too, Paige."

"Why didn't you?"

Because he needed the money, yes, but he also . . .

Nope. Not going there.

"It's the biggest job I've done. It's a challenge I can't decline. And you?"

"People told me you would do the best job, Sutton, and your passion for the project impressed me." She rose with a half-turn to leave, then swiveled to face him. "If it matters, I am sorry for leaving the way I did before. It wasn't fair or right."

Her apology caught him by surprise. No, it wasn't fair or right. Not much in his life had been, and that particular unfairness had cost him years of anger and resentment.

Sometimes, it seemed a granite shell of protection had hardened around his heart, growing thicker each year. From the moment she left, he'd refused to allow anyone to chip away at that shell, exposing the organ to that kind of pain again.

"Will our working together be a problem for you?"

He owed her honesty, but how could he give it when one look at her made him question what honest was for him? "No problem."

She put on her coat. "Then I'll expect an estimate from you in a few days."

Sutton could blame his accelerating pulse on the caffeine in the Red Eye he drank, but the true source just walked out the door with that oversized tote dangling from her shoulder and slapping against her hip.

No problem? Big problem.

What he needed was a buffer between them. And he had one in mind.

Eleven

Sutton removed the Vance Farm cap and ran a hand over his head before he realized what he was doing. That last haircut had sheared him like a sheep, leaving him with hair too short to smooth. What did it matter how he looked, anyway? This wasn't a date. He was only at Paige's place to drop off the estimate he'd prepared.

Even so, he glanced at his reflection in the truck's rearview mirror. Worried eyes. Suntanned, furrowed rows that ran across his forehead. Every hour he'd spent working and reworking numbers to arrive at a fair price for Paige and earn enough money to set the farm back on track showed in his face.

He slapped the cap on his head and climbed out of the truck. She didn't care about his appearance. He rolled his shoulders to loosen his muscles and walked around to the back side of the house. When he called earlier, she'd said she'd be working in the studio.

Sutton tapped on the door. Hearing a muted "Come in," he stepped inside to find Paige bent over a little girl, tickling her. The screech of the girl—a blonde like Leyla—threatened to poke a hole through his eardrums. She squiggled with glee, and Paige laughed so hard, she could barely stand. For a moment, an odd emotion blanketed Sutton. He'd call it enjoyment, but that was too simplistic. It went deeper, so deep he chose not to put a name to it.

"Don't you know that's dangerous?"

Paige glanced at him. She let go of the giggling girl and straightened, the laughter gone, but a smile lingered. "Tickling a child is dangerous?"

"No, but an unlocked door and a call to come in without checking identity first isn't safe."

"It's only been a few minutes since you called to say you were coming. Besides, we're talking about Hidden Veil."

"It isn't a crime-free zone."

"Who are you?" The little girl, whose giggles had filled the room when he arrived, stared up at him.

"Cassie, honey, this is Mr. Sutton. He's the one who's going to make our house pretty."

The girl smiled up at him. "I want to help make it pretty."

Great. That was all he needed—children running around, getting into his tools and materials, thinking they could help.

"Maybe Mr. Sutton will let you watch once in a while. Otherwise, we all should stay out of his way while he works."

The little girl looked like she was about to argue until Paige pointed to a cardboard box in the corner. "Right now, you can help me by taking your toys out of the box and putting them in the basket. You know where they go."

"Okay, Mommy." Her little legs skipped to the other end of the room.

Mommy. That hit Sutton harder than hearing Leyla call her Mom Paige. Sure, Paige no longer had that fresh-faced teenage look—not that she didn't look great—but in spite of their ages, he struggled to imagine her as a mother of three.

Sutton studied her closer. Shadows darkened the skin under her eyes, and her eyelids drooped with fatigue. She looked like she hadn't slept last night. Rather than ask about it, Sutton focused on the room.

Though vacant for a while, Paige had turned the building into a usable space for her studio. Bright. Clean. No cobwebs or dust. Three out of four cement block walls freshly painted in a neutral cream. The bright blue wall along the back added a boost of cheerfulness and emphasized the differences between them. Sutton would have painted it cream also.

Rows of shelves, most still empty, covered the back and side walls. A huge metal can with a lid occupied a corner. Aprons hung on pegs. Boxes stacked along the walls filled a good portion of the space. Some were unopened moving boxes that obviously contained things she'd brought with her from Georgia and had marked "Fragile."

She might run from him under certain circumstances, but once he'd completed the house renovation and she had set up her studio, she would have a harder time taking off without a word. That thought shouldn't have brought him even a smidgen of comfort, but it did.

Paige glanced at the girl, who was trying to pick up a cardboard box far larger than she could manage. "No, Cassie. Put it down."

The girl lowered it to the floor.

Paige turned back to him. "She's my little helper."

Something hit the floor, and they both glanced at the little girl as wailing filled the room. Evidently, the little helper didn't understand the word no, because she'd tried to pick up the same box again and dropped it on her foot.

"Excuse me." Paige ran over and lifted the child, cooing soft words in her ear, inspecting her toes, and kissing her cheek.

Sutton frowned. No "I told you not to" speech?

While she was occupied, Sutton whipped out the estimate and contract, centering his attention on the reason he'd come rather than the temptation to say something he'd regret. Again. Once the kid's sobbing stopped, Paige returned, and he handed the papers to her, ready to leave.

After perusing the estimate, her eyebrows shot up. "Are you sure about this?"

Where she was concerned, he wasn't sure about anything. "I priced it out."

"But it's—"

"Too much?" He knew better than that, but he'd left some wiggle room for surprises.

"Not at all. I'd imagined it to be much more."

"Don't get your hopes up. It may be more if I find problems we didn't expect. You'll notice I put in the contract that you're responsible for any unexpected costs and existing repairs."

"That's fair."

"Since you haven't chosen all of your materials, I tried to overestimate the costs for things like counters and fixtures." She'd proven she had fine taste, but it wasn't over the top, not even in the choice of quartz for the countertops.

"Good. I still haven't finalized decisions about some things."

He pointed to the papers. "Let me know when you've signed the contract. I'll pick it up, then get the permits and work out a schedule."

"I'll read it tonight and call you tomorrow." She rubbed the tip of her nose, then dropped her hand. He braced himself for what was coming. "I know I asked the other day, but do you really think we can do this? Work together, I mean."

The easy answer was no, but for the sake of the family and the farm he had to make this work. "Yeah. Why not? That's in the past, and there's nothing between us anymore." Nothing for her, anyway. She'd moved on, gotten married, had kids. And him? "Nothing. Right?" He held his breath and awaited her answer. It was crazy to tack on that question, but he couldn't help himself.

"Right." She smiled, her voice as cheerful as that blue wall, too cheerful for his ego. "Before you go, there is one more thing."

"What's that?"

"The sink you looked at in the store?"

"The farmhouse sink." He'd only looked at one.

"Yes."

"What about it?"

"I want it for the kitchen."

He nodded. "I'll add it to the list. What about the bathroom sinks?"

"I'm not ready to tackle renovating the existing upstairs bath, but for the downstairs and the new en suite in my bedroom, I'll make the sinks."

"You'll make them?"

She patted the rim of what resembled an extra-large oil pan on the three-legged pottery wheel. "Ceramic sinks are a thing. For the downstairs bath, I'll make something reminiscent of the bowls people once used with pitchers and washstands. The ones in the master bath upstairs will be more modern." His doubt must have shown, because she added, "Don't worry. They'll be beautiful."

"Yeah." Sutton turned to leave but something held him in place. Literally. He looked down. The little girl—Cassie—had grabbed hold of his legs. Surprise jerked him back a step. Had he not caught himself, he would have taken them both down.

Paige's low chuckle only added to his embarrassment. "She wants to say goodbye."

Sutton's gaze fell on the child. He pried her arms from his legs and moved away before she could grab him again. "Gotta go."

The little girl's crying followed him from the building. He was well over six feet and sturdy in a hurricane, but the howling made him want to march back inside and tell Cassie goodbye like a decent human being.

Sutton escaped to his truck. Contrary to what he'd said a couple of minutes ago, between Paige and her children, he saw no hope of getting through this job without losing his mind.

"I'm a couple of days behind." That was an inaccurate answer to the inquiry by Paige's VA. She was more than a couple of days behind. She hadn't even finished unpacking her boxes of supplies.

Her gaze slid from Shellie's image on the laptop screen and zeroed in on the studio shelf holding a dozen bisque pieces ready to be glazed. At least, she'd gotten *some* work done in the two weeks she'd been in Hidden Veil. "I'll call Carol after we finish here and talk her off the ledge." Who would talk *Paige* off the ledge?

"I don't know how you've done all you have lately, Paige. I'd be crazy by now. Can I call her for you?"

Shellie, Paige's Atlanta assistant—now virtual assistant—was amazing. She kept Paige organized and sane. "That's tempting."

It would certainly save her time, because Carol liked to talk, but . . . "I'll handle it myself. I haven't spoken with her in months, and you know I like to give that personal touch when I can."

Cassie climbed onto Paige's lap and waved at Shellie. "Hi, Miz Shell."

"Well, hi there, darlin'. How was your nap?"

Cassie rubbed her still-sleepy eyes. "Good."

Paige ran a hand over her girl's silky hair. "Are we finished, Shellie?"

Shellie looked down, probably to consult one of the endless lists she kept. "That's all I have for now. Don't forget the order for the Charlotte boutique."

Paige checked her list of projects pending. It was due at the end of December. "I see it. Thanks for the reminder."

Once her meeting with Shellie ended, Paige gave Cassie the lunch she'd made and called Carol Eaton at her shop in Savannah. She updated the woman on the status of her order, then they talked for another twenty minutes about various things. Carol's store had been one of the first businesses to carry Paige's work, so it was good PR to talk with her. Plus, she was a sweet woman.

Paige checked the time on her phone. *Oh, no.* "Carol, it's been great talking with you, but I have to go so I can run a few errands and be home when my kids get here."

"Okay, hon. You bring those sweeties to Savannah one day. I'd love to meet them."

"I will try to do that." Although, no time soon. "Bye."

Paige ended the call and scrambled to clean up the studio. When done, she slipped a coat on Cassie and snatched her purse from inside the house. "Let's get going, girl, or we won't beat the bus home."

"Let's beat the bus."

With another glance at the time, Paige figured it wouldn't be a problem.

They stopped at Johnson's to pick up a week's worth of groceries. With no place to store everything once the kitchen renovation began, she couldn't buy too much at one time.

While pushing the basket with Cassie down each aisle, people she had known years ago stopped her to say hello and welcome her back to Hidden Veil. Not wanting to be rude, she chatted with each of them for a few moments.

Thirty minutes after her last errand, she turned into her driveway. The trip home had taken three times as long as normal because of an accident, so she cringed at seeing Liam and Leyla sitting on the front porch steps.

Leyla jumped up and skipped toward the car. Liam sat stone still, staring at Paige with a black look—one she'd seen from him too often. She prepared herself for the upcoming clash.

After removing Cassie from her booster seat, Paige gave Leyla a one-armed hug and followed the two girls toward the house. "I'm sorry I'm late. There was—"

Liam continued to scowl. "It's cold out here."

"It's cold, Mom Paige." Leyla hugged herself and bolstered her brother's sentiment. She must be wearing her hearing aids for a change.

"I know. I'm so sorry." Actually, the December day felt more like late September, but Paige ran her hands up and down the girl's well-covered arms in a show of warming them. She climbed the porch steps and unlocked the front door. "I would have been back by the time the bus dropped you off, but an accident held up traffic for twenty-five minutes."

The girls ran into the house. Paige looked back. Liam hadn't moved. “Come in and warm up, Liam. I’ll make you some hot chocolate.”

“I don’t want hot chocolate.” He crossed his arms over his knees. “School got out early.”

“Early?”

“I reminded you about it this morning.”

Paige’s chest tightened. “That was today?”

“Yeah, and we’ve been here for hours.”

They must have arrived shortly after she left for town. “I’m so sorry. With so much going on, I forgot about the early dismissal. It won’t happen again.”

“Mom wouldn’t have forgotten. She’d have been home, waiting for us. She’d already have the hot chocolate made.” Liam rose, scowled at her once more, then bolted into the house, leaving the front door wide open.

Paige’s stomach bottomed out at the echo of his footsteps stomping up the stairs, and her eyes stung. She should go inside and talk to him, but her legs wobbled like the round-bottomed toy in Cassie’s toybox.

Liam was right. How could she have been so careless? Why hadn’t she scheduled a reminder of the early dismissal on her phone? Instead, she’d messed up . . . as usual. This time, she had allowed her children—her greatest and most cherished responsibility—to sit alone in the cold. They had needed her, and she wasn’t here.

Not even an apology made up for what she’d done.

As much as she wanted all three kids to think of her as their mother, she had never tried to dull their memories of Marissa. She never would. But oh, how she wished Liam could at least think of her as Mom Paige. But why would he if she didn’t act like a mother?

Nothing and no one on earth should come before the children entrusted to her care. Home renovations and work should take second place to family. And they were a family, even if two members preferred to deny it.

Twelve

Early Saturday, Paige opened the door to In Harmoni and breathed in the luscious scents of the handmade candles and soaps that were artfully arranged around the shop. They brought to mind Christmas cookies and candy canes and gingerbread houses.

She picked up a bar of soap wrapped in white paper decorated with silver snowflakes. After reading the ingredients for the "Winter Dreams" scent—all natural—she held the bar to her nose and breathed in the cool, fresh scent. Bri would love this.

"Hi, Paige." Shaina walked into the front room from the back, trailed by her aunt.

Harmoni smiled, adding to the jauntiness of her pixie cut, dyed a pale pink today.

"Hey, ladies." Paige held up the bar of soap. "This is wonderful. How did you capture the crisp bite of winter?"

Shaina laughed. "Harmoni won't reveal her secrets, not even to me."

"Well, I want it for my sister."

Harmoni ducked her head and held out her hand for it. "I'll

ring it up for you."

Paige laughed. "I'm not done shopping yet."

"Okay."

"I had to beg, but my sisters allowed me to try some of your creations, Harmoni. They were fantastic, especially the lotions, so I came this morning to continue our discussion from Thanksgiving."

"Let me put the soap on the counter while you two talk," said Shaina.

"Thanks." Paige handed her the bar, then eyed her surroundings.

"What do you have in mind, Paige?"

Paige studied Harmoni's angelic face. Not knowing one another well, could she trust the woman with her products? Then again, Harmoni might wonder if she could trust Paige. "If you're in agreement, I'd like to give you a few appropriate pottery items to sell here on consignment. In exchange, you'll receive a percentage of the sales, of course. I hope to boost both of our businesses, but if we find the arrangement isn't an advantage for either of us, we call off the agreement."

Harmoni's sweet face brightened. "It sounds like a win-win."

As they discussed the details, the siren from an emergency vehicle stopped Paige in mid-sentence. The noise grew in strength until it sounded like it had stopped in front of the building. Then the piercing noise died on a whine.

Paige stepped outside with Shaina and Harmoni on her heels. "It's parked in front of Jo E's."

"Oh, no. I hope Vera didn't have another heart attack. It would crush Jo and Bobby Goodwin." Shaina brushed past Paige, who whispered a silent prayer for the person in need.

Together, the three of them joined over a dozen other business owners and customers on the sidewalk near the coffee shop. Possibilities and theories surrounded them, whispered as if to say them louder would make them true.

A few minutes later, an EMS worker exited the shop, pulling a gurney. His partner pushed it from the rear. On the bed lay Jo Callahan, covered by a blanket pulled up to her chin. Her hand cradled the mound that was her unborn baby, and her face contorted into a combination of fear and pain. The men loaded the gurney into the ambulance.

Shaina broke through the crowd and hurried to Vera, whose age lines had deepened. A few moments later, she hugged the woman and returned with news. "Jo is in labor, but her blood pressure is low. They're taking her to the hospital."

In her normal hushed voice, Harmoni asked, "Does Kyle know?"

"Vera called him. He'll meet them at the hospital."

Pastor Jim from the church Paige's sisters attended—and she had attended since returning to town—stood next to Vera at the door to the coffee shop. "Anyone who wishes, gather around and we'll pray for Jo and the baby."

About two-thirds of the people on the sidewalk pressed forward, including Vera, Paige, and her two companions.

"We come before you, God, to ask you to watch over and heal Jo and her baby. We ask that you give the doctor wisdom and give her family and friends peace of mind."

Paige tried to "Amen" everything the pastor said, but her throat tightened with the thought of Jo losing her child. At their Thanksgiving dinner, Paige had seen the happiness in Jo's face when talking about the baby. She also recalled her own shameful envy.

Thoughts of her children blocked the sound of the pastor's words. Negative thoughts slipped in to remind her of the most recent argument with Liam and his resentment of her as a parent. She had prayed to be a mother in the worst way. But honestly, was it in God's way?

She couldn't remember praying about taking in Marissa's children. When asked, she had said yes without hesitation. Had she jumped ahead of God in her acceptance and, as a result, lost a husband, as well as Liam's love and respect?

With a hand on her stomach, Paige hoped to calm the sudden queasiness. Surely, losing her best friend hadn't come about through a selfish, opportunistic agreement?

"Whoa, Paige, are you all right? You're pale." Shaina laid a hand on her arm, bringing her back to the moment. "Jo will be fine. I believe that."

Paige turned her wrist as though consulting a watch that wasn't there. "I should go. My kids are expecting me."

Ha! What a lie. And what a travesty. They should expect their real mother. Marissa's entire world had revolved around her children. She wouldn't have forgotten that school let out early. As Liam said, Marissa would have had hot chocolate ready for them.

"I'll come back another time to make my purchases, Harmoni. We can discuss a collaboration then."

Paige left the two women staring at her. No doubt she had ruined that relationship, leaving Harmoni to consider her a flake who couldn't be trusted with her soaps and lotions.

Just as she didn't trust herself to be the best mother for her children.

An advantage of living in a small town was the speed with which Sutton received permits for his work, and he couldn't have timed the job better. Within a week, he was ready to start work on the house.

He kicked the truck's heater up, and semi-warm air blew into his face, a weapon against the early morning chill.

Even though Sutton had lost the Johnson place—he still couldn't think of it as the Matthews place—the work would be more a labor of love than a paying job. Although he definitely expected to be paid.

Armed with coffee and tools, he drove down the farm's driveway, turning right at the road. The estimate had satisfied Paige. It should have. He'd waffled back and forth between regretting the small discount on his labor—she didn't need it, after all, did she?—and seeing it as a sign of his ability to move past what she'd done to him years ago. All was forgiven.

Maybe not all yet, but for his peace of mind, he determined to achieve it.

Another possibility nagged at Sutton. Had he provided a discount so she would think he didn't need the money? Why try to fool her? She must know better. The Vance family's financial instability was no secret.

Besides, her sisters had likely kept her informed about all the goings-on in Hidden Veil over the years. Was it too egotistical to think they might have mentioned him? He chucked the questions and stopped examining his reasons for the discount.

The advance Sutton had requested would have made him gag had their roles been reversed. She didn't bat an eye. Her indifference to the cost only emphasized the gaping divide between their economic statuses. But it gave him enough money to buy the initial materials and put the some away for the tractor payment.

At seven-thirty-five, he pulled into Paige's driveway and parked on the grass to the left side of her car. She would go to the studio soon, and he could work in peace until the older kids arrived home from school. Paige had told him she tried to finish her daily work before school ended.

Liam and Leyla burst out the front door. Leyla's pink backpack bounced up and down on her back, and she wore another pair of rubber boots—a pink and blue plaid today—even though the weather promised sunshine.

Liam's navy-colored pack hung from his hand and almost dragged along the ground. The scowl on his face hinted that he and Paige had probably butted heads . . . again.

Seeing the kids reminded him of his conversation with Kyle last week. The guy's happiness over the birth of his daughter could have bounced him to the moon and back, especially after the danger the labor had posed for both mom and baby. Kyle's outlook during the call had taken a one-eighty over the fear he'd experienced after the ambulance rushed Jo to the hospital. Fortunately, the doctor got her blood pressure under control and delivered the baby through a C-section.

Physical danger—one more reason not to have children.

Paige exited after the kids and stood on the porch, holding Cassie. Wearing form-fitting jeans and a Christmas-green sweatshirt with some kind of textured design on the front, she stared after the older kids, her face downcast.

The key to the house Paige had given him allowed him to come and go as necessary. It meant he could wait to get here until after she went to the studio. Yet he'd arrived early, looking at it as having a good work ethic.

Yeah, a good work ethic. Nothing more.

The two older children approached the driver's side door of his truck, not stopping. Leyla's grin showed off two missing teeth—one on top and one on the bottom. She waved at him, and he dipped his chin in acknowledgment. Although he could think of nothing he'd done to warrant it, he no longer scared her. In fact, she always smiled and waved. Liam ignored him in the same way Sutton's siblings did.

Sutton tracked them in the rearview mirror. They stopped at the edge of the road as the school bus pulled up. It swallowed them and moved on.

A knock shifted his attention to the passenger-side window.

"Good morning." Paige's muffled voice barely penetrated the glass.

This was one of those times Sutton wished he had electric windows. Rather than shout, he got out of the truck. "Morning."

"Are you sure such an early arrival isn't taking you away from important work at home?"

"You'd rather I wait until after you go to the studio?"

"No, it's fine. I just don't want you to get behind in your farm duties."

"I've left Dillon in charge of most of the morning chores." Sutton was trusting the boy to complete the list he'd left before school. Dillon had complained about getting up an hour earlier, but once awake, he whipped the others, including Jenna, into a griping frenzy of work. The responsibility was good for all of them. Sutton should have handed it out long ago.

"Little Dillon?"

"He isn't so little. Eighteen and almost as tall as me."

"Wow. I guess it's been a while."

"Yeah, it has." With the pinking of her cheeks, he added, "The family's grown since you've been gone. Jenna is sixteen.

Then there's Joel, thirteen, Ariel eleven, and Patrick seven."

Paige opened her mouth as though she wanted to say something and closed it again. She set Cassie on her feet but held the girl's hand. Smart. The road wasn't far, and young kids could vanish in no time.

Cassie looked up at him. "Hi, Misser Sudden."

He recalled the way she'd clung to him in the studio and his reaction to her. Determined to prevent her from crying this time, he said, "Hey."

Paige turned toward the house. "Have you had breakfast?"

"Yep." He pulled a thermos filled with hot coffee from the seat and grabbed his tool belt.

As they walked to the front door, she asked, "What will you do today?"

"I'll start with the repairs we discussed on Thanksgiving Day. I expect it to take me into next week. Then the demo work begins, which includes removing the present wainscoting. Later, if you want, I can hang a few of the old cabinets in the studio for use as storage." Sutton hated to see anything go to waste.

"More storage is always good. What about the farm? Can you use some there?"

Probably, but getting her leftovers didn't sit well with him. "We're good."

"Come on, Cassie. Let's make breakfast while Mr. Sutton gets to work."

Sutton followed the two of them up the porch steps. The first thing he noticed was the huge Christmas wreath on the front door. It looked like something sold by an expensive specialty shop, far nicer than the one Debra had picked up at a charity thrift shore.

Inside the house, the dining room resembled a storage unit,

not a formal room for eating.

"As you can see, they delivered the new appliances. I know I should have waited, but I wanted them available as soon as you were ready for them."

He eyed a massive refrigerator, gas stove, and dishwasher. Their presence still left room for piles of boxes and the odd piece of furniture.

He peeked to the left. She had removed most of the wallpaper in the room she called the parlor. The walls still needed prepping for paint, but the furniture and knick-knacks brought a sense of normalcy to the first floor.

Except . . .

Jenna would claim the room threw up Christmas. Another larger wreath hung above the fireplace. An eight-foot Fraser fir, so fresh he could smell it from the hallway, sat in front of the bow window at the side of the room, fully decorated with a mixture of expensive-looking ornaments and ones handmade by the children. She had set out five manger scenes. Santas, elves, a train set, evergreen garlands. How had she found the time to work, unpack, choose renovation materials, take care of three children, and make sure their Christmas had all the decorative trimmings?

"There are more decorations than house space this year. Leyla and Cassie insisted on putting it all out. This room received the bulk, but more merrymakings are scattered in the rest of the rooms."

More decorations than house? How big was her old home in Atlanta?

Once more, Sutton compared Paige's decorations to the ones in the Vance house. His mouth compressed. No comparison to the fake greenery and dollar store ornaments. Clearly, she thrived after running away years ago. Had they married and become parents, his background promised that the odds of him being a good father and provider were next to nil, and her ex-husband had given her more than Sutton ever could.

She had asked if he thought they could work together, and he'd lied, denying any problem. Yet the sooner he got this job done, the better, because seeing her day in and day out, dreaming about what might have been as he'd done last night, could cause him more damage than her sudden disappearance fifteen years ago.

Paige cracked four eggs, dropping them into a bowl. She added milk to prepare scrambled eggs for herself and Cassie on the old stove. Sutton would begin work in the kitchen in a couple of weeks, leaving them to eat meals made in the microwave or countertop convection oven.

She had just flipped on the burner under the pan when he returned to the kitchen after examining the plaster in her bedroom ceiling. The tree limb had done a boatload of damage to the roof, but the insurance company had come through.

Sutton stood next to her, shrinking the room size—in her mind, anyway.

Paige beat the eggs while the pan heated, her fork clinking against the bowl. His closeness left her brain as scrambled as the breakfast. "What do you think? Do I need to replace the whole ceiling with drywall?"

"No. I can fix it." He leaned against the counter he would eventually remove and sipped the coffee from his thermal cup.

"Are you sure you don't want some eggs?"

"No, thanks." Sutton stared at his cup, his brow a mass of wrinkles.

Paige poured the eggs into the pan and set the bowl down. She hadn't liked the look on his face. It warned of something serious. More money than he'd mentioned to fix the plaster ceiling? "What's wrong?"

"Nothing is wrong. Just wondering."

"What?"

He pushed away from the counter. "Why did you buy this particular house, Paige?"

"You know I always liked it."

"Me, too."

She stirred the cooking eggs, then glanced at him. "Why didn't you buy it?"

"Someone beat me to it."

At the snap in his words, she turned back to the stove and ran the spoon through the eggs to cover her wince at his tone. Her sisters had told her about his family life these last years—his struggle to provide for them, a responsibility that wasn't his. She didn't blame him for being angry, but it wasn't her fault he hadn't acted in fifteen years. "I won't apologize for moving back to Hidden Veil and choosing this house as the place to raise my children."

"I never asked you to."

She beat the spoon on the edge of the pan to shake loose the scrambled eggs and some of her own anger. "Then why bring it up?"

"This place has always meant a lot to me."

Paige whipped around, the spoon held in her hand like the Statue of Liberty's torch. Was he saying he'd wanted the house, not simply for its convenience to the farm, but because it held the same sentimental value for him as it did her?

Before she could think of how to respond, he released a sigh and walked toward the doorway. "I'd better get to work."

"Mommy." Cassie tugged on her pant leg.

"Yes, sweetie?" She stared after Sutton as he walked out the door. "What is it?"

"There's eggs on the floor."

Paige looked down and groaned at the bits of pale-yellow scrambled eggs that had fallen from the spoon onto the small rug she kept in front of the stove.

As she cleaned up the mess, a lump bigger than the ones in the frying pan clogged her throat. First, her penchant for running away from her problems had taken away the future she and Sutton might have spent together . . . here. Second, she had taken this house from him.

Maybe she should have stayed in Atlanta.

Determination pushed Paige to her feet and straightened her spine. Why should she feel bad when he hadn't bought the house in fifteen years? Someone beat him to it? Yes, and that someone planned to stay.

Even as her resolve grew, regret settled over her at hearing the crushing disappointment in his words. If it hurt him to see her in the house he had wanted for himself, why agree to renovate it for her?

Thirteen

The more he worked on Paige's house, the more Sutton liked the idea of specializing in renovations.

Growing up in an old farmhouse, he'd had plenty of practice patching plaster walls and ceilings, as well as working with old plumbing and settling floors. Still, that goal was down the road. He'd done his homework but had a lot to learn about historical preservation if he eventually moved into that area of expertise. For now, Paige required less preservation and more modern comfort.

Sutton had spent the week tackling minor jobs on the house. A week ago, the roofers repaired the hole caused by the limb that crashed through the roof. Today he had finished repairing the water-damaged plaster in Paige's bedroom. He imagined her lying in bed and looking up to see an area of missed paint or a chip in the plaster. It pushed him to seek perfection.

When his thoughts lingered on the image of her lying there in those ridiculous unicorn pajama pants, he shook his head, scattering the provocative mental image to the winds.

Sutton double-checked his work, looking for anything that might be improved. He enjoyed farming, but construction of any type provided a unique sense of pleasure. Both required hard physical labor that let him work with his hands. Both allowed him to be outside, no matter the weather. And both left him exhausted by the end of the day.

Accomplishing a good day of honest work satisfied him. If he had his way, though, construction would be his sole profession.

But he was stuck.

As they grew, his siblings had become more expensive to raise. Jenna and Dillon each wanted a car. Even a junker they could share required gas, insurance, and frequent repairs. He and Debra had discussed the older ones finding jobs, but how would they get back and forth to work? Sutton couldn't take time out of his busy schedule to drive them, and he didn't trust his dad to take on the responsibility.

Now, his brother continued to bug him about learning the finer points of running a farm. He'd throw out "You promised" whenever Sutton told him he didn't have the time. It was true. He'd had little time to do more at the house than eat and sleep lately. He also hoped for more for Dillon—for all his brothers and sisters—than struggling as a farmer.

He should have aspired to bigger things himself and gone to college to study something like accounting or marketing. Even going part time, he'd have a better-paying job by now, one that provided greater financial security for his family.

Enough self-pity.

Sutton concentrated on cleaning up the mess in Paige's room. His phone buzzed. He dug it out of his pocket and checked the caller ID. Kaine Abbott. Good.

Kaine rolled into town about seven months ago after quitting his job as a smokejumper for the Forest Service in Idaho. At first, Sutton hadn't taken to the brash, moody brother of his friend

Trey. Over time, he'd learned of Kaine's loss and the grief that drove him back to North Carolina, so he'd cut the guy some slack and learned he wasn't so bad. Eventually, they became friends.

"Hey, Kaine."

"How's it going, Sutton?"

"Busy. Thanks for calling me back."

"Sure. You left a message saying you've started the reno on Paige's house."

Sutton appreciated how quickly Kaine picked up on his lack of time for chit-chat. "You've talked about your construction experience."

Paige's kitchen renovation was a large project that would run smoother and faster if he hired someone to help him, not to mention Kaine would be a buffer between Sutton and Paige. Thankfully, he'd worked employee labor into the cost he'd given her.

"Summers during college, work around my grandfather's farm, and in the down time from fighting wildfires. From what I hear, Paige's house is a big project."

"Big enough that I could use some help. I can't employ you full time, and you have your job at Harley's, but I thought we might work something out."

"Sounds like you haven't heard. For the next few months, Harley is limiting the number of jobs he takes. He plans to care for his wife while she goes through her cancer treatments and not worry about the business."

Harley's garage stayed busy, but a stranger wouldn't realize his success by looking at him. He was a bearded bear of a man, a tobacco-chewing throwback to the mountain men of the nineteenth-century American West.

"He's scheduling everyone for a couple of days a week only, so I can use any hours you provide."

"Send me your schedule and we'll work around it."

"Will do. Thanks, man."

Sutton jammed his phone into his back pocket.

"I can help."

His glance shot to the doorway where Liam stood, still dressed in his school clothes and dragging that poor backpack on the floor. "Help with what?"

"Fixing the house." The boy stepped into the room. "I can help you."

"I don't think so." Sutton reached down for the tarp he'd used to cover the floor and protect it from any plaster that fell. "This is adult work."

Liam dropped the backpack and entered the room. He grabbed one end of the tarp and handed it to Sutton, then grabbed a second end. "I may not be an adult, but I can fold this and hand you the tools you need. That's how I helped Aunt Paige's dad fix the porch."

The defiance in the boy's tone had Sutton thinking he was listening to Dillon. "Don't you have homework?"

"Nope."

Sutton took the ends of the tarp from him and finished folding it. "You're not working for me."

"Why not? You need help. That's what you told that Kaine guy."

"First a trespasser, now an eavesdropper."

"An eavesdropper who can help you."

Liam was nothing if not persistent. Even though Sutton admired the boy for standing his ground, that wasn't always a good thing. Look where his own stubbornness had gotten him with Paige years ago.

"Fine. If your mom doesn't object, you can help clean up sometimes."

"What about my pay?"

"You'll earn experience." Sutton brushed past him intent on cleaning up the mess before Paige saw it. "You can start now. Grab that bucket with the leftover plaster."

"Okay." Liam followed him out of the room, carrying the bucket. "And she's not my mom."

The bell Paige had installed over the studio's door jingled. She straightened from bending over the pottery wheel, pushed the stool back with her foot, and peered through the wire rack holding bisque pieces that were drying before being fired.

She had used two five-shelf metal racks to divide the front area with the kiln and the rear area with her pottery wheel, so she couldn't see all of him, but she would recognize those long legs and boots anywhere. Sutton had a way of standing tall and straight, his bearing reflecting his pride—a little too proud for his own good sometimes.

When he stepped clear of the shelving, she said, "Good morning."

"Hi." He pointed at the shabby golden bell over the door. "What's that for?"

Wiping clay from her hands, Paige walked toward him. "Someone left it at the back of a closet. I thought it would be fun to use. Besides, it will let me know if Cassie opens the door while I'm working." She pinned him with a stare. "Or if I have an intruder."

"Funny, Paige." As she'd hoped, he must have recalled their previous conversation about safety.

"You can be way too serious, Sutton." She couldn't help but tease him, even though she had come here from a large city where crime wasn't rare. Residents considered Hidden Veil a safe place to live. Still, as he'd said, it wasn't a crime-free utopia.

"Serious gets the job done. I've removed the two hanging cabinets in the kitchen you asked me to save." He looked around. "Where do you want them?"

"The only place available is over here." She led him to the wall next to the workbench. "They can go above the small rolling table."

He measured the spot to be certain they would fit, then looked around. "You have quite a setup here. I never knew a potter needed so much stuff. The last time I was here, you hadn't organized the space."

She glanced at the room, trying to see it through his eyes. It overflowed with the tools of her trade. Shelves held paints and glazes, buckets, and dozens of items in various stages of completion. Two smaller tables, a rustic work cabinet, and a cart hugged the walls. Aprons hung from hooks. Other than the muddy-looking pottery wheel, dirty sponges and rags, and a large bucket of gray water, the place was clean and organized.

"I use it all. The shelving, the large freestanding worktable, even the six-foot workbench left by the previous owner." The wheeled cart under a side window held containers with hand tools for trimming, scoring, and cutting, along with more buckets, sponges and rags. Instruments and equipment needed to create her pottery pieces filled almost every inch of the building.

Sutton veered around the worktable on his way to the pottery wheel. "I guess I interrupted your work." He studied the flat piece of clay, not yet formed.

"It's fine. I'm not far into it."

He continued to scrutinize the clay. "What will this one be?"

"I'm making a baby plate, part of a set with a cup and bowl. I gave the only other set I had available to Jo as a baby gift after Rose was born."

According to Reagan, Jo and Kyle had wanted to name their little girl after Jo's grandmother, but rather than Vera, the woman suggested they use her middle name. Again, a little voice swooped in to convince Paige she had been cheated. In this case, cheated of the pleasure of naming her own children. Why, when God had given her three lovely children to raise, wasn't she satisfied with the blessing?

She was. It was just—

"Paige?"

Sutton's voice broke through to free her from the shame of discontent. He'd moved closer, and his raised eyebrow accused her of zoning out on him. Guilty. "I'm sorry. Did you say something?"

"Now who's being too serious?" The small quirk of his mouth told her teasing could go both ways. "Is tomorrow a good time to hang the cabinets? Kaine will be here to help."

Paige had lost her desire to work on the baby set. "You can do it now. I'll help." At his doubtful expression, she flexed her arm. "I work out." *Sometimes.*

"Yeah, I see that." His smirk said he appeased her.

"You let Liam help." Oh, wow. Now she'd parroted what Leyla had said to him yesterday.

"Liam has done a little cleanup." He sighed. "I'll probably

regret this, but I wouldn't want anyone to accuse me of wasting that bit of muscle I see. It will take time to prepare before I hang anything. Why don't you go back to work? I'll let you know when I'm ready."

Once he left the studio, Paige shook her head. What was she doing? She hired Sutton to do the renovation, and she had more work than she could keep up with. To avoid examining her motive too closely, she returned to the drying clay sitting on the wheel.

With a cabinet loaded onto the dolly, Sutton rolled it out the back door of the house. Paige had put a sticky note with "Save" on this one and one more, so he and Kaine had taken extra care when removing them from the wall.

So far, Kaine had proved a wise choice. He worked as hard as Sutton and, knowing what needed to be done and how to do it, needed little supervision.

A wealth of volunteers lined up to help with this job. Liam wanted to help. Leyla wanted to help. Paige wanted to help. Only Cassie hadn't volunteered. Come to think of it, the child had volunteered to make the house pretty. Customers had never offered to assist him in the past. It was almost like . . . like they were a family and everyone pitched in to get the work done.

An expelled breath formed a cloud in the cold air. What would he know about families working together? For years, pretty much anything that needed doing around the farm he'd done alone with the idea he couldn't depend on anyone but himself.

Dillon's behavior over the past couple of weeks called him out. The kid had taken on the farm chores with an energy Sutton hadn't seen since the boy was five. So far, his brother had listened to instruction and done everything Sutton asked of him. How long would that enthusiasm last? Time would tell.

He did know the past few weeks had opened a crack in the protective granite he'd built up. The crack allowed in something that felt too much like dependence on others.

Paige must have heard him roll the dolly over the crisp, winter-dead grass, because she opened the studio door the moment he arrived at the building. He set the cabinet on the floor and let the heat from the portable heater warm his wind-chilled face.

After carting over the second cabinet and his tools, he attached the units to the back wall of the studio as Paige had requested. She put those mini-muscles to work and held each cabinet in place while he screwed it into the concrete block wall. He was glad he'd changed his mind about accepting her help, but didn't she know she could have helped him more by remaining in Hidden Veil after high school?

Within moments of having finished installing the cabinets, the bell over the studio door jangled and Leyla burst inside the building. She dropped her backpack between the shelves and scuffed across the concrete floor in a pair of lime-green plastic boots.

The kids were home from school.

"Hi, Mr. Sutton."

"Are your hearing aids in?" Man, he sounded like Scrooge himself, but he'd started asking her that question every time he saw her.

"Yes, sir." She pulled out the extra stool Paige kept in the studio and scrambled onto it. "We're going to the Christmas Eve service tomorrow night. Are you?"

"Nope."

"Why not?"

"Leyla, honey . . ." Paige knew his attitude toward religion. Did she think she should protect him from embarrassment?

"Because I don't go to church, Leyla."

The little girl gasped. "Don't you know Jesus?"

That's what his smugness got him. How would he extricate himself from the probing question and his own stupidity for stepping into the trap? "I—"

"Mommy and Daddy knew Jesus. They're with him right now in heaven. Don't you want to be with Jesus when you die, Mr. Sutton?"

Aw, man. How was he supposed to answer that with upsetting the child even more?

Sutton braced himself when Leyla nodded as if she'd made a crucial decision. "It's okay. Mom Paige says the best way to know about Jesus is to go to church and read the Bible." Leyla hopped off the stool and grabbed her backpack. "We'll pick you up, and you can sit next to me. That way, I can tell you when the pastor says something important."

The bell jangled as Leyla opened the door and disappeared outside, leaving Sutton speechless, his mind spinning with the ways he'd lost control of the last few minutes.

Paige's raised eyebrow issued a challenge, daring him to disappoint her daughter. "Looks like I'm picking you up at six-fifteen tomorrow night."

She followed Leyla out the door. Sutton stood alone in the studio. He wasn't sure which threw him most, feeling ambushed or this foreign sense of anticipation.

Fourteen

Sutton stood in the parking lot, next to Paige's SUV. The double front doors of The Rock Community Church brought to mind the doors to a dungeon. Step inside and disappear.

His throat tightened. He hadn't attended a regular church service since his mother died. Weddings, yes. Funerals, yes. But not a straight-up worship service. Would they sing songs he knew? He didn't even own a Bible.

He glanced around the parking lot. It was too late to back out now.

Or was it?

He was a grown man capable of making his own decisions about whether to attend a church service. Why think he had to kowtow to a little girl's whims? In another six months, she wouldn't even remember he'd come here tonight.

Warm lights shone on the building. Overall, the old Quonset hut turned feed store turned place of worship seemed inviting enough. And with the upbeat music coming from inside, he questioned whether he was attending church or a rock concert.

At least he had ignored Debra's suggestion to wear his suit coat. Meeting his friends for an occasional lunch after church had taught him that a nice pair of jeans and a dress shirt was as formal as the occasion demanded.

Unless this special night demanded something dressier. He glanced down at his clothes, then at the others filing inside the building. Lots of red and green sweaters, but he was good.

"Sutton?"

He blew out a breath at the sound of Lane calling his name. He had hoped to sneak inside without attracting the attention of anyone he knew, especially his friends. Instead, he'd stood around gawking, wasting time and trapping himself.

Here we go.

Sutton did his best to rid his expression of the dread that twisted his insides. He felt like the beaters of a taffy-pulling machine curled and tugged on his insides like it formed a rope of candy.

Lane and Macie stopped at his side. Lane glanced from him to the other side of the SUV, where Paige ushered the kids out of the vehicle. First, his eyes lit with surprise, then humor.

Sutton crossed his arms. He lowered his voice and said, "Don't get any ideas."

Eyes wide, Lane tried for an innocent "Who, me?" appearance. "No ideas here."

"Then stop looking like you swallowed a clown."

Lane laughed and slapped Sutton on the back. "I've been trying to get you here for years, but I guess I wasn't the right one to tempt you."

"Don't get your hopes up. I came tonight because I got out-maneuvered."

Thankfully, his friend didn't ask for the details of that sad tale. He'd never hear the end of the teasing.

Paige moved to the front of the vehicle. Holding Cassie, she and Macie talked while Liam and Macie's son Alex bolted into the church like best buds. During the drive, Sutton and Paige had said little to each other. No need to, because the kids gabbed non-stop about the service, Christmas morning, their friends. Whatever entered their minds turned to words.

"Are you ready, Mr. Sutton?" Leyla stared up at him. She looked at Lane and said, "I brought Mr. Sutton to meet Jesus, so when he dies he can talk to my mommy and daddy in heaven."

Sutton wanted to crawl into the nearest hole and let someone shovel dirt over him. He should never have agreed to ride with Paige. If he'd driven his own truck, he could leave whenever the inclination struck him . . . like now.

Rather than laugh as Sutton had expected, Lane said, "I'm glad you brought him. You must be Leyla. I'm Lane."

She looked the horseman up and down. Her grin revealed the start of a new tooth to replace one she'd lost a couple of weeks ago. "Both our names start with L. It's my favorite letter in the alphabet."

"Mine too."

Sutton's back teeth clenched. "Can we take this inside before we miss the show?" Before his other friends arrived to pile on with the "Sutton and Paige sitting in a tree . . ." rhyme.

The girl leaned toward Lane and in a loud whisper said, "He isn't very nice sometimes."

Lane's bellowed laughter drew the attention of the women. "Don't worry. He's more bark than bite."

Paige laid a hand on her daughter's shoulder. "It's getting cold. Let's go inside."

Leyla grabbed Sutton's hand and tugged him forward. The church was almost full. A teenager drew candles from a basket swinging from her arm and handed one to each of them. His confusion must have shown, because Paige said, "It's for the end of the service. You'll see."

They couldn't find enough empty seats to sit with the Beckers, but Paige found four near the back of the room, enough for her, Cassie, Leyla and Sutton. Liam and Alex had already settled into a row closer to the front.

Sutton hadn't entered the building since Lane and Macie's wedding in August. This visit was completely different. Already at least ten people had welcomed him with smiles, handshakes, and—when necessary—introductions.

Once the music changed to something softer, conversation halted. Kyle walked to the front and gestured for everyone to rise. The band played, and words flashed on a large screen. Standing beside Sutton, Leyla belted out the words to "O Little Town of Bethlehem" as loud as her little voice could manage.

Sutton nudged her with his elbow and tapped his ear. Leyla frowned and dug into her backpack for her hearing aids. Paige glanced at him, her smile warming him more than the combination of the central heat and the packed church.

Over the years, he'd missed her smile and those eyes that sparkled with humor . . . and love.

To keep himself from being smothered by the past, he focused on the song, listening but not singing, which brought up another memory. His mother would walk around the house at Christmastime, singing at the top of her lungs as she cleaned—a little like Leyla without her hearing aids. He could still hear her voice when she told him the Christmas story and prayed with him at bedtime. She talked about God's love for his children—how no one on earth could match its greatness and depth.

Almost as if she knew the future, she would say, "God loves

you, Sutton. Never forget that. People will fail you. They'll disappoint you. If you ever feel abandoned by others, remember that God is faithful. He'll always be there waiting for you to reach out."

Guilt stabbed him in the gut. He had forgotten his mother's words from years ago. How? She'd said them with such conviction, such certainty, begging him to remember. And he'd let her down, just as Paige and his father had let him down.

"Are you okay?"

Sutton blinked to find Paige had leaned over Leyla and whispered in his ear. "Yeah. Sure. Why not?"

"Because you looked like you'd seen a . . ." She reached out to place a hand on his arm, then drew it back. "Never mind."

They both faced forward as the pastor started speaking. "Tonight, I won't focus on the typical scripture in Luke that we associate with this time of year. As I prayed about what we celebrate—of course, the birth of Jesus—God led me in a different direction. I want to talk about God's love for his children."

The muscles in Sutton's neck and back turned to steel, and he crossed his arms. The last thing he wanted to hear was a sermon reiterating his mother's words. But he couldn't turn away, couldn't shut out the confident voice coming from the front of the sanctuary.

As the pastor—Pastor Jim to his congregation—held an open Bible, Paige pulled out her phone and tapped, probably bringing up a Bible app like Lane and Trey kept on their phones. She held the phone in front of Leyla, so the girl could follow along as the man read the words that appeared on the screen behind him, words from 1 John that drew Sutton's attention.

"'This is how God showed His love among us: He sent His

one and only Son into the world that we might live through Him. This is love: not that we loved God, but that He loved us and sent His Son as an atoning sacrifice for our sins. Dear friends, since God so loved us, we also ought to love one another. No one has ever seen God; but if we love one another, God lives in us and His love is made complete in us.'"

Sometimes, Sutton didn't feel as though much love lived inside him.

Afterward, Pastor Jim waxed on for twenty minutes about the real reason Jesus was born. About how much God—*the Father*—loved his children and provided a way, not only for them to join Him in heaven, but for them to be that embodiment of love in this world. It all started with the birth of a baby.

This is love: not that we loved God, but that he loved us and sent his Son as an atoning sacrifice for our sins.

Nowhere in there did the pastor talk about the grisly death Jesus ultimately suffered. What loving father would do that to his child? It made Sutton's dad look good.

"As you celebrate this Christmas, remember that God sent his Love to the world. He'll always be there waiting for you to reach out."

Reach out? Wasn't it up to God to make the first move? Then again, according to the pastor, He had.

Okay, God, if You care so much, work out my family situation and maybe we'll talk.

As Pastor Jim finished and walked away, Kyle stepped onto the stage. "Take up your candles and stand, everyone."

Sutton wasn't sure what the candles were for, but knew he was about to find out.

A lot of shuffling and rustling went on as people rose, clutching their small candles in plastic holders designed to catch any dripping wax. To Kyle's right, a man played "Silent Night" on a violin, and Kyle led the congregation in singing. As he had earlier, Sutton simply listened.

One candle lit another, which lit another, the flame being passed down row after row until at least a hundred flickering lights glowed throughout the room, including Sutton's. The peace in the ritual called to him—drew him like a moth to the flames being held high on the last verse.

Silent night, holy night,
Son of God, love's pure light
Radiant beams from Thy holy face,
With the dawn of redeeming grace,
Jesus, Lord, at Thy birth,
Jesus, Lord, at Thy birth.

With the close of the service, everyone quietly filed out of the building. In the parking lot, people trotted to their vehicles. During their time inside, snow had fallen. Paige's three kids shuffled around the SUV, making footprints in the snow. They let the flakes land on their hands and opened their mouths to catch them as they fell. While they wanted to stay and have fun, Sutton wanted nothing more than to go home.

Minutes later, Paige pulled into the farm's driveway. He reached for the door, and Leyla said, "We have something for you, Mr. Sutton."

Twisting in the seat, he watched as she dug through her backpack. She pulled out a small but heavy rectangular box wrapped in Christmas paper and handed it to him.

He glanced at Paige, who shrugged. "Leyla insisted."

Sutton unwrapped the box and opened it. "A Bible?" Really? Not even Lane had gone this far in his effort to see Sutton "saved."

"Everybody needs one."

He closed the box's lid and opened the car door. Once he left the vehicle, he turned back, holding up the box. "Thanks."

As Sutton walked into the house, he weighed his options. He could toss the book, box and all, into the kitchen trash can. He could read it, but didn't see himself doing so. Or he could hide it in a drawer until Leyla forgot she had given it to him.

"He'll always be there waiting for you to reach out."

For now, he would go with the last option.

Fifteen

Paige stood next to her mother in the row at the front of the church designated for the bride's family. In the background, a woman played the "Wedding March" on a keyboard. Like all the guests, Paige's attention was on her sister as she walked down the aisle in a frothy white gown.

Correction. Reagan bounced toward her groom, who stood with a goofy grin on his face and adoration in his eyes. Dad did his best to keep up with Reagan, but to the amusement of the wedding guests, reached the altar a step behind her.

Paige leaned toward her mother and said, "Next time, we get Dad running shoes."

Her mother's shoulders shook as she tried to keep the laughter inside.

Trey and Reagan had decided on a small wedding party with only one attendant each—Brianna as Reagan's maid of honor and Kaine as Trey's best man. However, family, friends, and townspeople packed the church.

Paige and Dustin had eloped, defying his family's wishes, adding another reason his parents hadn't liked her. They believed the elopement was Paige's idea, even after Dustin took the credit. At the time, eloping sounded romantic, especially when Paige dreaded the social spectacle his mother would have made of their special day. But after attending the weddings of friends, she realized what she'd missed. What her parents and his had missed.

If she had it to do again . . .

No reason to waste time on "if only," since she couldn't see herself marrying again.

Lane slipped in next to Macie on the groom's side. Kyle and Jo had found seats a couple of rows behind Paige. Since Vera wasn't with them, Paige assumed Jo's grandmother stayed home with little Rose.

And Sutton? He had ushered in Trey's mother, but Paige hadn't seen him since.

As discreetly as possible, she scanned the guests. There. In the back. He stood near the door of the sanctuary. The last time she saw him in a suit, they attended their senior prom. He'd looked good then, but tonight . . . She caught the admiring sigh before it escaped.

Paige's gaze swept the room. He probably brought Blondie as his plus-one. She didn't see Nicole. Unless the woman declined the date. A spark of hope flared, throwing Paige's emotions off kilter.

Since he stood there alone, why couldn't she motion to him to sit with her?

No, that wasn't a good idea. She sat in the family row, which would cause all kinds of rumors to spread. Of course, after he attended the Christmas Eve service with her, it was too late to avoid rumors.

Something had happened to him that night. Paige had seen it in his face. Now, she prayed for him often, something she should have done years ago. Like Leyla, she would love to see him find Jesus.

Oh, that shocked expression on his face when her little girl presented him with the Bible, as though he didn't know whether to accept it or give it back. Pride over her daughter's caring heart had welled inside her.

Fingers gripped Paige's arm, and she looked down at her mother. Too late, she realized the music had stopped and everyone had taken their seats—everyone but her. She dropped into the chair, staring straight ahead, her face ablaze. On her other side, Liam and Leyla chuckled.

Thankfully, the ceremony proceeded with the bride and groom wholly unaware of the way Paige had embarrassed herself. Their focus centered solely on each other.

Before Paige knew it, her sister and Trey had said their "I do's." She swiped at the moisture under her eyes as the couple walked back down the aisle, clutching one another and smiling at the people they passed.

"That was beautiful." Paige's mom dug a tissue from her purse.

After an endless number of photographs, Paige herded the kids into the crowded fellowship hall—an addition built onto the main body of the church—for the reception. She'd spent hours since Christmas helping her mother and sisters prepare food and set up decorations. It had helped to have Macie donate a couple of scrumptious dishes. Although good advertising for Macie's upcoming catering business, the Hartwells believed she did it out of friendship and a good heart.

Between the wedding, the holiday activities, and the renovation to the house, finding time to fill her pottery orders was like a treasure hunt for Paige, a precious commodity that often came late at night. Work piled up—literally. Pieces sat on tables and the workbench, waiting to be fired or packed for shipment.

Mom reached out for Cassie's hand. "Come with me, sweetheart. I want to show you off to my friends." She looked around. "Where are Liam and Leyla?"

Paige stood with Brianna, Shaina, and Harmoni. "They ran off to play with friends."

"I guess I'll introduce them another time. Let's go, Sassy Cassie."

The child giggled at the name and grasped her grandmother's hand.

Paige had met Brianna's date, Tucker Fleming, at Thanksgiving. He was a soldier—the brother of Brianna's close college friend. As much as her sister played it down, the relationship appeared to be serious, and Paige was glad he'd been able to attend the wedding.

Tucker and Ethan, Shaina's date, excused themselves to get their dates some punch. Paige had declined their offer to bring her back a cup. So did Harmoni.

Shaina asked, "How's the renovation coming?"

"It's slow, but I can't complain, and Sutton and Kaine are doing a terrific job."

Shaina glanced at something behind Paige. "I would expect it of Sutton, but—"

"But not of me?"

Hearing Kaine's irritated voice, Paige turned her head to see him standing a couple of feet away. During the Thanksgiving get-together, she had sensed the friction between the two of them. Today, Shaina had gotten in the first dig.

Shaina raised her chin. "Did I say that?"

"You don't have to say anything to be toxic, Shayla."

An unladylike snarl rose from Shaina, and the two of them peeled off in different directions, putting as much distance between each other as the small room allowed.

"Don't mind them." Bri chuckled. "They clashed the first day they met, and things haven't changed."

"Why did he call her Shayla?"

Brianna shrugged. "Who knows? It's part of their routine. They're like a comedy team without the laughs."

"Interesting."

"Nice wedding, but I'm going to give the bride and groom my congratulations, then go home." Harmoni's voice barely rose above a whisper. "I have pets to feed."

Paige turned to her. "Dogs or cats?"

"Both. Plus a lizard, two rats, a boa, and a ferret." After reciting the bizarre list of pets, Harmoni walked away.

Brianna laughed. "You should see your face. You look like you just noticed the lizard sitting on your shoulder."

"Not a good mental picture, Bri." Paige shivered.

They talked for a few more minutes. All the while, Paige's subtle gaze swept the room.

"Who are you looking for?"

Evidently, her search wasn't as subtle as she'd thought. "No one." No one but Sutton and his blonde.

"Lane said Sutton had to leave. Something about a family crisis."

Ignoring Bri's mind-reading capability, Paige asked, "What kind of crisis? Was someone hurt?"

"He didn't say so. With that family, it doesn't take much before they run to Sutton for help."

Paige hadn't realized the rigidity in her shoulders and back until the muscles relaxed after a short, silent prayer for Sutton and his family. The poor guy had his hands full.

Her body's reaction had calmed, but knowing of his absence left her feeling alone in a church building filled with people.

He couldn't get through a friend's wedding celebration without receiving a distress call from home.

Sutton drove down the country road at a speed that could get him a ticket, but figured the sooner he got to the farm, the sooner he would solve whatever disaster required him and be able to return to the reception. He slowed after hitting a pothole that threatened to send the truck off the pavement and into the grass. The budget held no room for a broken axle, new alignment, or worse, a new truck.

He parked next to the farmhouse, got out, and slammed the door. Even from the steps going into the mudroom the argument inside assaulted his ears.

Debra met him in the kitchen. "I'm glad you're here. Dillon and your father . . . I've never seen them so angry with one another, and they won't listen to me." Hoarseness kept her voice low. "Your father has threatened to kick him out of the house."

"Sit down and relax. I'll handle it."

Sutton marched into the living room to find the two combatants standing a foot apart, eyes locked on one another, bodies stiff, and jaws tight. Dad complained. Dillon shouted his defense. Ariel, Patrick, Joel, and Jenna stood on the stairs to the second floor, watching the action.

"What's going on?"

Without breaking eye contact, his dad and brother attempted to explain their positions at the same time. It only sounded like a loud and garbled buzz to Sutton's ears. He put his fingers to his mouth and released a screeching whistle that had them both wincing and turning to him.

"What the . . ." His dad rubbed his ear. "What was that for?"

"My sanity." Sutton propped his hands on his hips. "Dillon, you first. Tell me what's going on." When his father protested, Sutton raised his hand. "You'll get your turn."

Dillon took a step toward Sutton. "First, he tried to tell me I'd added too much feed to the trough for the cows." He pointed to Dad. "What would he know about it? I can't remember the last time he fed the livestock or fixed anything around here."

"I've been working around the farm since I was a toddler, boy. I know how to spread feed."

"Oh, yeah? When was the last time you stepped foot in the barn? You're too interested in your bottle to care about what's going on!"

"That's enough, Dillon." Sutton ran both hands through the waves of the short hair on his head. "He has a point, Dad. You haven't helped out—any meaningful help—in years."

His father's whisker-stubbled chin dipped, and his lower lip trembled. The look of shame lasted all of two seconds before he straightened. "We shouldn't waste feed. You know that. You're always getting on to me about wasting money. Besides that, the boy drove the tractor around like he was some hotshot NASCAR driver. I tried to—"

"Wait a minute." Sutton turned to Dillon. "You took the tractor out today?"

The defensiveness returned to Dillon's voice. "Yeah. So?

What's wrong with that?"

"The snow the other day left a muddy mess when it melted. Driving that heavy tractor over slick wet ground leaves ruts we'll have to smooth out. I just made a payment on that equipment. We can't afford to wreck it. What were you thinking?"

"I thought I needed to learn how to drive it if I'm going to help you around here." Dillon took a breath. "I was thinking you promised to teach me, but like him," he cocked his head, gesturing toward Dad again, "it turned out to be an empty promise."

"I've been busy, Dillon. You know that."

"Yeah, busy putting Paige and her kids above your own family."

He dared to tell Sutton how to carry out his business? "Busy making money to pay for your food, Debra's medical bills, Christmas presents, Dad's beer, the utilities that keep this house warm and the lights on, and supplying the feed you wasted!" His gaze hit on each person in the room. "If anyone else wants to take on the responsibility, be my guest. Right now, I've had it with all of you."

Let them argue it out themselves. He'd had his fill of drama for the day.

He spun to escape the room only to find Debra standing in the doorway to the kitchen, standing in his path to freedom and a sound mind.

She moved aside to let him through. The touch to his arm as he passed stopped him. "I'm sorry. I shouldn't have called you today, Sutton. You have a right to be fed up with all of us. I am sorry your father and I abandoned our position of authority in this house." She drew in a deep breath as though filling her lungs so she would have enough air to continue. "I am as much to blame as anyone for forcing you to be the stronger member of the family." Another deep breath. "You should have lived your childhood as any other young one, as your brothers and sisters have had the privilege of doing. Go back to the wedding and enjoy yourself. It's time your father and I handled our lives ourselves."

For a moment, he stood frozen, staring at the newfound strength in her expression, the determination in her smile. Could she do it? She couldn't a few minutes ago. Part of him wanted to stay to see if she would succeed, but he decided she deserved the chance to try.

Possibly, he'd gone too far in assuming responsibility for the lives of everyone else in his family. He may have even made things worse by not forcing his dad and stepmother to step into the roles of providers and mentors. The only way to know for sure was to stand down and let the parents take over.

He bent forward and kissed her cheek. "Thanks."

Sutton crossed the kitchen and paused at the mudroom when the volume of her hoarse words rose. "Now, you all listen up. Things are gonna change around here. That goes especially for you, John."

"But, Debra—"

"I'm done hearing your excuses and pleading 'Debra's,' and I'm not done talking, John Vance."

Sutton walked out the back door, his steps sluggish and his emotions dazed by his stepmother. A gradual grin lifted the corners of his lips. He would either come home to peace . . . or total destruction.

Questions stopped him on the way to his truck. Was this the start of a different way of life for the Vance family? He recalled his off-the-cuff challenge to God on Christmas Eve. Had God heard and answered?

Sixteen

No. No, no, no. This can't be.

First, another argument with Liam that morning. Now this.

Seated behind her desk at home, Paige studied the order form from three months ago, then reread the email forwarded from Shellie. It referenced a purchase scheduled for shipment by the end of December—products she hadn't created yet. The purchaser demanded Paige "ship the items in three weeks or consider the order canceled."

A small and somewhat simple order, she could throw the pieces in a day, but she also needed time for drying, firing, glazing, and another firing.

She had never dealt with this particular business before and had no history with the owner, but the haughty tone of the email indicated the woman had little patience for errors and even less grace for those who committed them.

How could she have let this order slip through the cracks? And it wasn't the first. Since starting her business, she had never missed an order until she moved here. This was her second one. She couldn't afford to gain a reputation for being unreliable.

She reread the sheet she'd printed and placed in her order

binder. This requisition had become priority number one, and she was thankful it was only five scalloped lace soap dishes and five simple spoon rests. Still, she made it a point to treat each customer the same, whether they ordered one piece or fifty.

Thankfully, the business, a specialty boutique in Charlotte, was close enough that she could deliver everything herself if necessary. It was for the best. She could ensure everything arrived unbroken—undoubtedly, damage would send the woman into a tailspin—and she could apologize in person.

Her concentration broke with the sound of a cheerful whistle outside her office window—a prelude to the *whir* of the saw Sutton used to cut the lumber for the new board and batten wainscoting in the kitchen.

Over the past few days, Sutton had taken to whistling as he worked. While no one would confuse him with Snow White—Grumpy, maybe—it was nice to know he enjoyed his job.

Paige jumped from her seat, ready to go outside and ask Sutton to be quieter, so she could think. She sank back down in the chair, realizing she shouldn't stop him from doing the work she'd hired him to do. Like her, he had a job to finish.

Paige picked up her phone and moments later said, "Hey, Mom."

"Hey, honey. What's going on?"

Thankfully, the noise had stopped. Paige didn't have to strain to hear her mother's voice.

Not wanting to wear out her or her children's welcome, especially after Reagan's wedding had worn them all down, she had worked hard to give her parents a reprieve from grandchildren over the past week. "Is it all right if I bring the kids over after school?" She barely recognized the meekness in her voice.

"Sure."

Relief surged through Paige. She had returned to Hidden Veil for help with the children, but didn't want to burden her parents.

"Do you have plans for tonight?"

The expectation in her mother's voice left Paige figuring Mom hoped she had a date. Paige wanted to laugh. With whom? She'd met few people since returning, except for her sisters' friends. The men were married, aside from Kaine Abbott—too young—and the guy working outside.

"No, it's work, a rush order." A late order.

"Oh, I thought you asked me to watch the children for a special reason."

The saw began again. Paige got up from her desk and escaped into the hallway.

Did Mom assume that she and Sutton were together again? Paige couldn't blame her for jumping to conclusions after they attended the Christmas Eve service together. On second thought, her mother's interest could have come from catching Paige staring at Sutton at the wedding. She couldn't recall a recent time when she'd so thoroughly embarrassed herself.

"No personal plans, Mom. The move, the renovation, and the holidays put me behind in my work, and I'm on the verge of losing an order. Are you sure you don't mind? It may be late before I pick them up."

"We'll manage. In fact, I've missed seeing them since the wedding. I can come for Cassie now. If you'll call the school, I'll pick up the other two this afternoon and take them to Locke's Soda Fountain."

Great. Hyped up on sugar and ruined appetites. But her mom was doing her a huge favor, and this once, a pre-supper treat wouldn't hurt them. "Thanks. You and Dad have been a tremendous help."

After the call, Paige emailed Shellie, asking her to respond to the boutique owner with word that Paige would personally deliver the order at the end of the month. Afterward, she rushed upstairs to check on the napping Cassie.

Once her mother had left with the little girl, Paige grabbed her binder with the order information. On her way to the back door, she peeked into the kitchen. Since Sutton and Kaine had torn out the cabinets and removed the appliances and counters, the room was a blank slate. Empty and dusty from all the work being done.

"Sutton!" She walked outside and yelled over the noise from the saw—a shout that had no effect. "Sutton!" She ventured closer, reached out to tap him on the shoulder, and caught herself before touching him. The sudden disruption could have ended in disaster. As though he sensed her presence, he shut off the saw. She jumped back when he turned. Not that she stood close enough for him to bump into her, simply too close for her comfort.

"What's wrong?"

"Nothing's wrong."

He raised the eye protection he wore, settling it on the top of his head. Paige clutched the binder closer, like a shield. Despite the fine dust clinging to his plaid flannel shirt and forming raccoon rings around his eyes from the safety glasses, he looked amazing. Had she ever seen Dustin dirty? He'd often been fastidious to the point of making her feel like a slob.

As she stood there, lost in admiration, Sutton's brow creased, a silent request to know the reason she'd stopped his work. She shook some sense into herself. "I'm headed to the studio. Mom's picking the kids up from school. I wanted to let you know I won't be back inside the house until late, so I'd appreciate it if you'd lock the front door when you finish today."

"Sure."

Paige ventured another gaze into Sutton's face. She had thought she could handle working with him, that they would adapt to a new, more amiable relationship, maybe an eventual friendship. They had, but these last couple of weeks left her asking whether she could settle for being a friend to him. Years ago, she'd realized the difficulty of it and left town. That couldn't happen now. She was stuck.

She backpedaled. "I'd better go. I have a lot of work to do."

"Yeah. Me, too." He pulled down the eye protection and rotated away from her, ready to return to cutting the lumber to panel the walls . . . without so much as a goodbye. If they were indoors, he might well have said, "Don't let the door hit your backside on the way out."

Why should she expect a goodbye after she hadn't given him one years ago?

By the end of the day, Sutton had finished cutting the pieces that would form the panels for the kitchen wainscoting. With all that had interrupted his work since mid-December, he'd upended his schedule and stayed at the house longer than he would have liked.

Paige had opted to remove the plaster and lath from the outer walls of the kitchen to add more insulation and replace the original plaster with sheets of drywall. He'd begin tackling that messy job tomorrow when Kaine was around to help him. The work would expose the wiring for the electrician to come in next week.

His stomach rumbled, and he checked the time on his phone. Six-twenty-seven. He'd skipped lunch, so it was no wonder he was hungry. Had Paige eaten? He hadn't seen her since she left the house for the studio hours ago. She'd seemed frazzled.

He phoned the farmhouse.

"Yeah?"

Sutton recognized Joel's sullen greeting. "Hey. Tell Debra I won't be home for supper."

"Okay." His brother hung up.

Sutton frowned at the phone. Joel needed to work on his communication skills. Then again, Sutton wasn't the one to teach his brother, not when his skills weren't much better. He grinned. The new Debra could handle teaching Joel how to answer the phone.

Jenna told Sutton that after he walked out of the argument between his father and Dillon the day of Trey's wedding, Debra had lit into all six of the remaining Vances, whipping them into shape like a drill sergeant. Even his dad had taken to towing the line—for the most part. She allowed him two beers a night, with the goal of cutting it back to one, then none. She also forbade him to gamble. Only time would tell how long the prohibition would last, but for now, her taking charge was a load off Sutton's shoulders. Stronger in willpower, she also seemed physically stronger—and happier.

Two weeks had passed since Christmas Eve. He hadn't forgotten the message he'd sent to the God he wasn't sure existed.

. . . work out my family situation and maybe we'll talk.

Was that what had happened? Had this unseen deity that Lane believed was active in his life instigated a change in the Vance family? It was possible he owed God that talk, after all.

Later. For now, he made one more phone call before packing up his tools, locking the front door of the house as Paige had requested, and heading for the truck.

Twenty-five minutes later, he returned to Paige's house and parked in the back, his headlights shining on the building that had become The Potter's Hand studio. He snatched a plastic bag from the passenger seat, turned off the lights, and exited the truck that now smelled of the grilled hamburgers and French fries he'd ordered from the Red Dog Diner.

After closing the truck door, he froze. This was crazy. He ought to get back in his truck and drive off, leaving her alone to work. What did it matter to him if she stayed there until late tonight without eating?

Had she already eaten? Didn't want to be disturbed?

Maybe he'd leave the food in the truck and feel out the situation first. Or maybe he'd eat both meals.

He could see Paige through a window, bent over her pottery wheel. So focused on her work she hadn't seen the headlights? She straightened on the stool, flexed her back, and rolled her shoulders. How long had she sat there without a break?

As though she realized he was watching, she turned her head toward him, her expression puzzled. Too late to back away, to eat his hamburger alone and in peace.

Sutton arrived at the door at the same time Paige opened it. She peered around him. "Is something wrong at the house?"

"No problem. You didn't see my lights when I pulled up?"

She shook her head. "I guess I was too engrossed in my work."

He held up the bag. "Have you stopped long enough today to eat?"

"I've been busy." She sniffed the air. "Hamburgers from the Red Dog Diner?"

"You know your hamburgers."

She smiled. "I know how to read the name on the bag."

He glanced at the plastic bag with the diner's name. "Hilarious, Paige." But he couldn't stop the grin that insisted on finding its way to his face.

"They're the best." She put her hands together in a gesture of begging. "Please say that's mine."

"One for you. One for me."

"Those bearing hamburger gifts are welcome to enter." She stood aside to let him in. "Let me finish the piece I'm working on. I'm almost done. Half of the long table is clean and empty. Don't wait for me. I'll join you in a few minutes."

"No, I'll wait."

Sutton pulled out the to-go boxes and placed them on the cleared end of the worktable. The other half held a couple of dozen unfinished pieces, most of them small. Although he saw a few mugs similar in style to the ones she used at home, the purpose of the rest of the pieces—especially the round ones with a lip—eluded him.

He watched as the wheel spun and Paige's hands continued to work the clay up and down with little visible effort. Soon, her wet fingers finished forming a small bowl. The concentration on her face demonstrated the seriousness with which she took her work. All the while she explained the process. Once she'd created lines on the outside of the bowl with what she called a rib tool and appeared satisfied with the look, the wheel stopped. She picked up a wire with wooden handles at each end. It reminded him of an instrument of death.

"You're not fixing to garrote me, are you?"

Paige laughed. "Only if you deserve it."

Several wrongs flashed through Sutton's mind. His Christian friends would call them sins. He preferred to call them errors in judgment. Lane's voice echoed in his head. *"Doesn't matter, man. Even the tiniest wrong choice is an offense to a holy God."*

In Sutton's opinion, none of his wrong choices rose to the level of deserving spiritual death as Lane claimed.

But what if he were wrong?

Seventeen

True to her word, Paige finished in a matter of minutes. She placed the newly-created piece at the other end of the table. "I'll cover these overnight, let them dry tomorrow until they're at the leather-hard stage, sign them, and let them dry again." She moved as she talked, cleaning up the pottery wheel. "After they're dry, I'll fire them."

"Then they're done?"

"No. They're at the bisque stage. Then, they're glazed and fired in the kiln again." She pointed to the silver metal box at the other end of the room—the kiln, he presumed.

"I didn't realize how many steps were involved to create the simplest piece."

She graced him with a low-watt smile. "Let's eat our burgers before they get cold."

When Paige reached for a box from the diner, Sutton held it back. "Since when did mud become an accepted condiment?"

Paige glanced at her hands, covered in a wet and chalky gray clay. She made a face. "You're right. Starvation made me forgetful. I'll be right back." She hung her apron on a hook and walked to the door. "I'll bring us back some drinks. Diet okay?"

Diet? He made a face behind her back but said, "Sure." He should have ordered drinks with the food. Starvation had made him forgetful, too. His mind had centered on the food itself and Paige's reason for working so late.

Paige returned from the house with two soda cans. She sat down on one of the stools he'd pulled up to the table and handed him his drink. "Thanks for doing this. Sometimes I get wrapped up in my work and forget to take a break."

Like he often did. If Debra didn't see that he ate and took breaks during his time in the fields, he'd either starve or suffer dehydration.

"Do you mind if I pray?"

Sutton had learned over the years that having Christian friends meant mealtime prayers, sometimes long ones. He braced himself and hoped his stomach didn't go off while she talked. "Go ahead."

"Father, thank you for caring so much that you provide what we need, whether it be time, money, or this food. You are the Great Provider. In Jesus' name, amen." She raised her head and opened her eyes, her mouth cocked in a grin. "And thank you, Sutton, for being His deliveryman."

Deliveryman? He did the work and paid the bill only for God to get the bulk of the credit?

He opened his to-go box and nodded to the pottery pieces that looked like shaped raw clay at the other end of the table, changing the subject. "Do you put your name on everything like other potters do?"

"Not my name. I use 'Isaiah 64:8.'"

Sutton recognized the reference to a verse in the Bible. He'd seen it on her website—a tagline under the name of her business. Something about clay and potters and a father's hands. "Clever way to come up with your company's name."

Paige cocked her head. "You know the verse?"

Given his well-known aversion to religion, he couldn't blame her for her surprise. "I didn't memorize it, but it's on your website."

"You checked out my website?"

Should he let her shock offend him? Sure, he'd checked her website. He saw the verse and the online shop that displayed her products. He also noted what she charged for things he could buy at Walmart for a quarter of the price.

Well, maybe not Walmart, but it was another reminder of how far his finances lagged behind hers.

After swallowing the bite he'd taken from the now lukewarm burger, he pointed to the pieces at the other end of the table. "What are those?"

Paige heaved a sigh she must have felt all the way to her toes. "My effort to catch up. It's why I'm here so late. With the move, the renovation, the wedding, and settling the kids, I've gotten behind in fulfilling my orders."

Her voice rose higher with each word, so he covered her hand with his. "But what are they?"

"Hmm?" Her eyes widened. "Oh. I'm sure you recognize the coffee mugs."

"I do. The others?"

"The scalloped oval pieces are soap dishes. The round pieces are spoon rests. Of course, there's a platter and four dinner plates."

"You did all this today?"

"As I said, I'm behind."

"It's a lot."

"I've done so many of these pieces, I could do them in my

sleep." She covered a yawn, as if the word sleep brought on the need for it.

"You've come a long way from making mud pies in the dirt, Paige." Sutton concentrated on the burger, hoping she hadn't heard the wistfulness in his voice.

"God gave me a certain amount of talent and a desire to be a potter." Paige bit into the burger and almost swooned. "Not even hot, this is so good. I didn't realize how much I missed Rick Burns's food."

"Maybe you should have come back sooner." The words slipped out of his mouth before he could catch them.

Paige set the rest of her hamburger in the to-go box, her appetite gone. This visit from Sutton—the sweetness of his concern that she not go hungry and him bringing her a favorite meal—had stirred her expectation over what prompted it. Now his remark that she should have returned to Hidden Veil sooner left her scrambling to decide how to respond.

Maybe it was best to ignore the comment. Then again, maybe it was long past time to address their history.

"Sutton, I've already apologized for leaving like I did, but I should have said it the first day I arrived back in town. So, I'm saying it again. It was cowardly, and I'm sorry."

His jaw tightened, and he pushed away the Styrofoam box with only half of the hamburger and French fries eaten. "I won't disagree."

Paige nodded, understanding his frustration.

"One day you were here. The next you weren't. I didn't even

know why you left, Paige. You gave me no warning."

"You knew. You had months of warning and an afternoon of argument."

"You only left because I didn't want kids?"

As always, that subject had led to their last quarrel. "You understood the importance I placed on having children, and I understood why you didn't want a family. But parenting your own children isn't the same as raising someone else's." Paige's voice dropped off with the last word. Oh, wow. She'd just repeated Dustin's excuse for leaving her.

Her ex had wanted his own children. He wanted to leave the considerable estate he would inherit one day to offspring he had fathered. She'd heard from a friend that he was engaged again. Had he insisted on a fertility test this time?

Sutton closed the lid on his box. "What I understand is that I wasn't enough for you."

Paige opened her mouth, then shut it. Was he right? "I never meant for you to feel that way. That never entered my mind. We wanted different things from our lives, and I couldn't see how we would work. Looking back, I understand that my younger self handled everything wrong."

Those brown eyes drilled into her. "So, Matthews shared your dream of having kids?"

The last person Paige wanted to talk about was Dustin and his rejection of her and the children. "In a way."

"Paige—"

"Dustin's idea of being a father meant having biological children, not adopted ones." She attempted a smile, but it fell flat. "If it helps, I've learned what it's like to be tossed aside for not measuring up."

Lines of confusion formed on Sutton's face. "Are you talking about the divorce? How did *you* not measure up?"

The outrage in his voice brought on an all-too-familiar blurred vision until the room swam. A good thing. She hated hearing the outrage in his voice turn to "Serves you right" on his face.

His expression softened some. "Paige, what happened?"

"I found out . . ." She cleared the lump from her throat and brushed away the tears that streaked down her face. "I can't have children of my own. I never could." She hiccupped a laugh. "Ironic, huh?"

Speechless.

Sutton sat speechless, unable to come up with a response to Paige's announcement. What did she expect him to say? How could take away those tears? It had always slain him to see her cry, and it seemed nothing had changed in fifteen years.

Which was the best reason he could think of to fortify himself against the intense urge to pull her off her stool and onto his lap, encircling her in his arms. Nothing had changed for him, but everything had changed between them.

Yet part of Sutton wondered. If they had known years ago that she couldn't have children, would she have still left him? Would agreeing to parenthood have kept her from marrying someone else? From going through a divorce? Images of Liam and the two girls carried with them the realization that his silence wouldn't have prevented her from hoping to adopt.

Back then, they were both rigid in their opposing ideas. They remained so today. He hadn't changed in his opinion of fatherhood and, biological mother or not, she came with three children.

Paige was right. It wouldn't have worked for them. So why was he even here now?

And yet . . .

She swiped trembling fingers across her face again. He curled his fists to keep from reaching out to comfort her but lost that battle when his hand disobeyed his desire to keep it to himself—to remain aloof. How could he pretend he felt nothing when she fought so hard to control her pain?

And who said he couldn't show some humanity, some support?

He covered her hand with his. Even with the cold weather and working with muddy water, her skin was soft. She had said a good lotion was her best co-worker.

"After Marissa's husband died, she reminded me I had agreed to adopt the children should anything happen to her. She was being cautious, of course, but we never thought . . ." Her throat worked with obvious grief. "Sometimes, I wonder if she didn't know."

The warmth of her skin and the quiver of her fingers penetrated through his calluses. "Dustin's family opposed the idea. We'd been married for a couple of years, and I hadn't gotten pregnant."

Sutton's chest tightened with the reminder that another man had touched her. Hypocritical given his own past.

"Because Dustin was an only child, I think they were afraid assets that had been in the family for generations would go to someone who wasn't a true Matthews."

He refocused his attention on the story.

"Plus, Marissa was *my* friend, and they had never approved of me. I came from a small-town, blue-collar family. They didn't think I was good enough for their son."

Everyone in Sutton's family had loved Paige, even his dad when he was sober enough to pay attention.

"At first, Dustin didn't mind signing the paperwork. He'd wanted a large family, too. I'll admit it was probably the most important thing that attracted me to him. But he drew the line at ever making Marissa's children his heirs."

When she stopped speaking, Sutton couldn't let it go without knowing more. "What happened to the marriage?"

"After we were told the news about my inability to have children, Dustin's parents continued to their campaign to convince him he'd made a mistake in marrying me." She huffed. "They circled like sharks and intensified their disapproval over our marriage. They put pressure on Dustin, and Dustin put pressure on me and the kids, especially Liam. He was hard on him, always finding fault."

An uncomfortable heat enveloped Sutton. The heat of guilt?

"I tried to compensate for Dustin's attitude by spending more time with the kids."

As far as he could see, she continued to overcompensate. But was that any worse than turning a cold shoulder to them like he'd done?

"I also put more time into my work." Paige glanced around the studio. "So, you see, it wasn't all Dustin's fault when he agreed with his parents. And that was that."

"That's when you came home?" Did she come home or run home?

"Not for a while."

At the note of defeat in her voice, Sutton had to harden his muscles, especially the big one in his chest. Everything in him wanted to reach out and take her in his arms. He wanted to console her, sure, but it went further. He longed to kiss her like he used to do, like it was all that mattered in the world—*she* was all that mattered.

That couldn't happen. He couldn't let himself get swept up in the story and carried away on a tide of fruitless emotion. He couldn't risk her leaving Hidden Veil a second time . . . leaving him.

And yet, what was life without risk? What was risk without the possibility of reward?

He rose from the stool and pulled her to her feet. Denying his common sense—that impulse to second-guess his next move—he drew her into the enclosure of his arms. His chin rested on the top of her head while he forgot the pain of the past and focused on the perfection of the moment.

Then it hit him. Home. She was home. Right where she belonged.

Sutton drew back only enough to look into her eyes to see the same anticipation buzzing through his veins. Those eyes reflected nothing but the promise of soft lips meeting his again after years apart.

Sutton's phone went off, jarring them both and threatening to ruin their moment. No way. He let it ring. And it rang. Over and over as he tried to recapture time.

"You should get that. It might be important."

"No."

"Sutton."

She was right. It could be family. Who knew what disaster awaited him at home?

He kept one arm around her, his gaze on hers, as he yanked the phone from his pocket. He hit the button. "Hello?"

"Hey, Sutton."

"Nicole."

Paige pushed away and moved to the other end of the table, standing near the pottery.

He should have taken his focus off Paige and looked at the phone screen before answering the call. If he had, it would have rolled to voicemail and the moment wouldn't have been ruined.

Nicole talked, but all Sutton heard was the "Wah wah wah" of Charlie Brown's teacher. He broke in. "I'm not at home. Let me call you later."

Paige halted in the process of covering the new pottery pieces with a light sheet of plastic. The pause lasted to a two-count, then she resumed her work.

Nicole said, "Don't forget."

"I won't." How could he? These calls had turned into nightly occurrences.

Sutton regretted the few times he'd taken her out since reconnecting with her. Lane wasn't shy in his opinion that Nicole was the wrong woman for him. It didn't take a mind reader to know who his friend would say suited him best, especially after Lane told him of Paige's awkward moment at the wedding. Too focused that day on the call he'd taken from Debra, Sutton hadn't noticed that Paige remained standing, staring at him, after everyone else was seated. Lane's story had sparked an involuntary smile on Sutton's face, giving the horseman more ammunition in his belief that Sutton and Paige belonged together.

He slipped the phone back into his pocket. By that time, Paige occupied the seat at the pottery wheel again. "Paige—"

"I'm sorry. I have work to finish, so I can bring the kids home."

Recognizing defeat when he saw it, he gathered the box holding his cold hamburger. "I'll see you tomorrow."

She looked up. Her wan smile testified to an instant in time that had wrenched their emotions. "Thanks for the food."

Sutton nodded and walked out, even as the voice inside him screamed for him to turn around, tell her Nicole meant nothing to him, and beg her for a second chance.

Until he saw his battered truck.

Evidently, Dustin had a hefty inheritance. Even though Paige said his desire for children attracted her to him, surely she hadn't overlooked his material assets.

Sutton forced his feet to carry him farther from the studio.

Eighteen

Just like that, Sutton disappeared, and the silence in the studio echoed her disappointment.

Paige slammed a piece of clay on the wheel head, centered it, and slapped it with her palm. Well, she had all but told him to go. What did she expect? He'd beg her to let him stay? A silent chuckle tickled her throat at the idea that Sutton Vance would beg for anything.

She splashed muddy water on the clay, bent forward, and placed her hands and fingers in position to mold a bowl for an online order.

If she hadn't insisted Sutton answer the call, she would have kissed him. If she hadn't insisted he answer the phone, she wouldn't know he still dated Blondie. She had almost made a fool of herself, mistaking his desire to comfort her with a desire to kiss her.

Her foot pressed the pedal, and the wheel head spun—faster and faster. She forced herself to ease up on the pressure before she lost control of the clay.

Paige added more drops of water, then guided her fingers to open the slab of clay. *Nicole.* She had once liked that name.

Now she despised it. Of course, that attitude was unreasonable. Not every Nicole was a bombshell airhead dating Paige's former love.

What was more unreasonable was thinking Paige's opinion should matter to anyone, especially to herself. She had ruined her chance with Sutton long ago, and he wasn't the type to excuse that with a simple "Oh well."

But he had remembered the hamburger meal she always enjoyed and brought it to her. Should she read anything more into it than kindness toward someone who worked late?

In exchange for food, she had revealed to him her biggest secret, something she'd told no one but her mother, who she'd sworn to secrecy.

Paige took her foot off the pedal and stared at the bowl, misshapen by fingers exerting too much pressure. Exhausted and finished for the day, she threw up her hands, releasing thoughts of Sutton to the air.

Sutton pulled a pre-measured-and-cut sheet of drywall across the floor of the trailer hitched to his truck. He carried it through Paige's back door and into the laundry room, a space Paige had talked of sprucing up in the future. Kaine followed him with another sheet.

After knocking out the walls to the old, tiny closet in Paige's bedroom, he breathed easier when finding no issues that would make the job more difficult and expensive. No one knew what surprises the walls of an old house held. This one had kept those surprises to a minimum so far, both in number and expense.

While they awaited the inspection of the electrical and plumbing, Sutton and Kaine had framed in a walk-in closet and bathroom in Paige's massive bedroom. Today, they would add the drywall to the inside of the closet, creating a space almost two-thirds the size of Sutton's bedroom in the farmhouse.

Liam trailed behind them. Being a Saturday, the kid had dogged their steps all day, crowding the area, at least for Sutton.

"There's nothing for you to do here, Liam. Why don't you go play or something?"

The kid gave him that sour look Sutton was getting used to seeing. "I'd rather watch."

Sutton shot him his own look, one that brooked no argument, and Liam's shoulders sank.

Kaine propped his sheet of drywall against the bedroom wall. "Hey, Liam, you can do me a favor. It's tough climbing the stairs while carrying those drywall boards. I have one more sheet to go. Why don't you guide me up the steps so I don't trip? That will free Sutton to put up what we've already brought inside."

Trip? Kaine needed no help. Surely Liam wouldn't fall for that. He had seen both men carry sheets upstairs without tripping.

The boy's face brightened. "I can do that!" He trailed Kaine back out the bedroom door.

Kaine Abbott could talk a dog into giving up a bone. Sutton frowned. What if Liam tried to carry a sheet, then dropped an end and broke it? The budget allowed little room for replacing materials because of carelessness.

Simple solution? He'd take the cost out of Kaine's pay, making it the last time the guy enlisted the help of a ten-year-old.

Sutton opened his mouth to shout out a veto of the idea that Liam help. Then Paige's description of her husband's—ex-husband's—treatment of Liam rolled through his mind. He snapped his mouth shut. How different was the man's attitude toward Liam from his?

Sutton shot a screw through the drywall and into a stud. Kaine may be a charming but bitter smart-aleck sometimes, but he wasn't irresponsible, and all it had taken was giving Liam a job to bring a rare show of happiness to the boy's face.

The same had applied to Dillon when Sutton let him work around the farm. So far—minus the tractor incident—his brother had done a good job with everyday chores, enjoyed the work, and had taken some of the pressure off Sutton.

Dillon had a lot to learn about farming, though—things that had nothing to do with equipment and tools. Things he'd begged to be taught. Up to now, Sutton hadn't had the time. Check that. He hadn't made the time.

He shot a few more screws into the drywall.

Liam's cheerful voice rose up the stairwell. "Okay, Mr. Kaine, pick up the bottom a little. That's good."

Kaine carried the drywall sheet into the room with a smiling Liam tagging behind. When the boy glanced at Sutton, that upturned mouth turned down in an instant. Yep. Kaine was the hero today. And, as usual, Sutton was the villain, just as he was often the villain with his siblings—a role he'd grown tired of playing. Why was that? It had never bothered him before.

"Liam!" Paige called to him from downstairs. The boy mumbled something and shuffled out of the room.

"He's moody, isn't he?"

Sutton chuckled. Kaine was the pot calling the kettle black. The humor faded when he realized he hung from the pot rack himself.

"I think I'll head out."

Sutton glanced at his watch. "Yeah, it's getting late."

Kaine eyed the unfinished closet. "I can stay if you need me. It's not like my social life will take a hit. I don't think I've had big Saturday night plans since Trey and Reagan's wedding."

Sutton relied on low-cost fun but found plenty to do, even if it only involved hanging with friends. Sometimes, he wondered why Kaine stayed in Hidden Veil. "No, I'm good. Go ahead. I won't be far behind. See you Tuesday."

"Okay. I'm out of here."

It didn't take long to screw the rest of the drywall to the studs, and Sutton finished with the wall at the back of the closet. Monday, Kaine had to work at Harley's, leaving Sutton to tape and bed the new walls by himself. Country music, a bucket of mud, and he could do the job on his own.

He picked up his tools and left the closet. Two steps into the room, he looked up, and his body jolted to a sudden stop. All three kids watched him from Paige's bed on the other side of the room. How had they sneaked into the bedroom without him knowing? It was the eeriest thing he'd seen since last Halloween's haunted house tour.

"What's going on?"

"Nothing," said Leyla. "Liam said it would be fun to watch you work."

The boy scowled at his sister. "I did not."

"Yes, you did." She raised the hair covering her right ear. "See? I have my hearing aids in. You said, 'Let's go watch Mr. Sutton and see how long it takes him to throw us out of Mom Paige's room.'" Leyla let her hair fall back over her ear and turned to Sutton. "Is this when you throw us out?"

First of all, he didn't care a bit for Liam's attitude. Second, the kid was undoubtedly right in his theory of what Sutton would do if he'd caught them watching him.

Normally, the situation would earn a low growl from him, but for a reason he would likely never understand, he laughed. Not a frustrated, wry chuckle. This was a full-blown belly laugh, one he couldn't stop. Must be due to lack of proper sleep and a hefty work schedule.

Or life had finally driven him over the edge.

Whatever the reason, it prompted laughter from Leyla and Cassie. Like him, the girls probably didn't understand what they found so funny.

"What's going on in here?" Paige stood at the door, a stack of folded towels and washcloths in her arms. She glanced from him to the giggling girls and back to him, her eyes wide. "Who are you and why are you using Sutton Vance's body to entertain my children?"

"You get funnier and funnier, Paige." Still, as much as he tried, he couldn't stop the grin that followed his words. "Just because I don't want my own kids, it doesn't mean I can't be civil to someone else's."

Leyla's laughter stopped, and her little mouth rounded with disbelief. "You don't like kids, Mr. Sutton?"

Great. He'd forgotten kids heard everything. How did he explain without digging himself a deeper hole with that explanation?

Before he could figure out a response that didn't make him seem like an ogre, Paige eyed the children. "I told you before. You all need to let Mr. Sutton work and not bother him."

"They weren't a bother." Now why did he say that? He ran a hand down his face. It had to be fatigue. That supposition didn't keep him from opening his mouth again, though. "And earlier, it was possible Kaine wouldn't have made it up the stairs with a sheet of drywall if it hadn't been for Liam's help."

Paige tilted her head, confusion obvious in her stare. She turned to her son. "What did you do to help?"

Liam stared at Sutton as if he saw a stranger. Had he even heard Paige's question?

What harm would it do to let Liam think he helped? "He made certain Kaine didn't trip. It . . . um . . . it saved me having to do that duty."

"I see." Although he didn't condone lying, the spark of appreciation in Paige's eyes made his stretch of the truth worth every word. Without breaking eye contact with him, she spoke to the children. "Why don't you kids go downstairs and set the table for supper?"

Liam frowned, and all three continued to sit like lumps. Sutton eyed the boy. The kid needed to know he wasn't in charge. "She told you to move."

After studying Sutton as though judging his authority, Liam hopped off the end of the bed. "Come on."

Energy flowed through each step as the boy slipped out the door of the bedroom. The girls followed, leaving Paige and Sutton alone in the room. Sutton waited for her to tell him he shouldn't have butted in regarding Liam's rebellion.

She set the towels on the bed and approached him. "Thanks."

"For what?"

"For making Liam feel important."

Sutton would throw Liam a parade just to hear her soft voice and see those grateful brown eyes turned on him. His heart roared like a rocket taking him to the moon, and any fatigue he'd felt burned away with the heat of the stares flowing back and forth between them.

For years, he'd assured his friends that Paige Hartwell would mean nothing to him if they ever met again. He thought he'd convinced himself of it. Turns out, he'd only tried to fool them and himself.

Almost two weeks ago, he'd brought her a hamburger. Ever since, he'd kept his distance, but now, this was like that night. His whole being begged to reach out and pull her to him, to hold her, and feel those lips on his. To be a better man than in the past, a better man than her ex. Maybe even a man who dedicated himself to raising a family alongside her.

His arms rose, intending to pull her to him.

But how could he be that man, knowing the problems and responsibilities that existed with his family? Paige had been through enough with Dustin's parents. Besides, she was used to a certain lifestyle and would grow tired of being the breadwinner in their relationship or scrimping to pay the bills.

The heat turned to ice, and his arms fell to his sides.

Whoa. Who knew that bringing a stack of newly laundered towels upstairs would lead Paige to nearly hyperventilate?

She had closed much of the physical gap standing between her and Sutton. What would happen if she stepped even nearer to him? If she attempted to close the chasm she'd opened when she ran off?

What would happen if they finished what they started nearly two weeks ago?

She slid one foot forward on the hardwood floor and drew it back. Something in his demeanor had changed. He went from looking as though he wanted to kiss her to hardening his features—his entire body. He'd become like a block of ice, and she could feel the cold from where she stood.

Evidently, she'd misread him. For the second time in two weeks.

Paige tore her gaze away and settled it on the new closet behind him. "It will be wonderful to have all that space. I still have clothes packed away for lack of room to hang them." Something in what she had just said brought a deeper frown to his face. "What's wrong?"

"Nothing." He reached down for the tool belt he'd laid on the floor inside the new closet.

"Did I say something you didn't like?"

"Nothing you said, Paige. Not exactly."

She swallowed with the sudden ache in her throat. "Are you afraid I'll leave?"

He ran a hand through the waves of his hair until his palm cupped the back of his neck. Then he dropped his hand. "I'm the same person I was fifteen years ago. I have the same problems, the same responsibilities, and the same financial issues. We shouldn't start something with no chance of going anywhere."

"But, Sutton—"

He held up a hand to stop her. "I've wanted to buy this house for years. Even if I had scrounged up enough money to buy it, do you know how long it would have taken me to do the renovations?" When an answer eluded her, he said, "I could only afford to do a little work at a time, so it would have turned into a never-ending process. You've seen my beater of a truck. You know I still live in my dad's house. I have a little savings. Otherwise, I own next to nothing. I was never the right man for you, Paige. I never will be."

He thought material things were more important to her than love? "Sutton—"

"And I'm dating someone else."

Her stomach lurched at that statement. *Nicole.* Until now, Paige hadn't fully realized the seriousness of their relationship. Well, that settled her previous concerns over the renewal of a romance between Sutton and herself.

Paige moved back to the bed and picked up the towels, avoiding a glance in his direction. "Are you finished for the day?"

"Yeah. I'll be back Monday?" He said it as if he questioned whether she would want him back.

She had a house in a disorganized, half-finished state and a business she needed to get back on track. Even if she wanted someone else to complete the project, which she didn't, when would she have time to find and hire another contractor? Somehow, they would muddle through this renovation and, maybe, learn to co-exist in their small town without her heart breaking each time she saw him. "Monday."

Once he walked out of the room, Paige flopped down onto the king-sized bed. She wasn't born to money any more than Sutton and had never rejoiced in landing someone of Dustin's financial status. Yes, she had benefited by it and even enjoyed spending the money. But money came with its own set of problems.

Paige surveyed the new walls—the closet and the bathroom. She pictured the plan for the new kitchen. Maybe she enjoyed the money more than she'd realized. On top of their mutual wish for a family, had his wealth drawn her to Dustin? What if Sutton was right in claiming a lesser lifestyle wouldn't satisfy her?

She pulled her phone from her back pocket and pulled up the group contact with her sisters. Her fingers skimmed the digital keyboard with a text.

Company and conversation tonight? Do you have time?

Is something wrong?

What's up?

Paige bit her bottom lip. Was this the wisest thing to do?

I need advice.

Okay.

Sure.

Just knowing she could count on her sisters settled the roiling inside Paige.

Let me get the kids fed and settled in their rooms. Here, about 8:30?

I'll be there.

Me, too.

Paige clicked off, then stored the towels in the hall closet and went downstairs. *God, grant all of us wisdom.*

Nineteen

Paige watched out the front window until she saw Reagan's car turn into the drive. Before her new doorbell could announce a visitor, she opened the door. "Come in."

She hated feeling weak and had almost canceled this sisterly confab. If she had, though, she wouldn't rest and would probably fall asleep during tomorrow morning's sermon at church.

Reagan stepped into the hallway and shivered. "*Brr.* It's cold out tonight."

Paige laughed. "It is still January." She took Reagan's coat and laid it over a dining room chair. "Bri should be here—" Headlights flashed across the dining room window. "Here she is."

Ten minutes later, all three Hartwell sisters settled in the front parlor with a cup of coffee or, in Brianna's case, hot chocolate. With the children's bedrooms on this side of the house, Paige would hear if they moved around too much. The girls should be in bed, but she allowed Liam to stay up until nine o'clock, a bedtime rule he didn't always abide by.

They spent about three minutes in small talk, then, ever the impatient one, Reagan asked, "Okay, what's up? You said you needed advice."

Brianna grinned. "Reagan is eager to get back to her new hubby."

"Oh, I'm sorry." Paige hadn't given thought to the newlyweds' need for alone time when she called.

Reagan waved off Paige's apology. "An emergency came up, and Trey isn't home. I got the idea through your text that this was important."

"Me, too."

Paige sipped the steaming coffee and set the mug on the coffee table. "I'm probably making too much of this, but I want to know if you think I'm the type to be . . . money hungry. Do you think I put physical comfort and material things before relationships?"

Brianna's brow puckered. Reagan sank back in the chair across from the couch where Paige sat and studied her.

Bri shook her head. "Absolutely not. Why would you even ask that?"

The blunt and tell-it-like-it-is sister remained silent. "You haven't answered my question, Reagan."

"I'm thinking."

"Oh, come on, Reagan. You believe Paige is money hungry?"

"I didn't say that, but she does like nice things—expensive things. Clothes and all."

"She can't help that Dustin insisted she wear clothes you and I couldn't afford even from a thrift store."

Oh, that's a ridiculous claim.

"And drives one of the higher-priced Lexus SUVs."

Sutton had commented on her expensive car with leather seats. *What is wrong with my car?*

"Hey," Paige waved her hand in front of her face to get their attention, "I'm here. Talk *to* me, not about me."

Both sisters mumbled, "Sorry."

"I don't think you are money hungry, but you got used to buying the best when you were married to Dustin." Reagan set her mug on the round table next to her chair and leaned forward. "Now, what is this really about?"

Paige stopped to listen when she heard footsteps overhead. Once the sound died out, she said, "Sutton and I . . ."

When she hesitated, Brianna's eyes lit up. "I knew it! You two got back together! I told Reagan that would happen." She turned to Reagan, a smug grin on her face. "Didn't I?"

"Bri, we're not back together, and that isn't the problem." Paige took a calming breath. Boiled down, it was one of her problems, but she needed to set her youngest sister straight before Brianna reserved the church for a June wedding. "He claims I could never be happy with . . . anyone . . . who had no money in the bank. Do you think he's right?"

"That's silly."

Paige appreciated Brianna's defense but focused on Reagan, who sat with her lips pinched. Clearly, she wondered whether to agree with Sutton or Bri. "Well?"

"Paige, guys are providers. It's how they're wired. They want to provide for the family. It's possible Sutton sees your car, your house, your successful business, and he feels like you wouldn't need him."

The business hadn't been so successful lately, but that was another problem for another time. "He's wrong. I would always need him." That came out differently than she'd meant it. Or maybe not.

Reagan's gaze drilled into her. "You said you aren't together.

Are you hoping to change that, because as far as I'm aware, his opinion about being a father hasn't changed. What if you married and became pregnant?"

Paige's skin warmed with the reminder that she had never informed them of the real reason she and Dustin split. "I haven't been up front with the two of you. Mom knows, but—"

"What do you mean?"

"I told you Dustin walked out because he didn't want to raise Marissa's children. That was true, but it wasn't the whole truth. He wanted his own children, not someone else's, and we had none."

"You were only married a couple of years." Brianna huffed, her irritation with Dustin clear. "Was he that impatient?"

Paige rubbed her cold hands together. "It had nothing to do with patience, Bri. A few weeks before Liam, Leyla, and Cassie came to us, we learned we couldn't—I couldn't—have children."

Both sisters sat mute. Finally, Reagan said, "Why didn't you tell us?"

Paige shrugged, and she could barely see them for the moisture that built in her eyes. "For years, I bragged about how many children I wanted and the good mother I'd make. I'm embarrassed to say that neither of those things happened."

"Hey, you have nothing to be embarrassed about," said Brianna. "And Marissa wouldn't have entrusted her children to you if she didn't think you were the perfect one to raise them."

"She's right, Paige."

A half-laugh, half-sob, from both disbelief and gratitude, escaped. "Crazy how things turn out, huh?"

Brianna moved to the couch, wrapped an arm around Paige, and squeezed. She was always the most people-oriented of the three of them. "Not crazy, but you could have told us. We wouldn't have thought less of you. We don't now."

Not the touchy-feely type, Reagan remained seated in the chair. "Does Sutton know?"

"It came out in a conversation we had a couple of weeks ago." The laughter she had heard coming up the stairs this afternoon returned to haunt her. She had to admit, for a moment, it had sparked a flicker of hope inside her. "Getting pregnant is no longer a concern, but three children remain in the mix. Besides, he has a girlfriend. He emphasized that point to avoid any ideas I might get in my head."

"Do you have ideas in your head regarding Sutton?"

Of course she did, but Paige wouldn't give Bri more matchmaking ammunition. "You heard me say he has a girlfriend."

"Girlfriends come and go."

Reagan's nose wrinkled with displeasure. "You're not talking about Nicole, are you? If so, forget her. It won't last. They tried once before, but she dumped him for another guy. He isn't stupid enough to trust her a second time."

Then why did he take Nicole's calls? Why renew a relationship with her, something he had no interest in doing with Paige? "He isn't so stupid as to trust me, either."

Brianna returned to her chair and picked up the cup of hot chocolate. "Anyone with half a brain knows he's never stopped loving you, and I think he'll realize it one day soon."

The three of them concentrated on the drinks in their cups. Paige considered it a reprieve from the conversation about Sutton but not from her thoughts about him. Was Brianna right?

Somewhere nearby, a quiet rustling and thumping noise registered. She paid only enough attention to hope a family of raccoons hadn't moved into the crawl space under the house.

"Paige, you asked if we thought you were money hungry. No. You're not."

"Thanks, Reagan. I'm glad to hear it. I don't even know why it mattered. I do know it's crazy to worry about Sutton's opinion of me. I have three children. They come first. I wouldn't trade them for any man." By the frown on her face, Reagan had something else on her mind. "What?"

"Do you think your desire to be a great mom has led you to spoil the kids? How many pairs of boots does Leyla own? What about all the toys you've bought for Cassie? And Liam? Does he really need every new video game when it comes out?"

With the criticism, Paige wished she hadn't asked her sisters—Reagan, anyway—to come over.

"You can't make up for the loss they've experienced by buying them things or letting them walk all over you."

Says the woman with no children.

Since when had her sister become an expert on motherhood? Now Paige really wished she hadn't consulted them. "You've talked to Mom?"

"No, but it sounds like you've talked to her. I'm speaking from my observations and my experience with Quill." Reagan laughed when mentioning her Labrador retriever, the one she adopted after he ran out in the road in front of her car last year, almost costing Reagan her life. "Like your kids, he's a sweetheart, but if I had let him get away with some of the things he's done since I've had him, he'd be a spoiled monster. Believe me, I see them every day at the clinic."

"My kids aren't monsters."

Reagan rolled her eyes. "I didn't say that. I was talking about dogs and cats that come into the clinic. I may not be a mother yet, but I know what over-protected and over-compensated looks like."

"You two hold on." Brianna inserted herself into the conversation. "Paige, they're great kids." Before Paige could turn a smug look on the middle Hartwell sister, the youngest continued, "That doesn't mean they couldn't benefit by you laying down a few ground rules, one of them being that they show you respect, especially Liam."

Paige recalled asking the kids to set the table for supper. None of them obeyed, and defiance stood out on Liam's face . . . until Sutton's low, menacing voice convinced them to move.

First her mother. Now her sisters. She had returned to Hidden Veil to be near family who could help her with her children, and she respected each woman. They all agreed that the kids needed more boundaries and she should exert more parental authority. Would that make her a better mother, or drive Liam further away?

"I'll think about what you've said."

The inspector had approved the electrical and plumbing in the kitchen and bathrooms. Sutton decided he and Kaine would finish their drywall work in Paige's bedroom before tackling the drywall in the kitchen. While Sutton screwed the sheets to the bathroom studs, Kaine sanded the joint compound sealing the seams in the closet, preparing it for painting.

Paige appeared at the bedroom door. "Hello, Kaine."

"Hey, Paige."

Sutton's heart kicked up whenever she was near. This moment was no exception, even if she didn't address him.

Today, she wore faded jeans. Unlike his well-worn, naturally faded denims, these were modestly snug and probably bought already washed out. Placed side by side, the differences between Nicole and Paige shouted at him. One was heavy metal rock and the other a church hymn.

Even if he preferred the hymn, the heavy metal fit his circumstances better.

"The cabinet man called. The kitchen and bathroom cabinets will be ready in two weeks." After that announcement to the air, she walked away.

Less than the estimated twelve weeks. Time had gotten away from him. He wanted to refinish the kitchen floor before the cabinet installation.

Kaine appeared at the opening to the bathroom. His body shook with feigned shivers. "Is it my imagination, or did a cool breeze blow through here?"

Sutton ignored the bait, even though he'd felt the frost. He shot the last screw into a sheet of drywall. "If you're cold, wear a sweater."

"Maybe I will." Kaine positioned the next sheet on the wall and held it for Sutton to attach. "You and Paige are not getting along?"

"It's personal."

The guy had a point, though. The air had definitely cooled since he shut down the heat flowing between him and Paige last Saturday. She'd remained distant all week.

"I'll take that as a 'You're right, Kaine. We're not getting along.'"

Sutton shot a few screws into the drywall, catching the studs. Man, the way she'd looked at him Saturday . . . silently begging him to kiss her. He figured his face had reflected the same desire, because his mind had sure suggested turning back time and engaging in one of those make-out sessions from the past. What a disaster that would have been—for both of them.

Even though Sutton probably owed Nicole a thank you for providing him with an excuse he could use to back off and put some distance between them, he should break things off with her. The longer they dated, the more he realized why it hadn't upset him when she dumped him the first time.

Kaine shrugged. "I don't want to get caught in the crossfire of whatever is going on between you two. I've gotta hand it to you, though. I would find it hard to work with someone after the relationship broke up."

Not if you had no financial choice.

Sutton gave him the side-eye. "Trey's been talking?"

"Nah. I got the lowdown from Brianna during one of those rare times I saw her when she wasn't hanging with Trey's receptionist."

The Hartwells had kept Paige's whereabouts secret for years. Evidently, they had used her return to become chatterboxes.

"I may know little about what happened back then, but like I told Bri, you two give off enough sparks to start a forest fire."

Sutton paused his work. He agreed they gave off sparks. They always had. But he didn't need others to comment on it. "You're imagining things. I work for Paige these days. We get along fine, but we're not involved."

Kaine laughed. "Yeah. I saw how uninvolved you were last week. You're one of the hardest workers I've ever met, Sutton. You're also the no-nonsense type, but she walked by you last Thursday and you froze in the middle of screwing down a two-by-four. Then you sat back and watched her until she left the room."

"I did not. I paused my work to take a breath." Now, he sounded like one of Paige's kids or his siblings when they argued.

"Dude, you were so preoccupied with her you shot a screw into the ceiling!"

Sutton winced. True. He'd had to remove it and repair the hole.

He set down the offending screw gun and turned to Kaine. He'd learned long ago that if he wanted to avoid talking about a particular topic, diversions worked great. "There's something I've wondered about you, Abbott. What's going on between you and Shaina Weber?"

Twenty

Sutton waited for Kaine's answer to his question. Shaina and the man at his side had feuded since the day they met at Trey's clinic. When it came to her, anger surrounded Kaine like a force field, and he used obvious jabs at her like a weapon.

Shaina held her own with taunts and insults, but beneath her cool jibes, Sutton had noticed occasional anxiety, as though she feared Kaine would attack her physically. He couldn't imagine that happening, but if it did, the guy would have a whole gang of her friends to deal with.

Under the dark beard, Kaine's jaw worked back and forth. "Nothing is going on between me and Shaina. Believe me, it never will."

"A little touchy, aren't you? She's a nice woman. What do you have against her, Fireboy?"

"Don't call me that, and I'm not being touchy. She isn't my type."

"Why not?"

Kaine's face reddened. "I'm not into spoiled divas."

Spoiled diva? Shaina? She was no mouse like her aunt, but Sutton would never use the word diva to describe her. "What does that mean?"

Kaine raised his dusty hands in surrender. "Okay, I get the message. I won't pry into your life if you promise to never link my name with that woman's."

Sutton had his own problems and no time to care that Kaine's feelings for Trey's manager/receptionist were about as convoluted as his for Paige. At least he'd taken Kaine's focus off his own love life. "Deal."

Liam walked into the room and dropped his backpack on the floor. With the way he treated the bag, Sutton suspected it wouldn't last until the end of the school year. Didn't the boy care about the cost of replacing it? Still, Sutton kept himself from telling Liam to treat his possessions with more respect, that bookbags didn't grow on trees.

How the Matthews children treated their things wasn't any more his concern than his non-existent relationship with Paige was Kaine's concern.

He counted down. *One . . . two . . . three . . .*

"I'm here to help."

Right on time. The kid was nothing if not predictable.

Kaine glanced Sutton's way but, this time, didn't offer to find Liam a task. He left it up to Sutton, who struggled between coming up with one and telling Liam to go away.

Then Sutton remembered the boy's face when he told Paige that Liam had helped them. Only a few words seemed to give the kid a purpose. It straightened his shoulders with pride, and he looked like Dillon when doing farm chores. Ever since then, Liam had walked around like he considered himself a part of Sutton's crew.

After Kaine went back to his work in the closet, Liam glanced toward the bathroom doorway as though checking to ensure they were alone. He held up one side of the drywall sheet Sutton had placed against the bare studs. "Why don't you trust Aunt Paige?"

At Liam's question, the drywall sheet slipped in Sutton's hands, and he almost dropped it. Fortunately, his quick reflexes caught it before it hit the floor and broke the gypsum sandwiched between the paper. The sudden jerk would have pulled it from Liam's hands if the boy hadn't propped a hip against the material.

What had Paige told the kid? Whatever they discussed, he didn't relish anyone else hearing. It wasn't like he could close the yet-to-be-hung bathroom door.

"I could use more drywall screws, Kaine. They're in my truck. You want to bring them up?"

"Sure." Kaine left the room, wiping his hands on a rag.

Sutton leaned against a stud. "What makes you think I don't trust Paige?"

But did he trust her? Maybe he did. Maybe he didn't. He distrusted *himself* more when he was around her. Despite the separate lives each of them had led over the years, that spark Kaine spoke of remained—at least for him. After last Saturday, he believed she felt it, too, and he'd backed away from her.

"I never said I didn't trust her." Sutton pushed off from the stud, raised his gun, and fired a screw into the drywall.

"She did, and she told her sisters about it."

His gaze flashed to the boy. "When?"

"Saturday night when they came over. They said you weren't stupid enough to trust your girlfriend, and Aunt Paige said you weren't stupid enough to trust her either."

Sutton didn't know if he should be irritated that the Hartwell sisters gossiped about him or be glad to know they believed he wasn't stupid. And how did Liam know what they had said? "Where were you when this confidence in my intelligence took place?"

Liam stared at his shoes.

"Well?"

"I wanted a drink of water, so I came downstairs." A skinny shoulder lifted. "When I heard them talking, I . . ."

"You listened." Sutton shot off a few more screws. He was ready for Kaine to return. Where was he? "You know it isn't polite to listen in on someone else's conversation?"

"No, but it's good for learning some things."

"Like what?" Sutton could have bitten his tongue at encouraging a kid to spill what he'd overheard.

"Like you think she's money hungry, whatever that means." Liam shifted, but by this time, Sutton had fastened the drywall to the studs, so there was no danger in it falling. "She also said—"

"I shouldn't have asked, and you shouldn't be telling me about a private conversation between Paige and her sisters."

"Don't you want to know that she thinks you don't like her because of my sisters and me?" His expression challenged Sutton to deny it. "You know, Leyla might care that you don't like children, but I don't."

Sutton inhaled, preparing to answer the boy in a calm voice. No sense in escalating the situation. "I never said I didn't like children . . . in general." He kind of liked Macie's son Alex, and despite his grousing about the responsibility, he liked his siblings . . . most of the time. He may even grow to like this insubordinate child one day. "I don't want to raise any more of them."

"You have kids? Are you divorced like Aunt Paige? Did you

run out on your family like her husband did?" The boy shot out questions with the same speed and power as the tool in Sutton's hand shot screws. "She doesn't need you, you know." His eyes took on a sheen, and his voice rose on that last proclamation.

"Liam Matthews, that's enough." The voice, trembling with ferocity, drew their attention to the bathroom doorway. Paige stood near her bed. "Go to your room." When he continued to stand there, she said, "Go. Now!"

Liam brushed past her and out the door like his sneakers were on fire.

Sutton controlled the urge to whistle under his breath. In all his years of knowing her, he'd rarely seen Paige this angry. He felt a little sorry for Liam.

With the sound of pounding feet on the floor as background noise, Paige glared at Sutton. A storm cloud couldn't have looked darker than her expression. Maybe he should feel sorry for himself.

He waited for her to turn that wrath on him. Instead, she whipped around and disappeared out the door. Angry footsteps pounded the stairs. A moment later, Kaine moved into view.

"Where have *you* been?"

"She wouldn't let me come in." Kaine ambled across the room. "For what it's worth, I don't believe Liam meant it when he said Paige doesn't need you."

Oh, he meant it. What bothered Sutton most was that it confirmed his own belief about Paige. She had everything she needed, so why would she ever need him?

But beneath the storm of his doubts, he questioned the validity of that belief. Because Paige Matthews hurt. And, in spite of his circumstances, he wanted to be the one to help her heal.

"Let's get back to work."

Had she ever been more furious with Liam in his short life?

Paige sat at her wheel in the studio. A mound of clay waited on the wheel head while her mind drifted to yesterday's fiasco. What made him say those things to Sutton?

"You know, Leyla might care that you don't like children, but I don't."

She had approached the bedroom door as Liam's strident voice made that pronouncement. In thinking back on the scene, she felt sorrier for him than angry. He tried hard not to like any of the adults in his world. She didn't know why or how to help him get over his hostility.

Paige pressed the foot pedal, spinning the wheel and working the clay before adding more until she had enough to form the large basin that would be her bathroom sink. She continually checked the thickness of the bottom for the eventual hole to accommodate the plumbing.

She should have finished this personal project weeks ago. Sutton was expecting it. But paying orders came first. Now, even though she remained behind in her work, she couldn't put off this job any longer. A bowl this large took a long time to dry, and after this one, she had two more to throw.

With plenty of work in front of her, her mind still wandered.

When Kaine had tried to enter the bedroom with the screws, she waved him off and stood at the doorway to listen, eager to hear Sutton's response, yet fearful of what he would say.

"I don't want to raise any more of them."

That said it all, didn't it? To be honest, after spending weeks around her kids—around her—she had hoped he had changed his mind, even if only for Nicole's sake. But if what her mother and sisters said was true about her inability to set boundaries for the kids, she hadn't demonstrated a good example for him, so why should he change his mind about fatherhood?

"She doesn't need you, you know."

Eavesdroppers never hear good things about themselves. Liam's heated exclamation had sounded more protective than offensive toward her. Yet his presumption angered her.

No, Paige didn't need Sutton. But she could no longer deny she wanted him in her life, even more than when they were teenagers. Because her wish for them to be together wasn't based on a schoolgirl crush or first love kind of emotion. What she felt rose from maturity, life's experience, and the tendrils of a love that wound around her heart long ago and never set it free of him.

Yes, he could be grumpy.

Yes, he could be frustrating.

But he was loyal and capable and responsible to a fault.

And Paige had *never* loved any man more than she loved Sutton Vance.

"Look, Mommy. I made it pretty for you."

She startled at her little girl's voice and turned her attention to the child, taking in the dirty, wet clothes and the clay sticking to her face and shirt. Those big blue eyes shone with pride, and her hand clutched a muddy rib.

A rib?

Paige's eyes widened, and she glanced at the bowl on the wheel. Large indentations scored the clay in various places after the girl had run the rib tool along the outside of the bowl. Indentations not meant to be there.

"Oh, Cassie."

Twenty-one

Sutton grabbed a cone lying on its side in the corral dirt. He stacked the prop on top of one he'd already picked up. Lane used the cones in exercises to help those who suffered from PTSD. Once he'd finished gathering all six, he carried them to Lane's barn and handed them off to his friend. Lane added them to the rest of the equipment in the tack room.

This was Sutton's Saturday to volunteer at Healing Springs. He did little more than prepare and groom the horses, but he made time to work at the equine therapy center because he believed in Lane's mission.

Lane opened the dorm-sized refrigerator he kept in the tack room and handed Sutton a soda, then pulled out one for himself. "Ron is already gone, so let's sit in the cabin where it's warmer."

With the daylight fading and a slight breeze kicking up, the past hour had brought a dip in the already chilly temperature. They headed to the nearby cabin where Macie and her son had lived until she and Lane married. Afterward, it became a place for clients to unwind and talk. It was also an office for the center's part-time psychologist, Ron Gregory.

Inside, they removed their coats and settled near the fireplace, with Lane taking the couch and Sutton a chair across from it.

"How's the work coming on Paige's house?"

"The work is fine." Sutton popped the ring on the soda can and inhaled the sweet and spicy Dr. Pepper.

"And the relationship?" Lane tipped the can back and drank the soda as though he hadn't just asked a provocative question.

Sutton stared at his friend. "You decided to sneak that one in under the radar?"

What was with everyone? Why couldn't they accept that he and Paige had no future? He accepted it. "There is nothing going on."

At his friend's "I know you better" look, Sutton sighed. This was Lane Becker, the guy who had known him almost all his life. The guy who long ago proved himself to be someone Sutton could trust and confide in. Lane had stuck by him through all his struggles with his mom, his dad, and Paige.

"Okay, it isn't so fine."

Lane pressed back into the sofa's cushions like he planned to stay there for the next decade. "I have time to listen if you want to talk about it."

No, not really.

Holding the cold aluminum can added to the chill in Sutton's fingers. It was nothing compared to the chill that he'd felt from Paige over the past week.

Yes, really. "We had a . . . a moment."

"A moment?"

"Yeah. One of those times when you think you might do something," *like kiss the girl,* "but you back off."

"Ah. A moment." Lane nodded. "Been there."

"Ever since then, she's been cool toward me." He hurried to

defend himself. "Not that I didn't want to kiss her. Under the circumstances, though, it would have been a mistake."

"Because you can't forgive her for leaving?"

Had he forgiven her? Sutton hadn't settled that question yet. He exhaled long and hard. "According to Liam, Paige thinks I don't trust her."

"After what happened, anyone would understand if you're hesitant to want to get involved again. Was Liam right?"

"It doesn't matter. We're no longer the same people, Lane." Sutton scowled at the Dr. Pepper can. "No, that isn't right. I'm the same person. She's different."

"We've all changed since high school, Sutton. We're adulting now and face a whole different list of problems."

Other people faced different problems after becoming adults. Sutton kept the same ones. "Regardless of whether I trust Paige, it's too late. I told her I had a girlfriend."

Lane groaned. "Not Nicole."

"What's wrong with Nicole?"

Lane set his soda can on the nicked-up old coffee table between them and leaned forward, elbows on his knees, hands clasped. "She's nice enough, Sutton, but don't you think she's a little too . . . unreliable? I mean, she dumped you for another guy."

"Are you forgetting that Paige ran off to avoid me, and then *married* another guy?"

"Okay, I can't argue with that. But I know you. Nicole is not someone you want to spend the rest of your life with. Besides, you said you and Paige had a moment. How fair is it to Nicole when you still have feelings for Paige Matthews?"

"I never said I had feelings for Paige. That ship sailed. What happened was—"

"A moment. I get it. What you're saying is that you acted on impulse—a physical thing, nothing emotional."

"No, I—" The twitch of Lane's lips stopped him.

Lane straightened and shrugged. "Why go to the Christmas Eve service with Paige and her kids?"

"I told you. I got out-maneuvered by the middle munchkin." Sutton clenched his molars. "You know my situation, Lane. She and I are no longer on the same level, if we ever were, which means I'm no good for her. She's better off with someone who fits her lifestyle."

Lane frowned. "You believe Paige is too good for you?"

"She has a successful business. An expensive car. The renovation. It all adds up to buying what she wants. She doesn't scrimp and save to pay for something that determines her livelihood."

"Sutton—"

"Don't tell me there's more to life than money. It isn't just the money. It's the kids and the faith and, yeah, the trust. It all adds up to no future for us."

Lane studied him as though he saw a rank horse and plotted his course of training. "Do you remember the first night we took Alex and Macie to watch us in the team roping competition?"

Sutton beamed. "You told me not to call her a buckle bunny."

"I almost laid you out flat." Lane's smile dissolved. "You were great with Alex . . . showing him how to take care of the horses while Macie and I talked."

"Then he had his panic attack, and I beat it out of the barn as fast as I could. What is your point?"

"My point is that most women are more attracted to a man's heart than his wallet. You'll never admit it, but you have a heart bigger than your boot size. If you didn't, Sutton, you would have beat it out of Hidden Veil years ago."

A breath of disbelief escaped Sutton's lips. "I stay because I have responsibilities."

"Which is admirable." The wheels in Lane's mind clearly churned. "Did you know Paige told Macie that you're the reason Leyla wears her hearing aids most of the time now? She wants to please you, and that pleases Paige."

Leyla wanted to please him? He pictured the little girl's big smile every morning as she passed him on her way to the bus. It coaxed one from him in response. Her invitation to the Christmas Eve service and her wish for him to get to know Jesus so he could meet her biological parents someday warmed him. It was as though someone had filled his stomach with hot fudge.

Then he recalled her shock and disappointment when she learned he didn't like kids. "It isn't that I don't like kids." Why had what he'd told Liam slipped from his mouth now?

"I think you like them better than you know, and that scares you."

"You've hung around Ron too long. You're beginning to think you're Freud."

Lane laughed. "Ron's a smart guy."

True. The man had helped Alex and Reagan get through their fears and guilt.

"I didn't think Macie and I had a future, either. You remember. I believed I didn't deserve to be happy with anyone, but the two of us worked and prayed our way through our individual problems."

Sutton's prayer of Christmas Eve came back to him. The Vance family dynamics were far from perfect, but was it a coincidence that life had improved some? Or did God care enough to answer a challenging prayer from someone who had gone out of his way to ignore Him for years? And what about Paige's renovation? It came when he needed the money for the tractor payment. Had God known his situation?

"How do you talk to Someone you can't see, Lane? It seems like talking to God is like talking to air."

His friend's eyebrows rose, and he gaped at Sutton, saying nothing. Finally, he blinked. "Sorry. I didn't expect that topic, and it threw me."

"I get it. It's thrown me, too." Sutton pictured Leyla's Christmas gift. "Did I tell you Leyla—all of them—gave me a Bible at Christmas?"

Lane chuckled. "I like that little girl. Have you opened it?"

"I put it in a drawer."

"All right." Lane tented his hands at his mouth. "Talk to God like you would talk to a friend you respect."

"Like I talk to you?"

"Thanks for the compliment, but maybe show a little more reverence." Lane laughed. "Seriously, He wants to hear from you, Sutton. That means your thankfulness, your devotion, your questions. Anything that makes you happy, angry, sad, confused. You can trust Him to hear."

Confusion? He had that in spades.

"You're saying I should trust God after he sent Jesus to die?" Sutton's voice reflected his anger. John Vance had sacrificed his eldest son's freedom for his own good, so the idea of accepting that God would sacrifice His Son's life rankled Sutton.

Lane's mouth pursed. Sutton waited while his friend apparently considered his answer before speaking. "I've listened to the veterans who come here as they talk to one another, and I've asked some of them if they would serve again. A few say no.

Others think about it before they answer. Some respond right away with a resolute yes. They say, if it meant saving others from harm, they wouldn't hesitate."

"Like Matt."

Lane's brother had saved his team from an IED, something the Becker family recently discovered.

"I think if he were still here, he wouldn't hesitate." Lane paused a moment, then said, "You can't equate God to your dad. God didn't send Jesus for His own gain or in a recklessness manner. He sent Him because He loves us. Jesus, who knew the purpose of his mission and the end result, gave up His life so we could experience that love and share it with others."

The tune to an old children's song he sang as a child ran through Sutton's head. The words came from memory. *Jesus loves me, this I know.*

"You've given up a lot for your family, Sutton. Sure, you feel a responsibility toward them, but no one does that for people—strangers, friends, relatives—without love."

Sutton shifted on the couch, no longer comfortable with the conversation. He wasn't sure why he'd even started it.

He stood and grabbed his coat. "Thanks. I'll give your words some thought."

Lane looked as though he wanted to say more but kept quiet. He followed Sutton onto the porch. "If you decide to dig that Bible out of the drawer, the book of John is a great place to start reading. In fact, if you want, we can study it together."

"Maybe."

His friend let the subject drop but said, "Give Paige a chance to prove herself, okay? She may surprise you."

Or she could run out on him once more. "That whole episode when we were teenagers seems like a century ago."

"Sometimes, it would be nice to go back to a time when we had no greater worries than beating the Hornets on the football field."

Sutton chuckled. "We gave them a hard time."

"We did."

"We can't turn back time, though, can we?" If he could, Sutton would go back to before his mom died and his dad fell apart.

"Not an hour. We need to learn from the past but move forward."

Forward. For Sutton, that started with ending things with Nicole. After that? He wasn't sure.

Jesus loves me, this I know.

The song accompanied him like an invisible passenger during the entire drive to the farm.

Twenty-two

Sutton pulled to the curb and parked. Three cars in the driveway of the house Nicole rented with two other women prevented his truck from fitting.

He peered at the tiny ranch structure on a residential street and compared it to Paige's house. There was no comparison. This place was more Sutton's speed than Paige's, so uncertainty crept in. If not for Lane's assurance that Paige would be more interested in him than his financial status—an assurance he wasn't sure he bought yet—he would forget about his plan for tonight and enjoy the evening.

But this had little to do with Paige and more to do with Sutton's self-respect and disgust over leading Nicole on.

After inhaling a calming breath, he left the truck and walked to the front door. Before he could ring the bell, it opened and Nicole beamed at him as if someone had announced she had won the lottery.

Nope. No enjoyment for this evening.

She bounced outside onto the raised concrete pad that served as a porch. Not wasting words, she wrapped her arms around his neck and greeted him in a way that left no doubt he'd have his work cut out for him tonight. Stay on the straight and narrow, or give it up for a winding path of temporary pleasure?

He eased her backward, breaking the physical connection to her. "Are you ready to go?"

Nicole's head tilted, and her lips pressed into a brooding pout. "Feeling okay?"

"I'm good." Sutton couldn't blame her for asking. When he first started seeing her again a couple of months ago, he hadn't been shy in his physical affection. That had waned over the past month until kissing her had become one more guilty nail in the coffin holding her appeal. "I'm also hungry."

"Then let's go. I wouldn't want to be responsible for your starvation." She winked and grabbed his hand, weaving her fingers between his. "Besides, we have lots of time."

Not as much as you might think.

A few minutes later, he held the door for Nicole, then followed her into a new family-style restaurant on the outskirts of Hidden Veil. His nerves grew taut. If his conscience had allowed, he would have done this the easy way—over the phone. Instead, he'd chosen a crowded restaurant.

He spent a stupid amount of time poring over the dinner possibilities and putting off conversation, when he'd known as soon as he opened the menu what he wanted to order.

After dithering for several minutes, Nicole shut the menu when the server arrived. "I'll have the fried shrimp with coleslaw and a baked potato."

Sutton ordered a burger and fries. While waiting for the food, he gave little more than brief responses to her small talk, seeking a good time to break the news.

Once they had eaten half their meals, he swished a fry through the ketchup on his plate. "Nicole, we need to talk about something."

She pushed her plate away and crossed her arms on the table. "Say it."

"What?"

"Look, Sutton, I've broken up with enough guys—"

Including him.

"—that I know what's coming."

With a deep sigh, he pushed his plate toward hers, his appetite gone. "I think it's for the best that we stop dating."

"I'm not sure we ever did date. Since we got back together, you've been different from last time. At first, I thought you were focused on that house renovation and your family and all. But you really changed around Christmas. You stopped calling as much and were less enthusiastic about our time together."

Had he ever been enthusiastic? He didn't think so, which only brought on more guilt over his behavior these past two months.

Nicole placed her hand over his. "It's her, isn't it?"

"Her?"

"The woman you kept watching during the Thanksgiving meal at Jo E's. She's the one whose house you're working on, right?" Nicole removed her hand from his. "I knew she was trouble for me the minute I met her."

"We used to be close. It was a long time ago. She left Hidden Veil."

"Now she's back, and you want to be close again."

"This is not about Paige and me renewing a romantic relationship. We haven't."

"But you want to."

"It isn't possible, but I can't keep dating you when my heart isn't in it. It isn't fair to you, Nicole, and you deserve someone who wants to be with you because their feelings for you are strong."

"You're right." Nicole pulled her plate back toward her and picked up her fork. "You're a great guy, Sutton, so I won't say I'm happy, but I am glad you were honest with me. I don't have time to waste on a relationship that will go nowhere." She stabbed another shrimp. "You also deserve someone with powerful feelings for you. I saw it from her at the coffee shop that day."

"Not that easy. There are obstacles." Three little ones and one big one.

"There are always obstacles." She stole a fry from his plate and popped it into her mouth. "You have to decide if you have the guts to defeat them."

Sutton processed Nicole's words while finishing his meal. He had always considered her a bit of fluff, a fun time when he needed one. He'd done her a massive disservice in both using her and dismissing her intuitiveness.

Paige opened the door and invited Harmoni into the house. "I'm sorry you had to come here, but Cassie has sniffles, and she's cranky. I didn't want to take her out in the cold."

"It was no problem. I don't live far."

Paige pointed to the objects packaged in the box on the entry hall floor. "I could have brought them later this week."

"Like I said Friday, the pieces you left at the store sold quickly. The soap dishes, the candlesticks, and the lotion bottles all helped to increase the sales of my products, too, so I'm eager for more."

"I'm glad to hear it. Why don't we go in here?" Paige led her into the parlor and gestured for her to sit on the couch.

Harmoni dug into the pocket of her heavy sweater and passed Paige a piece of paper. "Here's your check."

With their consignment experiment starting off small and minus Harmoni's percentage, the payment wasn't large. Right now, though, Paige could use any amount she received.

She sat beside Harmoni, the check in her hand. "Thanks."

"Are you sure I can't get double the pieces this time?"

"I'd like to provide them, but I'm running low on stock. With the renovation of the house and other things going on, I'm behind. Email me with a list of what you want, and I'll bring them to you as soon as I can."

"My customers will appreciate it." A small grin lit Harmoni's face. "Shaina will appreciate it. I think she bought at least one of everything."

"I'll have to thank her the next time I see her." Paige placed the check on the coffee table. "When I get a break, I plan to return to your store. I can't wait to sniff the fragrance combinations in your spring line."

"I'm trying some new herb and flower blends and would love to get your opinion." Harmoni looked around. "Your house is nice."

"It's coming along." Gone was the terrible, tattered wallpaper from the hallway and parlor. "I'm looking forward to the whole inside of the house being painted."

Paige had chosen a soft off-white paint for the hallway to brighten it and make it seem larger. She planned to use the same color for the parlor. For the dining room, she had picked a gray-green, a shade lighter than the kitchen cabinets and board and batten wainscoting.

"Would you like a tour?"

"Sure."

Harmoni followed her from room to room. When they reached the empty kitchen, Paige said, "As you can see, everything is a work-in-progress. The counters, cabinets, and appliances will be in soon, but Sutton wants to refinish the floor first."

For the next few minutes, she explained her plan for the kitchen and the work that Sutton had done and would do. When she'd finished, Harmoni said, "He doesn't like her, you know."

The change of subject threw Paige. "I'm sorry. Who doesn't like whom?"

"Sutton. He doesn't like that woman he brought to the Thanksgiving dinner, even though Shaina says he's still dating her. He doesn't like her in a romantic way." Harmoni spoke that last quiet statement as though it was nothing more than a simple comment on the weather.

"How do you know?"

"People treat me as though I wear a cloak of invisibility." Paige prepared to dispute her claim but closed her mouth when Harmoni raised a hand. "They're not unkind, but because I'm quiet, I'm easy for them to overlook." She smiled. "Except for Shaina, but she doesn't count since we're not only related but roommates and friends."

Harmoni piqued Paige's interest. From her interactions with the woman so far, Paige suspected she possessed an intelligence and depth that the others didn't seem to appreciate. "I hope you'll consider me your friend, too."

"I do. Anyway, silence gives me a chance to observe, and what I saw that day told me Sutton was uncomfortable around her."

"He looked comfortable enough to me."

"Because you saw through jaundiced eyes."

"Jaundiced eyes?"

"I have no interest in Sutton, so my vision is clearer than yours. It's dispassionate."

Harmoni was saying that Paige's vision was skewed that day because of her interest in Sutton? She couldn't deny it, but had anyone else realized she'd seen the couple through the biased lens of jealousy and longing? It didn't matter when he still dated Nicole and made it a point to inform Paige of it. "How did we get on the subject of Sutton Vance?"

"You've mentioned him ten or fifteen times since I got here, Paige, and your voice turns soft each time. Plus, I saw the way you looked at him at the wedding." Harmoni dipped her chin. "I know it's none of my business, but you have a history with him. Maybe it's time to let him know your history can be repeated?"

Did her sense about Harmoni now prove Paige right about her? Yet Harmoni didn't know some things. She didn't know Paige had made a move to repeat history, and he rebuffed her.

"Let's not talk about Sutton. I want to get to know you better. When did you move to Hidden Veil?"

"A couple of years after college."

Harmoni's gaze scanned the room as if she saw it for the first time, and Paige understood what dispassionate vision meant. Harmoni looked as uncomfortable as she described Sutton. "We don't need to discuss it."

A slight smile brightened Harmoni's face. "There's nothing much to discuss. I found the perfect place to open my shop in this town. That's my story."

And she would stick to it. But was it the complete story? Many people's lives were an open book with at least a few pages glued together and unreadable. Paige had a feeling many pages of Harmoni Basinger's life book were stuck together and unable to be read.

The final date with Nicole went better than Sutton had envisioned it. He'd expected her to either throw a fit or—he shuddered—cry. Overall, she accepted their breakup with a calm, almost indifferent mindset. Not flattering, but he'd take it over tears any day.

After dropping her off at her house, Sutton headed back to the farm, grateful he'd followed Lane's advice. But where did that leave him now? His situation with Paige remained the same. Did he have the guts, the desire, to defeat the obstacles that stood in his way? Did Paige have obstacles of her own?

Prayer and work. That was Lane's answer to the problems he and Macie had faced. Sutton could do nothing about the work tonight, but Lane said he could talk to God anytime, anywhere. And, with his off-hand Christmas Eve remark, Sutton owed God a conversation. What would it hurt to try out the trust Lane spoke of and follow through with that talk?

"Okay, God, I owe You thanks for the change I've seen in my family. We both know the Vances have a long way to go, especially Dad, but the effort he's shown so far has lifted some weight from my shoulders." He drew in a deep breath and exhaled, steam filling the air in front of his face. "I'll be honest. I'm not all in on the salvation thing yet, but I'm ready to hear more."

For the rest of the drive home, he laid out every pressing thing on his mind, abiding by the horseman's advice to talk to God like a friend—one who deserved respect and awe.

Once Sutton reached the farmhouse, he parked the truck but remained inside the cab. He spent fifteen minutes in the cold vehicle, talking about his family, the farm, and his financial concerns. If anyone looked out the kitchen window, they probably wondered why he sat in the truck talking to himself. He didn't care. It was good to get things off his chest. If Lane was right, God heard Sutton's words, and he didn't talk only to himself or the air.

"You know my feelings for Paige. I tried to forget, to move on with others, but seeing her again, working on the house, getting to know her children . . . At one time, she was everything to me. Now I'm not sure what to do. I'm not convinced that I'm good enough for her or good father material for the kids. I could use some input."

He paused. Time ticked by with no answer, no firm direction, no suggestions. Should he expect an immediate response? Yes? No? But every time he thought of Paige, it seemed right, even inevitable. Was that his answer?

"That's all I have to say for now. Uh . . . Amen?"

He entered the house through the mudroom.

Debra sat at the kitchen table, peeling carrots. "We'll be ready to eat soon."

Sutton hadn't told her about his date, just that he was going out. "I've already eaten, but thanks."

"Your dad should be home from work soon."

Even though Sunday was a workday for him, so far, John Vance had kept his job with the janitorial service. Sutton considered that in itself a miracle.

Once comfortable in his room with the door shut, Sutton

opened the nightstand drawer and pulled out the Bible Leyla had given him. He opened it to the table of contents and found John among the list of books. Lane had recommended he read it first.

After propping his pillow against the wall, he flopped onto the bed. He began reading with the first verse of the first chapter. It felt odd. After rejecting any mention of God for years, he—Sutton Vance—voluntarily read the Bible.

He paused when he reached the third chapter and the sixteenth verse. "For God so loved the world . . ." Even with the passing of over twenty years, he remembered that verse from his days in Sunday School.

By the time he finished the book and turned the page to see that a new one started—Acts—he had questions for Lane.

Twenty-three

Paige shut the studio door. Halfway across the backyard, she picked up Liam's soccer ball from the dead grass. The cold overnight temperature had deflated the air inside the faux leather. She had told Liam many times not to leave the ball outside. Now, it needed inflating to use it, and she couldn't remember where to find the little pump. Probably still packed in some box somewhere.

She stared at the concave soccer ball, seeing in its flat shape the deflation of her enthusiasm in being a mother. Every time she thought about the cold way her son treated her, Paige considered herself a parenting failure. After the incident in which Liam confronted Sutton, she could no longer deny that her mother and sisters were right, especially when she still hadn't summoned the courage to talk to Liam about his attitude.

A week had passed, and her son's rudeness had only worsened, mostly when Sutton was around. The looks he gave Sutton were toxic. For his part, Sutton ignored the situation and continued his work on the house.

As for Paige's relationship with her neighbor-contractor, nothing had changed. No one would ever believe they had once talked of marriage. It felt more like she had hired a stranger to renovate her house.

She had to face it. Instead of things getting better through her move back to Hidden Veil, they had gotten worse. In fact, more tip-toeing took place around here than through the lyrical tulips.

God, did I run ahead of You once more through all I've done since moving here? When will I learn?

Paige bundled closer into her coat. She couldn't wait for spring and warmer temps, for a warm-up between her and all the people in her life.

She opened the door to the laundry room and dropped the flattened ball into a crate containing outside toys for the kids. Two steps up and she entered the hallway of the house. Since her mom had taken Cassie for a playdate with the grandchildren of one of her friends, she only had to worry about lunch for herself.

Paige winced at the whir and grind of the floor sander but peeked through the clear plastic sheet Sutton had hung on both doorways to contain the dust to the kitchen. Masked and wearing protective eyewear, he ran the machine over the hardwood flooring in a straight line, forward and back, scraping off years of stain. He had the muscles to accomplish the job, but watching him work made her glad she hadn't tried to do it herself.

She took in the flat, dull planks devoid of the old stain and imagined the beauty of the hardwood after he applied a new, lighter stain.

Sutton looked up. He shut off the machine and waved her into the room. Dust floated in the air, visible in the beams of sunlight coming through the two windows. Heavier bits of stain and wood coated the floor.

"I wanted to see how things were going. It will look great. I still see the grain in the wood."

Sutton pushed the protective glasses to the top of his head and pulled the mask down. "The stain will bring it out more." He crouched and ran his hand along a board. "Come feel it."

She walked closer and imitated his action. Her fingers skimmed wood so smooth it left no danger of tearing her skin through splinters. "It rivals satin."

"I don't know how many coats of stain I'm removing, but the boards will look new when I'm done."

When he was done. She couldn't wait for her house to be a home rather than a disorganized, dusty mess, but when he'd finished the renovation, she'd have no reason to see Sutton every day. That should please him. No more being pestered by curious or belligerent children. No more time alone with someone from the past who had broken his heart. No temptation to cast his doubts aside and—

And nothing. What was she thinking? He had a girlfriend.

"How's Nicole?" Paige winced at the question that left her mind through her mouth. She turned away from him.

"In the past."

In the past? "I'm sorry." *No, you're not.*

"Nothing to be sorry about. It was a matter of time. She wasn't the one for me, and she accepted it well enough."

It was on the tip of Paige's tongue to ask who was the one for him. She captured that question before blurting it out and embarrassing herself for a second time in two minutes.

She flinched in surprise when his gentle grip encircled her upper arms. She hadn't heard him close the space between them.

"Paige. Look at me." His hands fell to his sides.

She turned, not sure what to expect, and raised her eyes to see into his face. Warmth rushed through her. She hadn't seen him display that soft expression, that vulnerability, in over fifteen years, and she nearly melted, leaving a puddle on his newly sanded floor.

Renewal. The word popped into her mind as soon as their eyes met. Maybe she hadn't rushed ahead of God. With her move back to her hometown, had God begun sanding away layers of old experiences to ready her for a renewal, a second chance at beauty? She'd expected renewal as a mother, but now, that expectation spread to the man before her.

"I only dated Nicole to prove to myself that I could handle you being back in Hidden Veil."

She stiffened at the admission. Was that some kind of weird compliment that should make her feel better about his seeing Nicole? She retreated a couple of steps. "Really? Because I didn't look for someone to date so I could handle seeing you."

"I didn't mean . . ." He ran a hand through his hair, knocking off the eye protection. The plastic glasses clattered on the floor, but neither of them picked them up. "That didn't come out right. What I did was unfair to Nicole, but I did it out of pride."

"Pride?"

He looked away a moment, then back at her. "I was afraid you would think I still cared. I didn't want that."

Her mouth opened. After a fruitless struggle for something to say, she laughed. "Why would I think that? You've made it clear you don't care."

"Paige—"

She raised a hand. "No. I get it. I do." She understood his need to protect himself from her.

Renewal.

Paige had prayed for things to come to a head soon—between her and her son and between her and Sutton. All she knew for sure was that she would not run again. No matter the threat to her sanity. Until God told her differently, she was here to stay. And Sutton needed to believe that, too.

She cupped the back of his neck, drew his face closer, and planted a quick but possessive kiss on Sutton's lips before letting him go and stepping back. Feeling more emboldened, and with no regret over the risky move, she said, "You were right. Nicole was not the one for you. Because it has always been me."

Sutton considered himself fairly unshockable, but that kiss—quick as it was—left him unable to think clearly.

No, it wasn't the kiss. It was Paige's words afterward that had his head spinning in a cyclone of possibilities for the future. She didn't exaggerate. No other woman had ever taken her place in his life, and he'd bet no other woman ever would.

Now, her claim coming out of the blue convinced him his words to God had not simply drifted off into the air. They had reached the ear of a God that listened. Amazing.

Paige whirled. "I'll get my lunch and let you go back to work."

She thought he'd let her go about her business after issuing an announcement that turned him inside out? Well, she had another think coming. But did he have the guts to defeat the obstacles between them, as Nicole suggested?

Sutton turned Paige around until she peered up at him. "Lunch can wait. We've danced around the past, the present, and the future for long enough. It's time to settle things between us, Paige."

A hint of a smile appeared, but anxiety in her eyes overshadowed it. "Let's sit in the parlor and talk."

He followed her there and perched on the edge of the sofa next to her. They both sat mute until he swiveled on the plush cushion to face her. "I didn't write 'Have a heart-to-heart with Paige' on my schedule for today. I'm not sure where to start, so I'll start when I first saw you in November."

"When I fell through the porch? Not my best moment." She rolled her eyes. "We talked about it a little the night you brought me the hamburger, but I'm sure you weren't happy to see me again."

Sutton didn't need the memory of that day to talk about how he'd felt. "I won't lie. I was angry. Everything rushed back. The blow of learning you'd left Hidden Veil without a word to me. Frustration because your family refused to tell me how to contact you. The shame of seeing pity in the eyes of my friends." His head pounded with the rush of memories from so long ago. "Worse was the emptiness, Paige. I lost the best part of me when you left and, you're right, I never found anyone to replace you."

Her eyes filled, threatening to overflow. The sight left him rattled, but he restrained his longing to catch whatever tears fell from her lashes.

"I'm sorry. My family told me I would regret not talking to you first. They said it was wrong, but after our last argument, I didn't listen. I wish I had, because I've spent years regretting the heartache I caused you."

He remembered that day and shouting that he should be enough for her. The way he'd turned his back on her and left her standing alone in Hidden Veil's downtown park.

He'd driven her away from the park, away from town . . . and away from him.

If he had known he wouldn't see her for over a decade, would he have agreed to what she wanted? "Back then, if I'd said I'd changed my mind about children, would you have stayed?"

Paige dipped her chin, and a tear fell onto her lap, spotting her jeans. "I thought about it then, but I never set out to change you, Sutton, and I was afraid you would have eventually resented me. And if you never changed your mind about having children, I would have resented you."

Her words were truer than he'd like to admit. "I didn't think I could be a father, Paige. You know I couldn't chance that I'd turn into someone like Dad. I couldn't stomach the risk of ruining your life and the lives of my own children."

"I understand, but you weren't like your father then and you're not like him now."

"I don't know."

"No doubts. I knew it with all my heart. I still know it. You were so determined to be nothing like him you missed the truth of who you really were—a strong, dependable teenager saddled with too much responsibility at too young an age." She brushed away the tears. "You would have made a wonderful father."

"I wish I had your confidence, Paige, but even my siblings think I'm too hard-nosed. They don't understand that someone had to step up and provide for them, to keep up the farm and keep them from following in Dad's footsteps."

"They'll understand one day."

That understanding couldn't come soon enough because, somehow, something had changed in him. He now saw his siblings—even his stepmother—as more than a burden, a responsibility he had to bear. He was learning to appreciate their good qualities, even their quirks.

Sutton recalled the game of Go Fish he'd grudgingly played

with Patrick and Ariel on Monday night. Patrick was funnier than he had realized, and they all ended up laughing over his childish jokes.

Something had changed, all right. He had seen the younger Vances as more than a group of strangers living in his boyhood home. They were family. His family. People who wanted to include him in their lives, not just rely on what he could do for them.

"I wish . . ." Paige rubbed her forehead.

"What?"

"I wish my kids saw me as their mother instead of a bumbling stand-in. Every time Leyla calls me Mom Paige, it feels like I'm a temporary substitute for the real thing. One day, I'd love to hear her call me Mom and leave off my name."

A blanket of guilt shrouded Sutton. Did Debra see his use of her name in the same way?

Paige gripped his hand. "She thinks you hung the moon and prays for you every night."

That little girl prayed for him? "Why? I haven't done anything to earn it."

"You don't have to do anything to earn heaven, either. It's a gift, like Leyla's admiration for you. She wants you to know Jesus as she does."

Sutton swallowed. He hadn't decided if he was ready to admit this to anyone but Lane, however . . . "You can tell her I've been reading that Bible I got for Christmas, and I'm getting to know Him."

Paige's waterworks began again. "I'll do that."

He took a chance and scooted closer, enveloping her in his arms. When she rested her head against his shoulder, he tightened his hold, her tears dampening his tee shirt.

She sniffled. "I don't suppose we could stay like this forever?"

"I wouldn't mind." He chuckled. "But it won't get your house finished."

A loud, prolonged sigh preceded her shove upright. She ran her hands over her face, wiping away the tears. She frowned at him. "You're no fun."

Sutton cradled that beautiful face between his hands, the remaining dampness on her cheeks moistening his palms. "That's where you're wrong."

He leaned forward until his lips met hers, gently at first. Testing her willingness. Then more insistent. Tempting her reaction.

When Paige's arms wound around him and the zeal in her kiss equaled his own, it was as if the past fifteen years melted away. Once more, they were in this house and in each other's arms.

She pulled away. "I take back what I said."

"Good." He nibbled at her ear and grinned when she sucked in a breath. "Let's make us last this time."

Paige leaned back. "I want that. But Sutton, we still have the same issue times three."

It took him a few seconds for his brain to focus on reality and comprehend what she said. He hung his head. How could he have forgotten? "The kids."

"Yes." She rose from the sofa. "I love you, but I won't allow them to go through what they did with Dustin."

Despite her admission that she loved him, for a moment, his backbone stiffened in a defensive mode, blaming the problem in their relationship on the children.

Cassie's sweet laughter and the way she grabbed his legs, hanging on as if she hugged a tree, reduced some of the tautness in his shoulders. Leyla, with her bedtime prayers and aversion to the hearing aids, relaxed his spine. Liam . . . Well, Liam wasn't much different from Dillon—struggling to find his place.

Sutton wasn't Dustin, but could he live up to Paige's confidence in him? Could he fulfill an implied promise to her children to be the father he had wanted for himself?

"I can't guarantee I'll be the man you think your children need, but I'm willing to try."

Her gaze probed him until he thought he'd jump out of his skin. She nodded.

"There's another obstacle we need to discuss."

She sat back down. "What?"

Sutton sought a good way to bring up what she would probably consider one more example of his lack of confidence.

"If this is about your crazy idea that you're not good enough for me, forget that right now, Sutton Vance."

Crazy idea? "It isn't crazy, Paige. There's a real inequality between us."

"One that means nothing to me. Yes, I have money in the bank, but after this renovation, not as much as you think. Yes, I drive a nice car, but Dustin bought it for me four years ago. I couldn't buy that car today. Yes, I make a suitable living with my pottery business, but if I don't concentrate on filling the orders in my binder, that business will crash and burn." She took a breath. "Maybe I shouldn't jump ahead with assumptions about the future, but I don't care whose money pays the bills, Sutton."

"I care, Paige. I care that . . ."

Care that what? That he prove his ability to provide for a family? Hadn't he done that already? Or was his real problem a concern that others would look down on him? Yet as long as Paige respected him, who else mattered?

"I know you possess a strong sense of duty and take pride in what you do." Paige laid a warm hand against his cheek. "You are a hard worker. I'm a hard worker. My faith is stronger than it was when I was eighteen and set on getting my way. I believe if we depend on Him, God will be with us through anything."

Her last statement had the biggest effect on him. It reminded him of Trey's outlook after the kennel fire. His friend had said that, even in his weakest state, God had shown His faithfulness and given him the strength to face his fear of fire.

"Okay. We'll move forward." He raised an eyebrow in mock gravity. "But what about Leyla? I'm pretty sure she'll want to add to her collection of colorful boots."

"Hmm . . . That is a priority for her." She laughed. "I'll just teach her how to throw a few pots to earn her *booty*."

Sutton's face scrunched. "That's your idea of a joke?"

When Paige laughed again, he pulled her to him for a kiss that left them both breathless.

Twenty-four

Sutton rolled his shoulders, sore from hours of jostling with the vibration of the floor sander. He yawned. Man, he was tired. How much longer could he keep up the hard, physical labor at Paige's house and the hard, physical labor around the farm?

After a quick shower, he had dressed in shorts and a tee shirt, then belly-flopped on his bed. The hardwood in her house looked good, though. So good. Once he applied the stain, he'd cover the floor to protect it when they installed the kitchen cabinets. At each stage, he took photos for future marketing. Everything was taking shape, and this job would bolster his hope to switch his career from farming to construction, maybe with an emphasis on renovation projects.

He yawned once more. Paige was pleased.

Thinking of her brought a smile and terror at the same time. He'd spent years adamant that he'd never build a family of his own. Did he even know how to change? More time with her like today, and he could see himself adjusting.

Sutton picked up his phone to text her.

You asleep?

Can't sleep.

Why not?

Thinking about today.

Me, too. There's something I didn't tell you.

What?

Sutton only pondered the wisdom of it a few seconds before adding . . .

I love you.

He waited for her response, his nerves ratcheting up when it took longer than he'd like.

Don't make me cry with happiness. But I think I can sleep now. Goodnight, Sutton.

He smiled with relief and closed his eyes, intending to spend a few quiet minutes thinking.

Something hit him on the shoulder. When it hit his back, his eyes popped open, and he blinked until he regained full consciousness. A sore spot throbbed somewhere near his spine.

He groaned at waking from a dream involving Paige and him. It was one of those weird dreams that seemed real in sleep but absurd when awake. Something about a beautiful spring day and a picnic. He and Paige and about a dozen kids running around—most he'd never seen before. Where did they—

Another shove to the shoulder. "Get up, Sutton."

He rolled over on the bed, the mattress sinking, and rubbed

his eyes. Jenna stood above him. Tear tracks ran down her cheeks, and a wave of fear washed over him. He bolted upright. "What's wrong?"

"It's Mom. She can't breathe."

Wide awake now, he paused halfway to the bedroom door. "Where is she?"

"In her room. Dillon called 9-1-1."

"Good."

It took him two seconds to dash down the hall and into his dad and Debra's room. His stepmother sat propped against the headboard of the bed, her face pale and chest heaving as she fought to fill her lungs with lifesaving air. Joel and Dillon stood on opposite sides of the bed, trying to comfort her.

Sutton pushed Joel aside. "Have you used your inhaler?" The slight dip and rise of her chin told him she had, but it hadn't worked. "What about your nebulizer?" Same answer.

They had been through this situation a few times over the years. Each time, he struggled to recall exactly what to do. He looked around at his brothers and oldest sister. The same fear that had his mind frozen had frozen on their faces. He couldn't stand there and wait for her to suffocate or the EMTs to arrive—whichever came first.

"Let's get you sitting straighter."

He clasped one arm, while Dillon clasped the other. Together, they helped her straighten up in the bed. It did little good for her breathing, so he grabbed the inhaler on the bedside table. "Here. Use this again."

She took a puff of the medicine, followed by shallow breaths. Took another meager puff, repeating the process. In the distance, the faint sound of a siren told him the ambulance was getting close.

"Joel, go downstairs and meet them."

The boy rushed from the room, probably happy to escape his mother's distress and the anxiety of everyone around her. Only the two youngest Vance siblings remained asleep in their beds. With the coming noise, they wouldn't stay there long.

"Jenna, Patrick and Ariel will wake up with the ambulance's arrival. Make sure they're all right."

As she slipped out of the room, Debra gripped his hand, fear in her eyes—fear and gratitude.

"You're going to be fine." She had to be fine. He couldn't lose another—

The piercing wail outside and the strobing lights that flashed on the walls of the bedroom announced the much-appreciated arrival of help. Within three minutes Joel had led an EMT upstairs and into the room. Sutton explained the situation and Debra's health history. A second EMT crossed the room and took her vitals while the first responder placed an oxygen mask on her.

Debra's breathing eased somewhat, but before Sutton could wrap his mind around what was happening, the men had placed her on a gurney. He helped them get the rolling bed down the stairs and watched as they loaded her into the ambulance.

As the driver backed the vehicle down the drive and pulled onto the road, Sutton breathed easier himself. Then the cold seeped into his body—first his shoeless feet, then his legs, his arms, his cheeks, and his nose. Like Jenna's earlier slaps and shoves, it brought him back to an awareness of his surroundings.

Sutton whipped around. He trotted up the porch steps and into the house to finish dressing. Dillon stood in the front room with his shoes and coat on. Sutton's truck keys dangled from his brother's hand. "Where are you going?"

"To the hospital."

Sutton reached out to grab the keys from his brother, ready to tell him to go back to bed. But how could he when Dillon was as worried about Debra as he was? He dropped his hand and nodded. "Go warm up the truck. I'll be there in a minute."

The front screen door slammed, and Dillon was gone.

"I want to go, too." Jenna appeared, also dressed and ready to step into the frigid night.

"What about me?" Joel stood on the stairs, his hands gripping the banister.

Dillon and Jenna could handle themselves at the hospital, but Sutton wasn't sure the hospital could handle all five of his siblings. He laid a hand on the boy's shoulder. "You have an important job here, Joel. You need to watch Ariel and Patrick. It's up to you to keep them from being scared. That means talking to them in more than one-word sentences. Understand?"

Joel looked like he wanted to push back, then nodded. "Okay."

Sutton bolted up the stairs two at a time. In his room, he pulled on a pair of jeans, snatched his shoes from the floor, and slipped into his coat. All the while, he thought about his words to Joel. Maybe if he talked to Paige's kids in more than one-word sentences, he could be that man who gained their confidence.

It wasn't until he reached the front door that he stopped and took stock. Someone was missing. He turned to Jenna. "Where's Dad?"

She grimaced. "I don't know. He left after supper."

Sutton shook his head. Leave it to John Vance to be absent during a family emergency. Once he made certain Debra would be all right, Sutton would go after the worthless man who called himself a father.

He hated hospitals. He hated waiting in hospitals.

Sutton sank into the chair with the blue cloth seat, the padding hollowed out by other people who had waited. Bright lighting and activity teased people into thinking it was the middle of the day until they looked out the window to see the yellow glow from pole lights breaking up the darkness.

With his elbow on the metal arm of the chair, he rested his cheek on his fist and fought to keep his eyes open. Debra had been in the emergency room for two hours, and his father had yet to show up. Either he hadn't returned home or he returned in a condition that left him unable to drive to the hospital.

"What do you think? Why haven't we heard anything?"

At Jenna's quiet questions, he sat up and cleared his throat. "They need time to get her breathing under control."

"I'm thinking they'll keep her for a while," said Dillon.

"We'll see." He wanted her to have the best care, but how would they pay the hospital bill?

Sutton got up. "I'm going for coffee. You two want anything?"

Jenna said, "Not for me."

Dillon bobbed his head. "I could use some coffee."

"I'll be back."

Sutton found a coffee machine in an alcove down the hallway. He slid in some coins and watched as dark liquid splashed into a thick paper cup. Once it had finished, he tasted the coffee and made a face. What he wouldn't give for a cup of

Jo's Red Eye. But at least this was hot.

While he waited for Dillon's coffee, he glanced around. The hospital looked better than he remembered when his own mother had been a patient. It smelled better, too. But looks and smell didn't change the fact that people here either healed or died. Before he caught himself, a silent plea rose in him for Debra's healing. Prayer was becoming almost second nature lately.

He returned to his seat in the waiting room. A short time later, a nurse came to the door, looking for them.

"Mrs. Vance's breathing is better, but the doctor wants to admit her for tonight. I'll let you know when we get her into a room. You can visit her then."

"Thanks." Sutton settled in for more waiting.

Jenna got up and paced. "Where's Dad? He should be here."

"I don't want him anywhere near Mom. He should have been home." Dillon's subdued voice was drenched in anger toward their father, an anger that matched Sutton's. "What if she'd had this emergency and none of us knew, because we were asleep? No one would have been with her." His throat worked with emotion.

His brother had a point. "We can't live on what-ifs, Dillon."

Jenna stopped pacing. "They argued, and he stormed out of the house."

"I think it was an excuse to leave," said Dillon.

She shot a glare at Sutton. "Can't you go look for him?"

"I don't know where to look, Jenna. Besides, I need to be here in case the doctor has questions."

They continued to wait. A few minutes later, footsteps sounded on the linoleum tiles, and Sutton turned toward the door. He expected to see a nurse who would guide them to Debra's room. He was wrong.

His dad stood in the doorway, looking haggard, his hair mussed. The graying beard added years to his age. At least he appeared sober. "Joel told me what happened. How is she?"

Jenna ran to him and hugged him. "She had a bad episode. She couldn't breathe." Sutton's sister pulled back and looked their father in the eyes. "Where have you been?"

Dad patted her arm. "I needed a little private time." He asked Sutton, "Well?"

"She'll stay here for a while. They're getting her room ready."

Dad eased farther into the waiting room. All the while, Dillon scowled at him, not saying a word.

"Did they say how long? I want to see her."

Dillon jumped from his chair and left the room.

Sutton understood his brother's frustration. Even a subtle whiff revealed the alcohol on Dad's breath, not as strong as usual, but it clung to him like farmyard on a boot.

He grabbed his father's elbow and yanked him into the hall, then out the emergency department door, away from his siblings and anyone else who might hear. "You haven't earned the right to see her, Dad."

"She's my wife!"

"She's my mo—" As Sutton stood there, stunned by what he'd almost said, he recalled Paige's misery over her children not calling her Mom. He was guilty of the same, wasn't he? The look of hurt he often saw on Debra's face, because of him, was the same as the one he'd seen on Paige.

Like a flash of lightning, the reason he'd never referred to Debra as his mother flared in front of him, and his jaw dropped. "You discouraged me from thinking of her as my mother."

His dad raised his chin. "How did I discourage you?"

"Whenever you talk about her in front of the other kids, you refer to her as 'your mom.' When it's only me, you've always called her Debra. I'm thinking you never wanted me to look at her as *my* mother."

"You had a mother, Sutton."

"She died, Dad."

His father winced.

"Couldn't you see I needed a mother, too?"

"I never stopped you from thinking of her that way."

"But you didn't encourage it, either. Why?"

His father leaned against a stone planter at the entrance to the building. Her shoulders sank. "I love Debra, Sutton, but she's always had health problems. When they got worse, I got scared. Losing your mom tore both of us apart. I didn't want you to go through that again. I guess I figured it would be best if you didn't get too attached."

"She wasn't a puppy." And he was attached. He realized that now.

Sutton rubbed his forehead. "How much have you had to drink tonight?"

"Only a couple of beers." When Sutton's doubt showed, he said, "I swear. That's all. I'm not drunk."

"Go home, Dad."

"Please, son, I—."

"Go home."

Sutton left his father standing in the cold and went back inside. He met Jenna at the door. She said, "I'll go with him."

"You drive." He handed her his phone since she didn't have one. "Call Dillon's phone when you get home."

She nodded and walked away.

He trusted his teenage sister more than their dad to get them to the farm safely.

Twenty-five

Paige's nerves jangled, and a plea for welcome slipped over her lips. Was she ready for this visit? Would Sutton approve?

She released Cassie's hand long enough to knock on the front door of the Vance farmhouse before she took hold of her daughter again. On her other arm, she balanced a warm casserole dish.

The inside door cracked open, revealing a teenage girl's face. "Yes?"

"Jenna?"

"Yes."

"Hi. I'm Paige Matthews. I live down the road." She swiveled and nodded toward her house.

The door opened wider, but Jenna didn't invite them inside. She was a pretty girl with Sutton's wavy hair but little else to resemble him. "You're the one who bought the Johnson house. Sutton's ex-girlfriend." She wielded those last two words like a knife.

Paige couldn't blame her for defending her brother. "Yes."

"Sutton isn't here."

"I know. He called this morning and let me know he wouldn't be working today." Paige had left Kaine at the house to finish sanding the kitchen floor in Sutton's place. "I'm sorry to hear about your mother, and I'm praying for her health."

"Thanks."

Paige held up the casserole dish. "With all that's going on and taking care of your younger brothers and sisters, I thought you might be able to use a ready meal. It's lasagna."

The girl's eyes lit up. Then, as though she realized she fraternized with the enemy, she frowned. "That's nice of you, but I've planned our supper for tonight."

"This is already done. I made another one for my children." She took a chance and opened the screen door, poking the dish inside. "Taking it would do me a favor. My refrigerator is full. You can eat it tomorrow."

Jenna took the lasagna. "Thanks."

A small boy crept up behind his sister, still wearing sky-blue pajamas with dogs on them. "It smells good."

With the emergency last night, it was probable that none of the Vance children had slept last night. She understood why they stayed home from school today.

Paige smiled. "You must be Patrick. I have a daughter your age. Maybe you've met her at school. Her name is Leyla."

His eyes lit. "You're Mom Paige."

It should please her to know Leyla mentioned her at all, but at the use of the vague name, her enthusiasm took a nosedive. "Uh, yes, I am. This is Leyla's sister, Cassie."

Jenna eyed Cassie as if she noticed her for the first time, then gave Patrick the casserole. "Take this to the kitchen." She pushed the screen door open and said, "Come in."

Paige thought of declining. She had work to do before Leyla and Liam returned from school. But she hadn't met the younger Vance children, and curiosity won out. She entered right into the front room with its old, plaid couch and even older, worn chairs. The furnishings might look shabby, but the room was spotless.

"Have a seat." When Patrick returned, Jenna told her brother to take Cassie to the mudroom to see the new kittens.

Jenna asked, "She isn't allergic, is she?"

"No." Still, Paige wanted to keep her child from getting the idea she could take home a kitten. More than enough chaos swirled around the house right now.

Cassie tugged on Paige's pants leg and gazed up at her. "I want to see kittens."

The set of her daughter's mouth said she was ready to throw a tantrum if Paige said no. Her mother's advice about boundaries returned to haunt her, but it wouldn't do to risk an outburst in front of Sutton's family. "For a few minutes."

Once the children were gone, Paige asked, "How is your mom? Have you heard?"

"She's fine." A grumbly male voice lifted Paige's gaze to the stairs at the other side of the room.

"Hello, Mr. Vance."

He approached, dressed in a tee shirt and a pair of cargo shorts that had seen better days two decades ago. Even leaving off his graying hair and beard, lines ran across his skin like ditches in the cornfield. He looked decades older than she remembered.

"Paige Hartwell."

She stood and reached out a hand, not correcting her last name. "Yes, sir. It's nice to see you."

John Vance ignored her hand. "Looks like you've got your hooks in my son again."

"Dad."

Paige's face burned. "He's renovating my house."

"I saw the texts he sent you last night. It isn't your house that's being restored."

Jenna stood alongside Paige. "Dad, you read Sutton's private text messages?"

"You left his phone on the table. I was looking for word on your mom."

And maybe more? He must have read her conversation with Sutton last night and the declaration of love. Clearly, his father didn't approve, but this wasn't the time to attempt to reason with him.

Paige turned to Jenna. "My schedule is full at home, so if you'll take me to Cassie, we'll get out of your way."

"Sure."

Sutton's dad blocked her path. "How long will you be here this time before you run off without a word to him?"

"I'll get your daughter." Jenna rushed away, demonstrating her desire for them to leave in a hurry.

Fine with Paige. She didn't want to argue with Sutton's father and couldn't blame him for his anger after what she'd put Sutton through. "I'm in Hidden Veil to stay, Mr. Vance. I want my children to grow up here."

"You say that now. In another few months, you'll change your mind and take off." His narrow-eyed scowl sent her back a step. "Keep out of my boy's life. He deserves better."

Jenna carried Cassie into the room. The child squiggled in her arms, so Jenna handed her to Paige. "Thank you for bringing the lasagna."

Paige mumbled, "It was my pleasure." She beat a retreat to the front door and onto the porch. The door slammed behind her.

After being buckled into the car seat, Cassie whined,

"Mommy, I want a kitten."

Paige slipped behind the wheel. "No, Cassie."

The child pounded on the arms of her seat. "I want a kitten."

"I said no, young lady, and you will *not* throw a fit to get what you want."

At her sharp response, Cassie didn't argue but, in a small voice, said, "Okay, Mommy."

Paige stared into the rearview mirror at her daughter. *Huh.* It worked. It seemed Mom and her sisters knew best.

But did Dad? Sutton's father believed she was wrong for his son, that she would run from Hidden Veil a second time. Not that it hadn't crossed her mind in the beginning. But it wasn't possible, not when she had children who needed stability. Not when she had discovered her feelings for Sutton hadn't changed.

But was John Vance right to say his son deserved better than her, better than being saddled with three children who weren't his? More importantly, three children he didn't want?

She and Sutton had one more obstacle to conquer before they could consider starting a life together.

After over fifteen hours at the hospital, Sutton lumbered into the house and tossed his coat across the back of the nearest kitchen chair, expending his last bit of energy. He craved a shower, food, and a good night's sleep—in that order.

Dillon followed him into the kitchen and laid his coat on top of Sutton's. He sniffed the air. "Smells great. I'm starved."

"Yeah. Me, too." Sutton peeked into the hot oven and peeled back the foil covering a casserole dish. "When did Jenna learn to make lasagna?"

"Lasagna? Let me see." Dillon peered into the oven. "Man, that looks good."

Jenna appeared in the kitchen and pushed Dillon aside. "Leave that alone. I'll let you know when it's ready." She slammed the oven door shut.

"I want to eat, then sleep for a full twenty-four hours," said Sutton's brother. "But for now, a shower."

Dillon bolted from the room. Sutton grumbled about not being fast enough to reach the bathroom first.

"How was Mom when you left?"

"Good enough that I should be able to bring her home tomorrow." Sutton pulled a chair away from the table and fell into it. "How's Dad been?"

"He's a mad dog, snarling at everyone, because you wouldn't let him see her."

"I let him talk to her on the phone, but she was too tired to deal with a visit from him, and the doctor said we shouldn't stress her."

"Speaking of visits . . ."

Based on the way Jenna picked at the crimson nail polish on her fingernails, something she never did for fear she'd mess up the DIY manicure, Sutton steadied himself for bad news.

She pulled his phone from her jeans pocket and handed it to him. "I'm sorry. I shouldn't have left it out."

"Why? What happened?" He checked his phone to be sure it wasn't broken. He didn't need to add a new phone to his list of expenses, not when a hefty hospital bill hung over their heads.

"Paige brought the lasagna this morning."

Her thoughtfulness ticked up his lips into a smile. "That doesn't surprise me."

"Yes, but Sutton—"

"What does that have to do with my phone?"

She glowered at him. "I'm getting to that."

"Sorry. Go ahead, before I fall asleep."

"Just before she came, I got out the phone to text you to check on Mom. Dad came into the room. He grabbed it and noticed your texts to Paige. When she got here, he wasn't very nice to her."

"He read what I texted Paige?" Sutton pulled out his phone, but didn't need to call up his words from last night. He remembered what he'd written. How could he forget?

"I told him he shouldn't have done it."

His jaw clenched. "What did he say to her?"

"Maybe you should ask Paige."

"Jenna."

It took that one low rumble to get her talking. "He asked her how long she'd be here before she ran off again. Then he told her you deserved someone better than her."

"Where is he?"

"In the barn."

Sutton snatched his coat from the chair, ignoring Dillon's when it fell to the floor.

"Sutton."

He strode to the back door. "Stay out of this, Jenna."

Long strides carried him across the yard to the barn, where he found his dad sitting on a stool, staring at Rocket.

"I remember when you brought home this horse."

His dad's quiet statement caught Sutton off guard and brought his angry march to a halt.

"Never seen a colt so skittish and thin. You said you couldn't leave him where he was and had to bring him home."

Sutton approached the stall and rubbed Rocket's head. Years ago, he went with Lane to look at a possible new stud for Crooked Creek. While his friend discussed the purchase of the horse he wanted, Sutton wandered around until he saw a skinny, wild-eyed two-year-old. Although he'd ridden a few of Lane's horses, he wouldn't call himself a horseman or even horse-infatuated, but something drew him to the metal-rail stall to get a closer look.

With ten minutes of soft words, Sutton had coaxed Rocket close enough to the rail to touch his muzzle, to connect. Knowing it was impractical and irrational, he decided he had to have that colt. After twenty minutes of hard bargaining, he spent another ten trying to load his stubborn new horse into Lane's trailer. His friend never said a word about the foolishness of the purchase. Instead, he offered to help train a horse that turned out to be invaluable to Sutton as both a roping horse and sounding board for his complaints.

Even now, Rocket's presence brought a calming effect to him, dissolving some of his anger. Some.

Dad pushed up from the stool and rubbed a hand over his face. "You chose well. *That* time."

Sutton's backbone tightened. "Do you have a point to make?"

"I used to like that girl until I saw what she put you through. She'll do it all over again, son."

"You don't know that." Sutton didn't either, did he? All he had was trust and a powerful emotion that never died. "You tried to run Paige off by being rude to her?"

His dad's eyes narrowed. "Why are you soft-hearted toward her? Soft hearts get broken, boy."

"So you shield yours with alcohol?"

Dad drew his fist back and swung. Sutton dodged the punch

to his face and grabbed his father's arm. It wasn't hard to subdue him. Even with his height—nearly a match for Sutton—the man's slim form couldn't compare with Sutton's work-enhanced build.

He balled a fist, ready to knock some sense into his dad. *Honor your father, as I honor mine.*

Sutton scanned the barn, even knowing he wouldn't find the source of the commanding voice that stopped him, because it came from inside, and that terrified him. *Jesus?*

Letting go of his father, he relaxed his hand and tempered his voice. "You're wrong. Hard hearts break because they're inflexible." Sutton backed away from his father. "I love you, Dad, but I can't live here any longer."

He walked out of the barn convinced that the Jesus he'd fought against most of his life had saved him from doing something he'd regret. He could also save Sutton from eternal death.

I'm sorry for doubting You and not believing sooner. I'm sorry for the things I've done that go against the holy God You are. I want to become Your child. I need it. I surrender.

And maybe one day Dad would do the same.

Twenty-six

With the ringing of the doorbell, Paige pushed up from the floor. "I'll see who's at the door. You two keep going."

Leaving the yoga video running on the TV, she patted Leyla's upraised behind in fun, as the girl did her best to manage the Downward Dog pose. Cassie tried but tumbled to her side, then started laughing, which brought a smile to Paige's face.

After pulling the elastic band out of her hair, she redid her ponytail and straightened her workout shirt before opening the door. Her eyebrows shot up at seeing her unexpected visitor. "Sutton. I thought you would be at the hospital." Paige stepped back. "Come in."

Furrows marred his forehead. She couldn't tell if it was fatigue or worry. "Debra hasn't had a setback, has she?"

"No. She's better and should be home tomorrow."

"Good."

He tilted his head, listening. "If you have company, I can come back."

"That's a video. The girls and I are doing yoga stretches." Surely, he could tell from her form-fitting yoga pants and the sleeveless tee shirt. But his focus appeared distant and slightly dark, as though she was no one more than a stranger on a street he didn't wish to walk down. "If you're here to tell me you won't be working tomorrow, I understand. Kaine made good progress on the kitchen floor and said he would add another coat of stain tomorrow."

"That's not why I'm here. Can we talk?"

"Sure." Paige suspected the talk would involve his father. Someone must have told him of her visit. Was he mad at her for going to the house, or at his father for what he'd said to her?

He peeked into the dining room. "Smells good in here."

"I assume you know I went to the farm today. Did you eat the lasagna I took to your family?"

"I knew but got sidetracked, so I haven't eaten."

Sidetracked by her interaction with his dad? "Come on. There's plenty left from our supper."

They washed up in the downstairs bath, then Paige peered into the living room to check on the girls. They rolled around on the floor, doing somersaults and laughing. Seeing them occupied, she led Sutton into the dining room. She pointed to a chair at the table, removed the casserole dish from the refrigerator, and placed a large, rectangular slice of lasagna on a plate. Once the food finished heating in the microwave, she set the plate in front of him. "I'll be glad when the kitchen is finished and I can use all of my new appliances."

"Soon, I hope." Sutton dug into the meal as though he hadn't eaten in a week. When he'd almost finished, he put his fork down. "That was delicious, but we need to talk about what happened today."

Paige had guessed correctly about the purpose of his visit. She had replayed John Vance's accusation over and over in her head. At first, she'd questioned whether Sutton's father was right about her. Would she desert Sutton a second time? Before Leyla and Liam got off the bus, she spent hours in off-and-on prayer for guidance. The type of prayer that rolls over and over inside a person. In the end, she was more convinced than ever that while she deserved his scolding, Mr. Vance was wrong. She had no plans to go anywhere, especially now that Sutton had told her he still loved her.

A new thought stilled her. Had he persuaded Sutton that she wasn't worth another chance? "Is this where you tell me you've changed your mind about us?"

He drew back as if she'd threatened him, then reached out and placed his hand over hers. "No. If I haven't changed my mind about you in fifteen years, why would you think I'd let him change it for me now? I'm not sure of everything he said to you, but I'm sorry he put you through it. I don't need his protection from you, Paige. I know what I'm doing. You didn't let him . . .?"

"Change my mind? No way. Don't be mad at him for acting like a caring father. He tried to protect you, Sutton."

The furrows visible since his arrival returned. "The guy picked a great time to decide to be a father."

Paige frowned. "Do you think he'll ever forgive me?"

"I don't know what goes through his mind." Sutton cut off another piece of lasagna. "I told him I'll be leaving the farm in a couple of days. I can't live there anymore."

Her breath held. "Sutton, you know—"

For the first time, his mouth fashioned a grin. "I'm not asking to move in with you, Paige."

She exhaled. "Then where will you go?"

"Lane offered me the second floor of the cabin until I find a rental." He raised her hand and kissed the back of it, sending tingles up her spine. "Don't worry. I'll finish the reno here and continue working at the farm, gradually turning more and more of the work over to Dillon. I plan to manage the financial end until he's older. In the meantime, I'll build my contractor's business.

"My brother and I had a long talk while we waited for news at the hospital. I should have known when Dillon took science and Ag classes at school that he wanted to take over the farm. He claims he tried to tell me several times, and I didn't listen."

Paige grinned. "You have your moments."

"I have other moments, too." He leaned toward her, and she met him halfway, ready for the kiss his dark eyes promised.

Leyla skipped into the dining room with Cassie running behind. "Hey, Mr. Sutton."

They broke apart, sitting straight up in their chairs. Paige laughed at the way he shook his head in frustration. "Get used to it."

Cassie grasped the edge of the dining table, peeking over the top. "Hey, Misser Sudden."

"I thought you girls were exercising."

Leyla tugged on Sutton's hand. "We need Mom Paige's help, but you can do it."

"Do what?"

"Show us how to do the Tree."

Cassie grabbed his other hand. "The Tree."

He resisted, staying seated. "Me? What tree?"

Paige said, "It's a yoga pose."

Sutton turned back to the girls. "I don't know anything about yoga."

"Then we'll teach you." With that decisive statement, somehow, Leyla coaxed Sutton out of his seat. With each girl holding a hand, they led him across the hall to the parlor.

Fascination bubbled up in Paige, and she tagged along to see what would happen next.

"Okay," said Sutton. He stood with his backbone stiff, his arms at his sides. "Here's a tree."

Leyla giggled. "That's not it, silly. Show him, Mom Paige."

Paige pressed her bare right foot flat against the inside of her left thigh and brought her palms together at her chest as though she were praying. "Easy." She bit her lip to keep from laughing.

"See, Mr. Sutton? It's your turn. I'll do it with you."

He shot Paige a pleading glance. When she ignored his silent appeal, he kicked off his boots and raised his right leg, doing his best to mimic Paige's form, but he just couldn't steady himself, especially after placing his hands together in front of him. When he toppled over, hitting the floor like a felled oak, both girls doubled over in laughter. Paige didn't know whether to laugh with them or cry with joy over his efforts. Bless him for trying to relate to her girls.

They spent the next few minutes striking various poses, some real and some made up. Leyla assumed the role of leader, instructing Sutton on the way he should move. He was an incredible sport before Leyla told him to lie flat on his back in the rest pose. He closed his eyes and refused to get up.

Paige took pity on him. "Girls, I think Mr. Sutton has had enough yoga for tonight."

"For forever," he muttered.

"Go upstairs and get ready for your bath."

When they were gone, he opened one eye. "Can I get up now?"

Paige reached down for his hand and tugged, helping him to his feet, not that he needed it. "Thank you."

Sutton plopped onto the couch and put his boots on. "For what?"

"For indulging them. They had a good time."

"Yeah, well, they aren't bad kids." He stood and placed his hands on her hips, drawing her closer. "Except when they interrupt this."

He dipped his head, and his lips met hers. She wrapped her arms around him, sinking into the kiss, deepening it, and savoring every moment of this demonstration of their renewed bond.

A couple of minutes later, Sutton pulled back, breathing hard. "I think you'll be the death of me."

"At least you'll go happy."

His shoulders shook with laughter. "And on that note, I'm out the door."

He turned to go, then stopped.

Paige glanced at the doorway to the parlor and the boy standing there, watching them. "Liam. I thought you were upstairs."

He scowled, first at Sutton, then at her. Had he seen them kissing?

"I'm thirsty." Liam turned around and walked away.

Sutton watched him leave, concern digging lines between his eyes. "He doesn't like me, Paige."

"He'll come around."

She snuggled up to Sutton. She had hoped to ease the children into the idea of Sutton becoming more than her contractor. Would she ever get used to her plans derailing?

Standing in his room, Sutton went through his things, preparing for his move out of the farmhouse. He'd piled his bed with the possessions he wanted to keep and chucked into a corner the rejects to leave behind.

He tossed a handful of tee shirts into a canvas bag. At his age, he had little more to show for his life than what fit in a small closet and the few drawers of a dresser. Pathetic.

Sutton continued to fill the bag with clothes. He didn't even own the furniture in the room but would leave that for Dillon, who would move in after him. To his glee, Dillon no longer needed to share a bedroom with Joel and Patrick.

A knock on his open door had him turning to find Dillon there. "Come on in. I'll be done soon, and you can begin moving your stuff in."

"I'm in no hurry." Dillon plopped down on an empty section of the bed, his weight bouncing the bag and other items sprawled across the bedspread. "You sure you want to do this? I mean, Mom is gonna miss you and . . ."

"And?"

Dillon played with a loose thread in the bedspread. "We all will, even Dad."

Sutton paused in the process of dropping a dress shirt into the bag. For years, he'd felt like nothing but a piggy bank to his family. They came to him for what they needed, then went about their business.

Then again, hadn't he acted like a piggy bank? He provided for their physical needs, and then placed himself on his own little shelf, ignoring their more personal needs, like warmth and affection. By moving out, was he doing the same thing now?

No. It was time—best for him, best for them.

"Thanks, man. I'm going to miss y'all, too. But I'm not going far, and I'll be here every day to work the farm . . . help you work the farm . . . until you're ready to take it over."

"And Rocket will be here."

"Yeah."

The mention of his horse reminded Sutton of Liam—all the kids in his world, really. They weren't so bad. None of them were. He wished he'd allowed himself to realize that long ago. It may have made things easier with his siblings and Liam.

He still tried to wrap his mind around Dillon's choice to farm as his living. "Are you sure farming is what you want? You're young. You may change your mind, especially when it means you and Dad will bang heads."

"Yeah, I'm young, but I won't change my mind. This place is special to me . . . always has been. I don't want to sound all sentimental and stuff, but it's been in the Vance family for too long to let it slip away. And I like the work. I'm as strong and stubborn as you, Sutton. I can do it, and I can deal with Dad."

Dillon said that now, but was he really strong enough to handle their father?

Perhaps, because it was Dillon's choice to stay and ensure the farm succeeded and remained in the Vance family. He made that choice, not out of responsibility, but out of a desire to be the full-time farmer Sutton never wanted to be. And Dillon would probably be better at it. He had already shown he was more knowledgeable than Sutton had grasped.

"If you ever need me, and I'm not here, you know my number. If Dad ever gets—"

"Yeah, I know, and I'm not worried about Dad. I'm more worried about Mom. She's become a tyrant like—" He clamped his lips shut.

Sutton raised a brow. "Like me?"

"Almost like you." Dillon grinned. "She still has a way to go."

Sutton laughed and punched his brother on the shoulder. "Don't forget it."

Dillon picked up the book Sutton had set on the bed. "What's this?"

"It's a Bible."

His brother rolled his eyes. "I know what a Bible is, and I can read the cover. Since when did you decide to read one?"

"It was a gift." Sutton took it from Dillon and added it to the bag. Whenever he touched the book, Leyla's face flashed before him. He heard the loud voice. Saw the gap-toothed smile and ever-present backpack. The variety of boots she loved so much. The hearing aids she hated wearing.

"From Paige?"

"From all of them."

"Which is why you're taking it with you and not throwing it out?"

"I won't throw it out because it's . . ."

Was he ready to have this conversation with his brother when he was so new in his belief and understanding of what it meant to be a Christian?

Being superficial in his response to Dillon didn't appeal to him. His explanation about why he kept the Bible could be his most valuable provision for his brother and, possibly, his whole family.

From the moment he opened the pages and read the first few verses in John, something had compelled Sutton to keep reading what he'd always considered fiction but now believed as fact. Late at night, while everyone else slept, he read for half an hour, seeking answers to questions that occurred to him. He still understood so little, but Lane and Trey offered to meet with him for discussion and study.

He held up the Bible. "This is important to me." *Get real with it, Sutton.* "To be honest, I began reading it because I was curious. The more I read, the more I prayed, which led me to believe God was out there, that He is that caring Father who keeps His promises. For the first time, I can relax, knowing He has my back. I may be an adult, Dillon, but growing up doesn't mean your need and desire for a parent's love, their guidance, and their strength goes away. In here," he touched his chest, "God is giving me what I couldn't get from Dad."

"But you can't see or talk to God, so how do you know He's there?"

Sutton smiled. "Actually, I've learned to talk to Him." He explained about his Christmas Eve prayer and how he believed it was answered through Debra's sudden strength.

"Coincidence."

"Lane said answers to prayers aren't always so bold or positive. Sometimes we don't get what we want. He said it's possible we won't recognize an answer for years, if at all, and sometimes we won't like the answer. I'm believing that what's happened to this family lately is a result of prayer and faith."

Dillon's chin rose. "Paige left years ago. Have you talked to God about that? Where was His care for you then?"

Dillon had a point. Paige had left him, and for years, he hadn't come to terms with it. He should have shaken off the memories of her. He could have settled for someone like Nicole. Thankfully, he hadn't. And settle? In his heart, he had always known he couldn't settle.

"I don't have all the answers, Dillon. That's why I'm reading this." He placed the Bible on top of his clothes and zipped the canvas bag.

His brother hopped off the bed. "Let me know if you get them."

"I will."

Dillon walked out of the room, and the clomp of heavy footsteps told Sutton his brother had gone downstairs.

Twenty-seven

Sutton finished packing, then carried the big bag and a smaller one down the stairs. He stuttered to a stop when he reached the living room. There, in a line from oldest to youngest, his family waited.

"What's this? I'm only moving a few miles away."

Patrick launched himself at Sutton and wrapped his arms around his legs. The boy's head tilted back. "Why do you have to go? You live here with us."

"Patrick, baby, we discussed this." Debra pried the boy's arms away.

Sutton waved her off and picked up his brother. "Hey, I won't be a stranger. In fact, you'll probably get sick of seeing me."

Patrick's head swung back and forth. "You promise?"

He would continue to help around the farm, but if not for the work, would he be able to keep that promise? His gaze bounced from sibling to sibling. "Yeah, I promise."

Sutton realized he had resented his siblings—all children—for experiencing the type of childhood he missed. The fun. The lightheartedness. The lack of adult responsibility. Now, he understood that no age came without concerns and worries, responsibilities and apprehension. With all he had done to provide for his family, not even his brothers and sisters had escaped the anxiety.

One-by-one they told him goodbye as he walked toward the kitchen and the back door. When he reached his father, the old man stepped forward, his eyes misty. "I'm sorry for all I put you through, son."

Sutton's breath caught as he reran the words through his mind to be certain he'd understood them. "I've waited years to hear that." Sutton waited now for Dad to reach out and hug him goodbye. Instead, the man stood with his hands behind his back. Was he not worthy of a father-to-son embrace?

"I shouldn't have said what I did to Paige. If she makes you happy, then I'm happy for you." Dad pulled out a six-pack filled with brown bottles from behind his back. "This is a going-away present for you."

That's what he held behind him? Beer? He thought the situation of his drinking was a joke? Sutton's jaw went rock hard. This was how seriously his father took his move, offering him beer to go? "You know I don't drink."

"I don't either. Not anymore." He pushed the carton at Sutton. "I'm not a naive little kid. I know it won't be easy, but I joined a group to help me. You keep this to shove in my face as a reminder if I fall off the wagon."

Sutton grasped the six-pack—the empty six-pack.

"I dumped the beer down the sink," a crooked grin lined Dad's face, "with Debra's help."

A chuckle lightened Sutton's mood. "Never forget how big a help she is."

"No, sir." His father wrapped his arms around him, something he hadn't done since Sutton's mother died. "I'm going to make you and all of my children proud of me."

Sutton tried his best to swallow the lump in his throat, but his voice came out hoarse. "I don't think I could be prouder of you than I am this day, Dad." He patted his father on the back and turned to Debra. "I know you'll be there to support him, too."

Her eyes widened and teared up. She simply nodded and handed him a paper bag. "Those chocolate peanut butter cookies you like."

"Thanks." He embraced her. "Mom."

And thank you, God.

Sutton crossed the kitchen floor in search of his tape measure, his footsteps muted by the protective covering over the refinished hardwood. While the cabinet installers worked to put in the new cabinetry, he and Kaine would install the pre-built closet fixtures Paige had ordered for her bedroom closet. "Hey, Kaine, have you seen my tape measure?"

Kaine paused in the hallway after bringing in the boxes with the materials they would need. "Not this morning."

It wasn't with any of his other tools. Where had he put it?

"You want to use mine?"

"No, I want to find mine. Go ahead and take that stuff upstairs. I'll be up in a bit."

Sutton tried to remember when he'd last seen the tape measure. Frankly, he was doing well to remember what day it was. When he wasn't working at Paige's house, he spent his time at the farm, returning to Lane's cabin only to shower and sleep.

From what he'd heard from Debra, Jenna, and Dillon, Dad struggled but took his sobriety and responsibility to the family seriously. He had attended the group meetings and shown no signs of falling off that wagon he'd mentioned.

As much as he appreciated Lane lending him the use of the cabin so he had a place to himself at night, Sutton missed the noise and activity of the farmhouse. Boisterous mornings with people pushing and shoving to use the bathroom and prepare for school. Comings and goings. Yelling and laughter. At Lane's cabin, about all he heard were the snorts and whinnies of horses and the prowling of night animals.

When he wasn't working, he and Paige spent hours together, getting to know one another again and cementing the knowledge that they belonged together—always had, always would.

It all made for long, exhausting, and fantastic days.

He walked into the dining room, where he thought he might have left the tape measure after double-checking the measurements for the appliances. At hearing childish shouts and laughter, he glanced out the window. With the teacher in-service day and mild February temperatures, the kids played outside.

Little by little, conversation by conversation, Sutton opened himself up to the prospect that he could be the type of father Paige's kids deserved. Would he be perfect? Never. But as Lane described it during one of their Bible study sessions, people couldn't use the excuse that only Jesus was perfect as a reason for their own imperfection.

The girls had accepted him. Liam was another story. Sutton had tried to talk to him about his relationship with Paige, but the boy gave him the cold shoulder every time. Liam had even stopped asking to help with the reno. Logic said he would never come around. But Sutton had experienced a bold impression to wait him out. Until then, Liam continued to push his buttons with snide remarks—one of the most cutting of those remarks shot at him this morning.

"My dad saved people. He wasn't some rich guy who liked his money more than people, or a farmer who pretended to like kids to impress Aunt Paige."

Liam tried to rile him, and so far, Sutton had held his tongue. Even though he understood the boy's painful past, he still fumed over the disrespect. No. What he fumed most over was Paige's refusal to address Liam's rebellion before he harmed himself or someone else.

"That's a black look." Paige appeared in the doorway to the dining room. "Something wrong?"

"I can't find my tape measure. Have you seen it?"

She grimaced. "Oops. I borrowed it this morning."

"You borrowed it?" On the heels of the irritating thoughts about Liam, her calm confession brought his temper to the surface. "Paige, how am I supposed to install the closet fixtures if you run off with my tools?"

She stiffened. "I said I was sorry. You weren't around to ask, and I only wanted it for a minute. Then a phone call sidetracked me, and I left it in the studio. I'll get it for you."

"I'll get it." He strode toward the hall.

"Sutton—"

"I said I'd get it."

As soon as he'd crossed the backyard, he regretted taking out his frustration on Paige. Ugh. It meant an apology when he went back inside the house.

He stopped inside the studio and scanned the room. Where would she have laid the tape measure?

Pottery covered the large table. Three pieces took up most of the space—two sinks for the master bath and one for the downstairs bath. He couldn't wait to see them finished.

Spotting what he sought on the workbench, Sutton grabbed it and returned to the house. As much as he dreaded apologizing, it had to be done. She was nowhere downstairs.

He entered Paige's bedroom to find Kaine bent over, opening a box. "Have you seen Paige?"

Kaine scowled. "Dude, I'm not the lost and found."

Right.

The apology would have to wait. "Let's get to work on this."

Sutton and Kaine hadn't gotten far when Paige stepped into the bedroom about twenty minutes later. He laid aside the screw gun, making sure he noted where he'd put it, so he wasn't forced to ask Kaine. "Hey, I need to talk to you."

"Good, because I need to talk to you, too."

That inflexible tone gave him pause. He hadn't formed his response before she asked, "Do you know who broke my sink?"

After the sharp discussion with Sutton, Paige had retrieved a bottle of Harmoni's almond oil lotion from her bedroom and gone outside to sit on the front porch steps, escaping the pounding and boisterous male laughter from the kitchen. Those few minutes in the cold air had allowed her temper to cool. She shouldn't have taken Sutton's tape measure. She blamed herself for the consequence.

She'd spent a few minutes in a text conversation with Shellie, then walked around the corner of the house and to the studio at the rear. Inside, her stomach had dropped to her toes at the sight of the destruction. Now, in the house, she wanted to know how it happened.

"One of the unfired sinks for the master bath is in pieces on the cement floor of the studio."

Her mind jumped to the way Sutton had stomped out of the house once he learned she had taken his silly tool. It was ludicrous to think he caused the damage on purpose, but could he have knocked into it and it fell? Wouldn't he have told her?

Sutton followed her into the hall. "Someone broke a sink? All three were fine when I went out there to get this." He held up the tape measure.

"Well, one is in pieces now."

His eyebrows arched. "Wait a minute. Are you accusing me of breaking it?"

Was she? "I didn't mean for what I said to sound accusatory, but you were the last one in there, and . . ." She quit talking before she shared that the thought had crossed her mind. Wouldn't she have seen a look of guilt on his face if he were responsible? But she hadn't. And how well she knew he wasn't the type to avoid responsibility.

"I get it. I shouldn't have lost my temper. I wasn't mad at you, Paige. I'm sorry."

"So am I."

Sutton enveloped her in his arms, and she sank into the comfort before he pulled back to look at her. "What do you think happened? Did something fall on it?"

"I don't see how. There was nothing around to fall on it, and I only saw the shattered pieces of clay, nothing else."

"Can you fix the sink?"

"The damage is too great." Paige shook her head. "It means

waiting longer for a new one to dry before it can be fired and installed."

"It's okay. When it's ready, I'll put it in."

The girls rushed up the stairs, laughing, their faces red from the cold, and their feet pounding the hardwood. Paige stepped out of Sutton's arms.

"Hi, Mr. Sutton."

"Hi, Misser Sudden."

Both ran past them and into their room. Seeing her girls happy took away some of the discouragement in finding the broken sink.

"Paige."

She focused on Sutton.

"Have you asked the kids about it?"

"You think the children are responsible? They know better than to touch my work." As she said the words, Paige recalled the way Cassie used a rib to make one of the sinks "pretty." But the little girl couldn't push such a heavy piece off the table.

Leyla enjoyed moving—dancing, skipping, twirling. Could she have entered the studio and run into the table, causing the piece to fall? Paige rejected that idea. The sinks were too heavy for any of the kids to knock off by accident. And the table held other pieces more likely to fall.

"What if it wasn't an accident?"

"Are you saying someone broke it on purpose?"

Until Sutton asked that question, Paige hadn't realized she had spoken out loud. "I'm not sure. Why would they?" Yet a suspicion pushed into her mind—a suspicion she wanted to shrink from facing but must meet head-on. "Have you seen Liam?"

"Where's Liam?"

They asked their questions in unison. If the situation weren't so serious and distressing, their simultaneous responses might have seemed humorous. As it was, there was nothing to laugh over.

"I saw him outside earlier."

She sighed. "I did, too."

They had no sooner mentioned Liam than he lumbered up the stairs, hands in the pockets of his jeans and shoulders hunched. At seeing them in the hallway, he paused, his gaze shifting from Paige to Sutton. A guilty gaze? It appeared that way to Paige.

She sensed Sutton's eagerness to confront her son, so she stopped him with a hand on his arm. He eased a step back, and she asked, "Liam, I went to the studio and found one of the new sinks broken. Do you know how that happened?"

Liam's glower landed on Sutton. "He did it."

"Wait a minute—"

Paige tightened her hold on Sutton's arm to restrain him. "How do you know that?"

"I saw him through the window."

Sutton spread his legs and pulled from her hold when he crossed his arms. To his credit, he remained quiet, even though she could see by the pinched lips and hard stare how difficult that was for him.

Paige observed Liam. The pace of his breathing increased, and his eyes darted between them. His defiance melted under the scrutiny of the adults, and fear replaced it. Seeing the change, her anger at her son faded. Yet she couldn't let him get away with the destruction and trying to lay it at Sutton's feet. "We need to talk, Liam."

"You're taking his side against me, aren't you?"

"No. I'm taking the side of truth against a lie."

Liam brushed past them, ran to his room, and slammed the door.

Sutton took her hand, led her downstairs into the parlor, and pulled the pocket doors closed. "Paige, something has to change. Until today, he's only mouthed-off, but if he continues to escalate . . ."

"I know."

"Do you want me to talk to him?"

"No." This was something she needed to handle, a task long past due. "I'll talk to him tonight after we've both calmed down."

"You're sure?"

Paige couldn't blame Sutton for his doubt. She'd lost her nerve plenty of times. This episode proved she had to strengthen her resolve. She was the parent, the guide, and the authority figure. But she couldn't go into it headlong and unprepared. "Pray for us?"

He pulled her into his arms and kissed her forehead. "Always."

How she loved seeing him practice his new, growing faith. How she loved him!

Twenty-eight

Paige exhaled, long and slow, dreading this conversation and facing Liam's insolent attitude. But her family members and Sutton were right. She could no longer let him hold her responsible for every bad thing that had happened to him. She could no longer let him treat other people—in this case, Sutton—with contempt. If he continued down this path, it would only get worse, to his detriment and everyone else's. And Leyla would follow in his footsteps.

She asked God to give her the words to set her son on the right path, then she knocked on his bedroom door. "Liam?"

No answer.

Paige laid a hand on the cool doorknob. "I'm coming in."

Still nothing.

While the girls played in the bathtub, Paige took advantage of the time to hold a private conversation with him.

She opened the door and stepped inside, letting her eyes adjust to the darkness. It was after seven o'clock, pitch black outside and not much better inside Liam's room. However, the hallway light shone bright enough for her to spot the lump on the bed in the far corner. Was he asleep? She doubted it. He probably pouted, waiting for her to apologize for blaming him, something she wouldn't do—for his sake.

In the past, she'd often apologized, believing it was her fault he behaved the way he did. Why? It wasn't something her parents had modeled for their daughters. They were fair, yes. They listened, yes. But they also emphasized that they were to be obeyed. In all her daydreaming about being a mother, she hadn't realized how hard it was to be fair and loving yet maintain that authority figure role.

Paige pulled Liam's desk chair to his bedside and sat down. "Honey, we need to talk about what happened today."

She reached over and turned on the lamp sitting on the nightstand, the one he'd had in his bedroom in Marissa's house. At the sudden illumination, Liam twisted and faced the wall. An emotional ache clutched Paige at seeing the damp spot on his pillow.

"Are you going to leave us, too?"

She had to listen hard to hear the soft, muffled question. Once she sorted out the words, that emotional ache became a physical pain that throbbed in her chest. Leave them? Was that the bottom-line issue that drove her son to act as he'd done?

"Absolutely not." Paige laid a gentle hand on his small shoulder. "Look at me, Liam."

For a moment, he didn't move. Then he swiped at his cheeks, sniffled, and turned over to face her. For once, disrespect hadn't changed his eyes to blue steel. No scowl tightened his mouth. He resembled a grieving, uncertain, and scared child.

Had she been so busy trying to be the perfect mom that she hadn't given him the time and space he needed to adjust to his new life with an outsider, someone who wasn't an official family member? She'd told anyone within earshot that allowances should be made, because her children—Marissa's children—had suffered such heartrending losses. All the while, she glossed over any consideration that Liam feared even *more* loss.

Paige slipped from the chair to sit on the side of his bed and opened her arms. She held her breath, not daring to move another muscle, fearful that he would ignore the invitation. Finally, he scooted toward her and allowed her to enclose him in her arms.

With her chin resting on the top of his head, she asked, "Why would you think I would leave you and Leyla and Cassie? Legally, you're my children, but more importantly, you're the children of my heart."

"Mom and Dad left. Your husband left. You like Mr. Sutton, and he likes you. My mom and dad looked at each other the way you two do." He shook his head. "You never looked at Dustin that way."

She'd heard that children were perceptive, but only now realized the truth of that wisdom. Until the children came into their lives, she and Dustin had a comfortable relationship that leaned more toward respect and friendship than romantic passion. Their common interest was parenthood. They just had two different definitions of it. No wonder the marriage fizzled under the pressure of barrenness and adoption.

But what about Sutton?

"Anyone with half a brain knows he's never stopped loving you, and I think he'll realize it one day soon." What a beautiful realization.

"When my sisters came here three weeks ago, how much did you hear? When did you go back upstairs?" Paige figured the rustling sounds she'd heard that night were not raccoons but belonged to a ten-year-old boy.

"After Brianna said Mr. Sutton . . ." Liam stiffened in her arms. "He doesn't want anyone's kids, Aunt Paige, so if you marry him, he won't want us any more than Dustin did."

Oh, Dustin Matthews, what have you done? What had *she* done to this boy?

After the way she treated Sutton years ago, Paige had no leg to stand on in blaming Dustin for running away from their marriage. Running had been a theme in her life, too. Either running from Sutton or running ahead of God.

She tipped Liam's chin up in order to look into his eyes. "There's an old saying that eavesdroppers never prosper. Do you know what that means for you?"

"I'm grounded?"

Her lips twitched. "We'll talk about consequences in a few minutes. What it means for you is that you didn't stick around for the whole conversation and missed an important part."

"What?"

"I told my sisters that whatever Mr. Sutton felt for me didn't matter, because I have three children who come first."

He broke eye contact. "I miss my mom and dad."

"I know you do, sweetie. I do, too." A tear rolled down his cheek. She wiped it away. "If I had a time machine and could bring them back to you, I would do it in a heartbeat. Not because I don't want you, but because it would make you happy. That isn't in my power. I don't know why God allowed what happened to your parents. I do know things happen in life that we can't change. That's when we lean on God to see us through. Even if things don't always go the way we'd wish them to, He has a plan for each of us, one that is ultimately for our good.

"Your mother believed that, Liam. She had a strong faith and prayed often about who might raise you and your sisters if she couldn't. She wanted the right person to be there for you, to love you and offer you a home and family. I'm blessed that she chose me. You are not temporary guests in my house. I don't care if you call me Aunt Paige or Mom. I love you, Liam. You are my family, and I am yours. Whether I ever marry again and to whom, that will never change."

She didn't flinch as he scrutinized her face, no doubt searching for truth.

"Are you willing to think of me as part of your family?" As she waited for his response, her heartbeat pounded in her ears so loud she hoped she wouldn't have to find Leyla to read his lips. In the quiet, she heard the squeals and giggles of his sisters as they played in the bathtub.

"Yes . . . m-ma'am."

For a second, she thought he'd call her Mom, but it didn't matter. Maybe one day. "I'm glad." She hugged him. "But we need to discuss what happened today."

His chin fell. "I broke the sink."

Relief flooded over her with his admission. "Why?"

"He was mad at you. I thought . . ."

Paige replayed their conversation and deduced the child's reasoning. "You thought if I blamed Sutton, he would go away?"

Liam's head bobbed.

"Honey, he was frustrated because I took something of his without asking. People have a right to their anger sometimes, but they don't have a right to be destructive. What you did was destructive and wrong."

"I won't do it again."

"I hope not, or we'll have a less pleasant conversation."

A tiny smile slid onto his face. "Okay."

"Mommy! The water is cold."

"Coming, Cassie." She released Liam and stood. "You owe Sutton and me an apology for your actions today. You owe my family an apology for your attitude since our arrival in Hidden Veil."

"I'm sorry I broke the sink and that I tried to blame Mr. Sutton. I won't do it again."

"You'll tell him that tomorrow. You will also clean the studio every evening after supper until you've worked off the cost of the clay used to make the sink."

"How long will that be?"

"About two weeks, but it depends on the quality of your work."

"Two weeks?"

"If you'd like, I could add the cost of my wasted time in throwing the piece."

"No, ma'am."

"Mom-my!"

At Cassie's cry, Paige walked to the bedroom door. She stopped and turned around. "Liam, a big part of raising children is teaching them right and wrong and how to interact with others. It's especially important to teach respectful ways to treat people, especially parents. There will be no more disrespect, poor attitudes, or disobedience without consequences. Is that clear?"

He took a sudden interest in fiddling with his bedsheet. "Now you really sound like my mom."

Her voice broke as she said, "Okay."

Two months later

Vehicles lined the driveway, and Paige's house reverberated with laughter and banter. To celebrate the blessings she had received since returning to Hidden Veil, she'd decided to throw a party after the completion of the kitchen and downstairs renovations.

Today, friends and family filled the house—the Hartwells and the Vances, including Sutton's father. A few days after Sutton moved out of the farmhouse, John Vance appeared on her doorstep with a sheepish smile and an apology. The man had slipped once in his goal of full sobriety over the past weeks, but Debra laid down the law immediately, and he seemed determined to obey it. To Sutton's relief, his father worked hard to become the dependable family man he was before Sutton's mother died, and he assumed the role of mentor to Dillon.

Paige smiled at the noise and activity in her house. This was what made a home—family and friends whose love and acceptance provided warmth and coziness.

Macie pulled the lid off a large casserole dish, exposing the sight and marvelous aroma of freshly baked scalloped potatoes. "You've turned this old place into a home to be proud of, Paige."

"Yes, you have great taste." Jo bounced four-month-old Rose on her hip.

"Thank you, ladies." Paige added more veggies to the ceramic tray she'd made a few years ago. Using it reminded her that her hard work over the past few weeks had caught her up with her orders. Her business now stood on better footing.

"Sutton and Kaine have done a wonderful job, but they have more work to do in other parts of the house." She laughed. "That's if I can retain their services. Since I helped him establish a website and we uploaded the before and after photos of this house, Sutton has a full schedule of jobs on the calendar."

Jo snatched a carrot stick from the tray. "I heard Kaine plans to continue to work for him."

"He'll still be part-time at Harley's until Sutton can afford to hire him full-time."

Macie wandered to the kitchen window overlooking the side yard. "Oh, wow."

Paige joined her at the window. "What's wrong?"

"Nothing is wrong, but I never thought I'd see Sutton sharing Rocket with anyone under twenty-one."

Jo peered over Macie's shoulder. "I never thought I'd see him so relaxed and *happy* around kids."

Sutton stood by while Liam led the horse around the yard with Ariel and Leyla on the animal's back. He had spent hours on Sunday afternoons teaching her son how to ride. Today, he shared his four-legged friend with her children, as well as his youngest brothers and sister.

One of Paige's most cherished moments came two weeks ago, when she'd walked out of the studio to catch Sutton and Liam laughing as they wrestled on the ground. She rejoiced to see Sutton living moments he should have known during his childhood.

Although he still experienced times of awkwardness around her children, Sutton had come a long way since Liam apologized to him. During that chat, Sutton told her son that, should he and Paige choose to marry, Liam and his sisters would be a part of their life together—always.

He just hadn't reached the point of asking her yet.

Once the get-together ended and everyone but Sutton had gone home, Paige gathered the dirty dishes and took them into the kitchen. She may have bought this house out from under him, but today, they entertained as if this was *their* house, and it couldn't have made her happier.

Through the window over the sink, movement in the yard caught her attention. Sutton and Liam stood near the studio, talking. Her brow tightened. It looked serious. They didn't appear to argue, though. Finally, they shook hands, as if they had come to an agreement. What on earth were they doing?

When Sutton approached the back door of the house, she moved away from the sink, not wanting him to know she had spied on his interaction with Liam.

He walked into the kitchen and stood behind her. With his arms wrapped around her waist, he kissed her neck, sending shivers through her. "It was a great day."

"It was." She turned and placed her hands on his shoulders. "You were wonderful with the kids."

"They're growing on me." He grinned. "Guess what."

"What?"

"Maybe you haven't heard, but for the past couple of years, someone has sent anonymous gifts to people in need. That person has donated money for surgeries, Lane's Healing Springs project, things like that. Anyway, Dad got a check in the mail a few days ago from a Virginia attorney. It will pay a good portion of Debra's hospital bill."

"That's wonderful. I know you all were concerned about it. You don't know who sent the money?"

"Nope. I called the attorney's office but couldn't get any information. Whoever it is wants to remain anonymous. Dad almost didn't cash it. He said Vances don't take charity. He raised me that way, but in this case, I convinced him to lay aside his pride and accept it."

"I'm glad you did. Not doing so would deny that person a blessing."

When a tremor ran through him, like nerves dancing, she pulled back. "What else is going on?"

"While your dad was here today, I asked him an important question."

"Okay." Then the probable meaning hit her, and she gasped. "Oh."

Sutton rested one knee on the newly refinished hardwood floor. Seeing the tough and masculine Sutton Vance in such a humble position, she snickered. He growled. "Don't be funny, Paige."

Paige sucked in her lips and shook her head, deciding to wait but wishing he would hurry and ask.

He took her left hand. "Paige Hartwell, there will be times when I'm not an ideal husband. There may even be days when you'll wonder if you should run again—"

"Never. I'm here to stay." *With you.*

He grinned. "Good to know."

Every nerve ending seemed to burn with excitement as she waited for him to get to the point. Of course, he'd do it faster if she kept her mouth closed.

"Paige, I can only promise you one diamond, a beat-up truck . . . and a love that never died and never will. Will you marry—"

"Yes!

"I memorized this scene, and you didn't let me finish."

Paige tugged on his hand until he stood, then threw her arms around his neck and kissed him. "Sorry. Go ahead."

He shook his head and chuckled. "I'm not sure there's much point now, but will you marry me?"

"Yes. The answer will always be yes."

His facial features relaxed. "You should know I'll probably blow the parenting thing sometimes, but I'll do my best to help you raise your children—"

"Our children."

He paused a moment, as though running those words through his mind. "Our children. We'll raise them to know they're loved by us and by God."

How could she ever ask for anything more?

They spent the next few minutes in a celebration that curled her toes. Finally, he drew back. "We're not married yet."

"No, but you have to admit, this is a great make-out house."

Sutton laughed. "Can't argue with that."

"Wait a minute. Are you marrying me for my house?"

"Hmm . . . Let me get back to you on that." She punched his arm, and he laughed once more. "Okay. Maybe not, but you have to agree it's a bonus."

"I do love this place."

"Me, too, but we could live in a tent and I'd be happy." He cocked his head in a way that asked if she agreed.

"As long as you're there, I'd consider it."

"You were always the best part of me, Paige, the sunshine to my cloudy day," he whispered.

Oh, that was sweet. "Poetic words from Sutton Vance?"

"Truth. I've spent too much time focusing on the darkness in my life. I'm ready to live in the light."

After more cuddling in the kitchen, she asked, "What were you doing with Liam earlier? I saw you shaking his hand."

"I . . . um . . . I asked each of the kids if I could be their dad."

Her breath caught. “What did they say?”

“Cassie grabbed me around the legs. Leyla squealed and pierced my eardrums, and Liam—”

“Shook your hand.”

“Yeah. I promised him I’d stick around and be the father I always wanted for myself.”

Liam finally had another man in his life he could look up to, one who wouldn’t run out on him. “You’re going to be great.”

She wiggled the fingers of her left hand. “I think you forgot something, mister. My diamond?”

Sutton snapped his fingers. He pulled a small box from his pocket and opened it. “You distracted me.”

He pulled out a gold band topped by a small but well-cut diamond, not even half the size of the one Dustin had given her. But she valued this one so much more. “I love it!”

“There’s something else. I’ll be right back.”

He hurried out of the kitchen. A minute later, she heard an army of footsteps in the hall. Like the Pied Piper, he led the children into the kitchen.

Liam handed her a wrapped box. “For you, Mom, from all of us.”

“From all of us, Mom,” said Leyla.

Paige didn’t think she would ever not smile when the children called her Mom. She took the gift to the island, unwrapped the box, and opened it. She swallowed against the tightness in her throat as she pulled out her gift. “Is this what I think it is?”

“Jenna helped us put it together from the pieces of the sink I broke. Sutton made the frame.”

They had taken the unfired pottery and broken it into pebble-sized pieces, painted them the color of the kitchen cabinets, then glued them onto a stained board, forming letters that spelled "Home Sweet Home." Then Sutton placed it in a beautifully crafted box frame.

She glanced around the room for the perfect place to hang it. From the Hoosier cabinet that served as a coffee bar to the island and newly painted walls, to the large gas stove. She finally propped it on the fireplace mantel, where the words would add warmth to the room, even when no fire blazed beneath it.

This was the house of her dreams, and she would share it with the family of her dreams.

Home sweet home, indeed.

Reader Friend,

I love to write stories with happy endings. But, you know, sometimes real life doesn't have the same positive outcome as a fictional story. Not all "plot points" in our lives are wrapped up in neat bows and in a timely manner.

While giving me her thoughts on this book, my author friend, Heidi Chiavaroli, reminded me that our prayers aren't always answered in the way we'd like. (Thank you, Heidi!) Sometimes that happy-ever-after doesn't materialize.

It's in those times when we should depend more on God and the belief that He does have a plan that won't harm us but give us a hope and a future. We don't run from God because life is uncomfortable, as Sutton and Paige did. That's the time we run to Him as small children run to their parents for comfort.

If you struggle with believing God hears or see you, remember His name: El Roi, the God Who Sees.

He sees. He hears. He loves.

Thank you for spending your precious time with Sutton, Paige, and the kids in *A Father's Promise.* If you wouldn't mind, I'd appreciate a review with your honest thoughts. If you don't have time to post a written review, a simple rating will do.

Thanks so much, and Happy Reading!

Sandra

Want a little mystery with your romance?

Return to the small town of Hidden Veil for a new series! Reconnect with old friends and meet new ones.

In the exciting new **Hidden Veil Intrigue** series, expect mystery, danger, and all the romance!

Look for the first book in 2027.

Get the latest news!

Receive Sandra's newsletter and stay up to date with sales, releases, and a few surprises.
Head over to www.sandraardoin.com/newsletter, sign up, and start reading *Unwrapping Hope.*

Don't miss the first three books in the
HIDDEN VEIL HOMETOWN SERIES

She's the woman of his dreams.
He's her worst nightmake.

She seeks healing for her son.
He's looking for atonement for his brother's death.

He's loved her for years, but he can't compete with a dead hero.

She ends her relationships before emotions become involved and lives ruined.

As an author of heartwarming and award-winning historical and contemporary romance, Sandra Ardoin engages readers with page-turning stories of love and faith. Rarely out of reach of a book, she's also an armchair sports enthusiast, country music listener, and seldom says no to eating out. Visit her at www.sandraardoin.com.

Connect with her on BookBub, Facebook, X, and Goodreads.

Stay updated by signing up to Sandra's Love and Faith in Fiction newsletter at www.sandraardoin/newsletter.

www.ingramcontent.com/pod-product-compliance
Lightning Source LLC
LaVergne TN
LVHW100519110826
845146LV00002B/704

* 9 7 9 8 9 9 0 5 8 4 8 3 9 *